Justine Elyot's kinky take — anthologised in *Black Lace*'s t— most popular online sites.

She lives by the sea.

Praise for Justine Elyot

'If you are looking for strings-free erotica, and not for deep romance, *On Demand* is just the book . . . Indulgent and titillating, *On Demand* is like a tonic for your imagination. The writing is witty, the personal and sexual quirks of the characters entertaining'
Lara Kairos

'Did I mention that every chapter is highly charged with eroticism, BDSM, D/s, and almost every fantasy you can imagine? If you don't get turned on by at least one of these fantasies, there is no hope for you'
Manic Readers

'. . . a rip-roaring, rollercoaster ride of sexual indulgence; eloquently written, at times shocking, and always entertaining'
Ms Love's Books

Also by Justine Elyot:

DIAMOND

JUSTINE ELYOT

BLACK
LACE

1 3 5 7 9 10 8 6 4 2

First published in 2014 by Black Lace, an imprint of Ebury Publishing
A Random House Group Company

The Random House Group Limited Reg. No. 954009

Addresses for companies within the Random House Group can
be found at: www.randomhouse.co.uk

A CIP catalogue record for this book is available from the British Library

The Random House Group Limited supports The Forest Stewardship
Council® (FSC®), the leading international forest-certification organisation.
Our books carrying the FSC label are printed on FSC® -certified paper.
FSC is the only forest-certification scheme supported by the leading
environmental organisations, including Greenpeace.
Our paper procurement policy can be found at:
www.randomhouse.co.uk/environment

Printed and bound in Great Britain by Clays Ltd, St Ives plc

ISBN 9780352347756

To buy books by your favourite authors and register for offers visit:
www.blacklace.co.uk

Chapter One

In many ways the place hadn't changed. There were some differences – the high rises were gone, replaced with nests of tiny newbuilds. The pit head was a museum, now, and there was a ring road encircling the town, keeping it in, separate from the old coalmining landscape that had been its life blood, as if to say 'This isn't part of you, any more'.

The signs of modernity were calculated to comfort, but they didn't do much for Jenna's mood, and she found herself in uncertain spirits as she parked the car and wandered down the lone, pedestrianised street that made up the 'town centre'.

Perhaps this had been a mistake, she thought, looking into the shop windows – those that weren't boarded up. The only businesses that seemed to be flourishing on this wet Wednesday afternoon were the bookmakers, the pound shops and the glorified pawnbrokers that had sprung up on every corner.

A big chain pub with a happy hour that lasted until teatime was full and bright, as if its façade of good cheer had sucked everyone off the street and left it empty. She thought about going in and getting a nip of something to keep the shivers off, but there was no guarantee she wouldn't be recognised, and conversation was the last thing she was after.

The high street drifted into nothingness: the old covered market was abandoned now, just a shed earmarked for demolition. She stepped under its dark, old awning and tried to remember it the way it was: the smells of overripe fruit and veg, meat and fish all competing to hit the back of her throat the hardest. The little stalls full of knitting wools or costume jewellery or model-making kits. The slow crowds of old ladies in five layers of clothing and kids in tracksuits. And at the centre of it all, Smash Records, where she had spent every Saturday afternoon. Where she had met Deano.

She made a sharp about-turn and walked swiftly to the end of the street and into the residential area beyond, her umbrella charging before her like a weapon. Densely-packed terraces gave way to more spacious environs, within a ten minute walk, and soon she saw the church tower that confirmed she had taken the right route and was near her destination.

She decided to walk through the churchyard rather than keep on the straight path. Something about churchyards in pouring rain encouraged contemplative peace, and she was in need of it. Among the lichened stones bearing names of people who had breathed their last centuries before, she stopped and looked up at the sky. Its grey threat was not the best omen for a day on which her life would change.

But she didn't believe in things like that. She believed in making your own luck. She had made hers, and now she could afford to buy the house that had fascinated her since childhood. And if she didn't get a move on, she'd be late to pick up the keys.

There it stood, just the other side of the churchyard, mostly hidden behind a high yew hedge. The grounds of Harville Hall had been the scene of many a childhood exploration, ever since the owners had abandoned it during the miners' strike, when she was five. She and the other kids from the estate had used its ever-more-overgrown gardens and woodland for innumerable games of A-Team and Robin Hood. She had never managed to get inside the house, though, because the walls had bristled with alarms and those new cameras that filmed you. The big, red, spray-painted 'TRAITOR' on the side gable hadn't been washed off for years.

Of course, it would be long gone now.

She went to stand by the padlocked front gate, looking up and down the street for signs of the keyholder. The house had been lived in again, since its abandonment, but little had been done to it in the way of renovation. Although structurally sound, it had a blank, neglected look.

Within half a minute, the door of a shiny, red sports car parked up the road had opened and a man in a very smart, dark blue pea coat stepped out and strode towards her. Having no umbrella, he held a leather satchel over his head to keep off the rain and he grimaced at her as he drew level. The grimace did nothing to disguise his handsomeness, though. Jenna was pleasantly impressed and couldn't help giving him one of her brightest beams back.

'Hi,' she said. 'Jenna Myatt.'

'Thank God for that,' he said, holding out the hand

that wasn't occupied with the satchel. 'Lawrence Harville. What a day. Shall we step inside? Or I could hand over the keys in my car, if you prefer?'

She shook his rain-wet hand and nodded, indicating that they might go inside the Hall in order to complete their transaction. She wasn't sure who was checking out whom harder – both of them trying to keep their cool at meeting a 'celebrity'. Old money meets new, she thought, and it's hard to say who's more impressed. It was nice, and novel, to be able to hold her own with a Harville now. He might have the history, but she had the stellar career, the amazing roster of celebrity clients on her books and the international reputation for being the best manager in the business.

He unlocked the gate, which was in dire need of oiling, and led her up the side path. The borders were so overgrown that the weeds brushed against her tights, wetting them. She would have to hire a gardener. What was the going rate around here? Much less than in London, she guessed.

The stone steps were still intact, and the front door's paintwork might have been peeling but it was still substantial enough and only needed a bit of a shove to open.

'It's the damp weather,' explained Harville, with an apologetic little smile.

'You'd think it would be used to it by now,' said Jenna. 'Living round here.'

Harville's smile brightened into brilliance and he laughed politely.

'Indeed,' he said, stepping into a musty but enormous hallway.

Jenna had been living in Los Angeles when she bought the place, and this was the first time she had crossed the threshold. Her assistant had tried to warn her, she remembered.

It's not in the best condition. You can get a modern mansion in Cheshire for just a couple of hundred thousand more.

But she had not been able to get Harville Hall out of her mind, and she had insisted on pressing on with the purchase. She'd made her bed, and now she'd have to lie in it.

It wasn't even like her to be sentimental. She put it down to the split and the stress of it. Three years in La-La-land had turned her gaga. She had yearned for home, but not the redbrick council semi home. She wanted a home that reflected her success in life.

'Must be a wrench,' she said, looking around at the dusty, black and white diamond tiles and the woodwormy walls. 'This house was in your family for years.'

'Not that long,' said Lawrence. In the semi-dark, his face was pale and rain-slick. 'It was built in 1836 for my great-great-great, add a couple more greats, you get the picture.' His smile was charming, and his teeth so white. She couldn't work out if he was older or younger than her, which made her feel at a disadvantage with him.

'I'd call that a long time,' said Jenna.

'Well, it is, I suppose, and times change, don't they? We aren't the big, bad landlords grinding the faces of the local widows and orphans any more. We've nothing to keep us in Bledburn.'

'Although Bledburn kept you very nicely for more than a hundred years,' said Jenna, more tartly than she intended.

'Well, yes, it did.' Lawrence looked a touch uncomfortable and she was surprised by her urgent need to see him smile again. He, of course, was far too polite to bring up anything he might know of her situation, and she ought to be grateful to him for it.

'Sorry,' she said. 'It was nothing to do with you, I know. So, where are you going?'

'Not far,' he said. 'Nottingham. I've still got some property in the area, so I'll be around and about.'

'Perhaps you'll, uh, drop in for a cup of tea.'

Why the hell had she said that? She was here to pick up the keys to the house off him, not establish a social connection. Now he would think she fancied him! It was a definite over-compensation for such a small slight.

At least the beam was back. 'I'd like that,' he said. 'Care for a tour?'

'Oh. All right. I'm guessing this is the hall.'

'Well guessed. If you come through these doors to the right, we have what we used to call the family room. The drawing room, to our more formal ancestors.'

He took her through three more similar chambers, plus the enormous kitchen, a few steps down from the reception rooms in a semi-basement. Each of the five bedrooms on the upper floor was faded and cobwebbed, the sash windows awry in their frames so that draughts blew in and raindrops collected on the sills. They were empty of furniture, but Jenna was not going to bring much into the house until her full refurbishment was complete. Until then, she would camp out in one of the downstairs rooms with a mattress, a suitcase of clothes and her laptop. The kitchen range was perfectly usable, so she wouldn't have to worry about cooking, and she would buy firewood to burn in the hearth. Not coal, she thought, wryly.

'You have plans for the place, I assume?' said Lawrence, pausing on the landing.

'Yes, a full renovation, I think. I need a project.'

She wished she hadn't said that. It meant that she had to think about how much he might know about her. Perhaps he pitied her.

'The devil makes work for idle hands,' he said, with a slightly too-knowing smile.

'Well, the devil won't be coming anywhere near me, at any rate,' said Jenna, as briskly as she knew how.

'I'm sure.' He paused. 'Well, a Bledburn girl returns to the fold. How long since you were last here?'

'Oh, you know, I don't even . . . Maybe fifteen years?'

'As long as that? You don't have family here?'

'My parents wanted to retire to Spain so I bought them a villa. Marbella. They love it out there.'

'You could have joined them. Sunny Spain or rainy Bledburn? Seems like a no-brainer.' He looked bleakly through the huge stained-glass arch above the stairs, on which rain blattered without cease.

'I used to dream of living in this house,' said Jenna softly.

'You know it's reputed to be . . . Sorry, sorry, I should think before I speak. Tell me to shut up.' Lawrence looked so stricken that Jenna laughed.

'Haunted? Of course I know that. Everyone does. But I don't believe in ghosts.'

'Good. Besides, what did they used to say? "The only good Harville's a dead Harville." So you should be quite safe.'

'Oh, come on. Those were bad times. You can't have been more than a baby then.'

'I was toddling, I think.'

So he was younger than her, but only a year or so.

'Funny how our lives have been shaped by something that happened before we could possibly understand it,' she said.

'I think that's the human condition,' said Harville. 'What can we do?'

'Our best,' said Jenna with a nod. 'That's what we can do.'

He closed his hand around the banister with a rueful little burst of something that was not quite laughter.

'You made your fortune,' he said. 'And now, here we are. Who would have predicted this over our cradles, eh?'

Jenna bit her lip. 'I'll take care of this place,' she said. 'I promise.'

'Thanks. Listen, here are the keys.' He took them from his pocket and handed them over. 'That one for the front door, that one for the kitchen door – well, I've labelled them anyway. I ought to get back to town.'

She followed his determined move towards the stairs, watching his pea-coated back and broad shoulders in descent.

'If you're passing,' she said, once he was at the door. 'Do call in.'

He turned, and gave her a long look.

'I'd love to,' he said, taking a mobile phone from his satchel. 'Give me your number. I'll call.'

Much later, after the van had delivered a rudimentary complement of furniture – all of it old and sturdy, from reclamation yards – and Jenna had finished her dialled-in Thai takeaway and got the butane gas heater on in the front parlour, she got out her phone and looked at the number she had been given.

She was sitting on a mattress in her temporary encampment. Once the house was done up and sparkling, she would have her half of the furniture from the LA house shipped over. It wasn't easy to picture it here, in this faded room, but she was sure its beauty and suitability would amaze her, when everything was in order.

Lawrence Harville, though. She lay back on the mattress and let out a long, loud laugh. Imagine what Deano would think if he heard about that. Everyone in Bledburn had hated the Harvilles, after they sold everyone out in the strike, but Deano most of all. He had even written a song about them. 'Lord of Plenty', track four on the *Bleeding Hearts* album. Jenna began to sing the chorus to herself:

'Fine clothes, fine house
Fine words, fine wine
And it's all paid for
By the men in the mine.'

It had been quite an anthem, at the time.

Yes, a few careless snaps of her with Harville in the sidebar of shame would be enough to get Deano launched into orbit. If he asked her out, she'd see that they went somewhere extremely and unavoidably public. To begin with.

She betted he was a charmer, a smoothie, a fast worker. She'd met enough of his type, over the years of glitz and glam. He'd be experienced, and probably decent in bed, even if he would have his hand up your skirt by the time the entrées were taken from the table.

Selfish, though. An egotist, probably. Just like Deano.

It was still worth the wind-up. If he called her, she would definitely show an interest.

And why wouldn't he call her? She might be a bit older than him, might be taking a sabbatical from her high-profile, high-pressure career in music promotion, but she was at her physical peak.

She was toned, honed, perma-tanned, coiffed, Botoxed, groomed, plucked, buffed and styled within an inch of her life. She was *never* going to be featured in one of those magazine spreads with a photoshopped circle around some less-than-perfect feature. She only wore tracksuits at the gym and she was only seen without make-up in bed. Sometimes not even then.

True, it wasn't going to be easy without her retinue of staff, all devoted to the greater glory of Jenna Myatt's image, but there was no need to let things slide. This house was evidence enough of that.

Don't you ever get tired of being perfect?

Deano's voice cut into her thoughts, still heavy with the local accent that he had never made any attempt to lose – unlike Jenna, who had hired an elocution coach the day she left Bledburn. Indeed, in latter years, Jenna had grown to loathe Deano's accent. It had become more an affectation than a genuine dialect, a shorthand way of showing that, however rich and famous and American he might look, he was still a Bleddy boy at root.

As if you didn't run as fast and as far as you could, the minute you had the chance.

She wanted to stop thinking, so she found Candy Crush on her phone and devoted her next half-hour to the cause of colourfully animated mindlessness.

Some kind of thud from above made her turn down the volume and sit up. What was it? The room had grown dark while she was playing, the moonlight not sufficient to cast much more than the palest wash on the uncarpeted floor.

She sat, almost too tense to breathe, for a good five minutes. No further noises were heard.

'A bird's nest on the roof,' she muttered to herself. 'Or, oh God, maybe rats in the attic. More than likely. Ugh.'

She got up to put on the light, opening the door to the hall in order to listen more carefully.

Again, nothing.

'It's nothing,' she told herself.

All the same, she put her phone on charge, to make sure it was fully topped up, and decided against wasting the battery on games any more.

It was getting late, and she was tired.

She couldn't have a hot bath or shower until the electrician came to fit a new boiler tomorrow. She would have to make do with cold water, baby wipes and body spray until then. And she had no mirror, except the tiny one in her compact! Why had she not thought to bring one?

Her makeshift bed felt cold, but at least it was dry. Tomorrow she would get some wood for the big fireplace; she'd have to buy it, since everything in the garden would be soaked and pulpy. She had practical matters to concentrate on. So much to do. No time to think, to mourn, to languish.

No time to dream . . .

But she did dream.

Footsteps overhead, creaking on the boards. A white

smoke, ectoplasmic in appearance, filling the room and hissing into her ears. How cold it felt, filling her lungs, choking her, pressing down on her chest. She tried to kick, to fight it off, but her limbs were weighed down and even her lips would not move to emit her silent scream.

After what seemed like hours of struggle, Jenna's eyelids opened and she was able to move her trembling arms. She lay still for a while, catching her breath, waiting for reality to chase the horrible traces of her dream away. It took a while and it still lay lightly upon her when she sat up and looked around her, identifying the dark shapes in the room one by one.

It was all right. She was in bed, in Harville Hall, in the front parlour. Outside, a wind blew, sending cold blasts down the chimney at intervals. It was late – when she checked her phone, she saw that it was five past three.

Lawrence's words about the place being haunted came back to her. She wondered what form the hauntings took.

But you don't believe in ghosts.

Easy enough to say so in the bright light of day, but now it was dark and late and lonely. She was far from home, she thought, and yet she wasn't.

I have no home.

It was a melancholy thought.

Don't start crying, not now. You've been so strong.

She thought about Deano, in bed with that girl right now, no doubt. Or was he? What was the time difference?

The calculation kept her level-headed, made her think that Deano was probably sitting down to eat, now, or in make-up for a personal appearance or interview of some kind. Or he might be in the pool. Or the gym.

He'd probably ditched her already.

How, she asked herself, already kicking herself for going down this well-worn, emotionally flagellating path, could Deano have done it to her? How could he have cheated on her with that . . . OK, she was younger, but she was *fat*.

She got that he had cheated on her. He was rich, famous, magnetic, attractive – temptation did more than get in his way. It literally climbed into his bed, on more than one occasion. So that hadn't shocked her as much as it might have done.

She got that he had cheated on her with a teenager. It was a rock star cliché. Boring, trite, predictable, unworthy of him, but . . . She could have forgiven it, in time.

But to cheat on her with a *fat* girl! It was an insult. It was beyond the pale.

You used to be the same size as her, he'd said.

'I was never that big!' she protested, but actually she had been. A British size 12 when they met, three sizes bigger than she was now.

'It's not even big!' Deano had said. 'It's a healthy size. Jesus, Jenna, you're as bad as the rest of them.'

She didn't know who 'the rest of them' were, but she wasn't sticking around to take the blame for her own husband's inability to keep his dick in his pants.

She ran her hand along her arm, checking for spare flesh. Nothing to pinch. Nothing but firm, taut, brown skin. Breasts, small but still high. Thighs supple and yoga-flexible.

If she was awake at this time of night, she might as well make use of it.

She stood by the window and began to warm up, jogging on the spot in bare feet.

Nothing stops me. I am unstoppable. One thing marks out

the success from the failure, and that is how much they want success. Make it your hunger, make it your thirst, make it your lust, subvert all your appetites into this one drive.

The mantras calmed and focused her.

She worked out until she was dizzy and her head pounded, then she fell back on the mattress and took a long drink from her flask.

Still only 4 a.m.

She was physically tired, but her brain ticked on. What would trick it back into sleep? What could she think about?

Lawrence Harville. She thought of that creamy-coffee voice telling her to do things. 'Take off your clothes, Jenna.'

He would be sitting, legs astride a wooden chair, shirt undone, tie loose around his neck, looking louche and lecherous after perhaps a couple of brandies. His eyes were heavy-lidded, his face a mask of sensuality and desire.

He would make her take off her cocktail dress, and underneath she would be wearing something daring. What would it be? Stockings and suspenders, and a tight bustier that lifted her breasts almost into her face. A tiny wisp of a thong. He would be able to see through the sheer lace triangle and, when she twirled for him, her bare bottom would be exposed, bisected by taut black elastic.

'Come and stand in front of me,' he'd say, and she'd pose, hands on hips, feet planted wide on the floor, trying to look insolently insouciant while his gaze raked her up and down and side to side.

Without warning, he would clamp a hand between her thighs, smacking down on her sex lips, holding them in an iron grip.

'What's this?' he'd whisper.

'None of your business,' she'd say, defiant, pretending not to want it.

'No? What if I pay for it?'

'You couldn't afford it.'

But he'd take a roll of banknotes from his inner jacket pocket and stuff them into the cups of her bustier.

'Now?'

Her knees trembled at the thought of being bought, of being property to be used.

She nodded, looked down, instantly humbled.

'OK,' she whispered.

'Money talks,' he said, pushing stubby fingertips inside the gauzy thong to rub at her clit. 'And money gets you wet, doesn't it?'

She nodded, all her defiance knocked out of her by this accurate assessment of who and what she was.

'What kind of woman gets wet when she thinks about money?' he asked.

She knew the answer that was required of her.

'A whore,' she said.

He laughed, running his fingers steadily over her nub, to and fro. With his other hand he reached behind her and smacked her bum.

'That's right,' he said. 'Get on your knees, whore.'

She obeyed, regretting the absence of his touch at her most intimate spot.

'Earn your money,' he said gloatingly, opening his trousers. 'Get that mouth to work.'

She reached for his cock and warmed it between her palms, breathing down on its tip. It was big and firm, ready to do all kinds of things to her.

She took it in her mouth and he held her hair and told her over and over that she was a cocksucking whore who lived to suck cocks until he filled her mouth with bitterness and she swallowed it down.

But Jenna couldn't come. The fantasy left her feeling desolate and empty and more than a little dirty. Was that what she was? Was it what she wanted?

Deano had said that money was her only true love. He had been wrong, of course he had. She loved music, she loved the cut and thrust of business life, she loved the moments of glory and the little luxuries of her daily existence. And she had loved Deano, once.

It did seem a long time ago now, though.

She stiffened.

Another noise – a muffled thud, two storeys up. It had to be coming from the attic or the roof. What was it?

Whatever it was, she didn't want to go up there. Every frightening urban myth she had ever heard crowded into her brain. Psychopaths on roofs, in adjoining rooms, making phone calls from feet away.

She lay utterly still, barely breathing, her ears listening for something to break the rush of black sound around her. No creaks, no taps, no footsteps came.

That's it, she thought. This was a terrible mistake. Tomorrow she would call the estate agent and put the place back on the market. Go to the London office. Forget about the sabbatical. Try and work through the humiliation of being left by her husband and biggest client until everyone was too intimidated and too polite to ever mention it again.

The room was not as dark now. Dawn wasn't quite breaking, but it was on its slow way. It wasn't too early to get up, she thought. She had got up at five for years, drunk a glass of wheatgrass juice, done an hour in the gym or pool before taking her calls. There hadn't been enough hours in the day, then. She strongly suspected that there might be too many, now.

She drew back the heavy, dusty curtain and looked out into the wet, dark garden. It was overgrown and needed a lot of tender care. She would have to hire a gardener.

But what was she thinking? She wasn't staying. She was going to pack up and get out of here, as soon as possible. The split with Deano had infected her brain. What on earth had made her think this was a good idea?

She pulled out one of the bottles of water from her bag and drank it on the mattress, letting its cold clear stream flow down her throat and revive her. She would have bags under her eyes. She needed to apply some gel. God, she needed a shower. This was just dire.

She put her head in her hands and began to sob.

Three hours later, she woke again, having cried herself into an exhausted sleep. Now it was light, quarter past eight by her watch, and things looked slightly less desperate, in that odd way they always did once the darkest hours were past.

She'd call the estate agent at nine, as soon as they opened.

She put on the same pair of 7 jeans and cashmere hoodie she'd worn yesterday – perhaps the first time she'd worn the same outfit twice in a row this millennium – and sauntered, barefoot, into the front hall.

Nothing was disturbed. Everything was as it had been the last time she saw it.

So what had caused the noise up above her? She peered

up but the staircase held no clues. Harville hadn't shown her the attic. He hadn't even mentioned it.

Perhaps she ought to check it. Or perhaps she should just leave its rats, or birds, or whatever were up there, for the next lucky owner.

She sat down on the bottom stair, overwhelmed by a need for some human contact – a voice, a word, anything. Before she could stop herself, she was keying in Lawrence Harville's number.

'Hello?'

'Hello, God, I'm sorry, I forgot it was before nine, have I disturbed you?'

'No, no.' But he sounded as if he was still in bed, with that thick, slightly drugged tone to his voice. 'Sorry, who?'

'Jenna. Jenna Myatt, the new owner of the Hall.'

'Yes, yes, of course, forgive me. Brain hasn't kicked into gear yet. More coffee needed, I think. What can I do for you, Jenna? Is everything all right up there?'

'Oh, fine, I think. Just wanted to ask you about the attic space.'

'The attic?'

'I don't remember looking around up there. Is it boarded? Insulated? Is there a step ladder anywhere so I can go up and look around?'

'The attic? You know, I really couldn't say. I don't think I've been up there in my life. It used to be servants' quarters, years ago, so I suppose it's got flooring.'

'It's just there were . . . funny noises. They seemed to come from there.'

'Oh, dear. How unnerving. I hope they didn't keep you awake all night.'

'No, no.' Jenna wondered why she needed to give the

impression that strange noises in a strange house in the dead of night when completely alone were no big deal. His voice, alone, seemed to make everything all right, and convince her that she had been fussing over nothing. 'But I did want to check. Could be a family of squirrels or anything.'

'Squirrels! They'd be company for you. Must have been rather lonely in that rattling old place on your own.'

'Well . . .'

'Listen, would you like to meet up for lunch? There's nowhere much in Bledburn itself, but some smashing country pubs in the area.'

Jenna didn't want to bite his hand off but she couldn't keep a note of almost hysterical relief from her voice when she said, 'That might be nice – thank you.'

'Shall I pick you up at twelve?'

'Perfect.'

Lunch, then London, she thought. The attic could go fuck itself, along with the whole of Bledburn.

She put on socks and boots and climbed the stairs to the first floor, walking through each of the bedrooms in turn. Her visions for the rooms came back to her and she began to regret that she would never see them transformed. She had been full of plans. Renovate the house then turn it into an exclusive boutique hotel and five-star restaurant. Put Bledburn on the map. Perhaps make it the first of a chain, buy other property in the Nottingham and Sheffield areas.

She looked up at the ceiling, but she couldn't see a hatch or any obvious access point. There was clearly a room, or rooms, up there, but how the dickens did one access them?

But, then again, she didn't want to. It was pointless, after all. She was going to go downstairs and call the agent.

She could hear the chirrup of her phone from the parlour. Probably one of the offices, unable to cope without her, already. It was a strangely cheering thought, and she headed back to the stairs. But before she could take the first step, a huge clatter from overhead was succeeded by what sounded like a cry of pain.

A voice. It sounded very like a human voice, or that of an animal that counterfeited human voices exceptionally well. An adult male voice.

She could run down to the phone, but instead she ran back until she was standing beneath the ceiling and shouted, 'Who's there?' Instead of fear, she felt a sudden and growing outrage that somebody was in her house, ruining her sleep and her nerves. That somebody needed to know who he was dealing with. He needed to know that she was furiously angry with him.

There was no reply, so she shouted again. 'Who's there? Answer me or I go straight to the police.'

Again, silence. The clatter and cry had been accompanied, now she thought about it, by a huge thud. Perhaps whoever it was was hurt. Or perhaps he was lying in wait for her, and when she went downstairs he'd creep out, find her and clobber her.

She had to call the police. It was the only option. Whoever it was had no business there – probably just some old tramp with nowhere else to shelter, but all the same, she wasn't the Salvation bloody Army, was she? There was a hostel in Bledburn, surely.

She was on her way to the stairs yet again when she was surprised by the unmistakable miaow of a cat. There was a *cat* up there! Was it possible that the cry had been of an animal? Sometimes she had heard cats making the most remarkable noises, like children crying. That was it. Relief showered down upon her, drenching her. It was just a silly cat, or cats. Maybe kittens.

They couldn't stay there – they'd starve. She would have to let them out.

She began a close examination of the landing, thinking as she did of Lawrence's assertion that he had never been in the attic. Well, clearly someone had, or how had the cat got up there? Perhaps the estate agent or the surveyor?

She pushed and thumped at the wood panelling until she felt something give beneath her hand and a section of wall was revealed to be a hidden door. It opened, without grinding or creaking, to reveal a small dark staircase. Even now, her heart was thumping wildly and she half-expected to be coshed by an unseen hand, but there was nothing looming overhead when she got to the top and peered ahead. It was too dark to see much, but a smoky grey cat ran over quickly and stood miaowing at her head with an air of righteous indignation.

'All right, kitty,' she said, lifting the animal down and letting him jump on to the landing. 'I expect you're starving, aren't you? Have you been mousing up here? Are there any more of you?'

She made a kissing noise with her lips, but no more cats appeared.

Now the attic was attained, she wanted to investigate. She went to get her phone and put on the torch app, returning to the attic. The cat bounded around her feet, still mewing, in a fury.

'I'll feed you in a moment,' Jenna promised, although

she didn't think she had anything a cat might be interested in. She'd have to nip to the shop for some tins, unless the remains of the Thai takeaway were acceptable.

She climbed the hidden stairs again and shone her torch into the big dark space.

'What the fuck?' she breathed, staggered by what met her eye. The wall in front of her was painted as intricately and beautifully as anything she had ever seen on her trips to Italy. But instead of cherubs and saints and churches the scenes were of local landmarks and people, the hills outside and the mineshaft, the high street and the working men's club. They were executed by the hand of a master, and Jenna could not do anything but haul herself up, into the attic to look more closely.

'Harville Charity' read the title of the closest panel, and on it were painted scenes of the Victorian bigwigs of the town cutting the ribbon in front of the old workhouse – now a sheltered housing development. All around the well-dressed, well-fed men in top hats were thin men, women and children holding up wooden soup bowls. Many of the men had coal-blackened faces along with crutches or bandaged heads, indicating that they were workers fallen on hard times. And the Harville version of charity had been to send them to the workhouse, where they would be separated from their wives and children and set to harsh, futile labour for the rest of their days.

Jenna brushed a tear from her eye at the image of the queue of hopeless, helpless people. She had studied local history at school, but care had been taken not to point any fingers at the Harvilles, even though it was open knowledge that they had never done a working man a favour in all their lives.

'Bledburn's Lost Heroes' was the next panel. It was a depiction of the famous Harville Pit disaster of 1869, when twenty-seven men were killed after a seam collapsed in on them. The bodies were brought up from the shaft, one by one, while weeping women and children were provided for and comforted by their fellows and neighbours. Meanwhile, in the distance, Harville Hall stood remote, no representative of the family to be seen amongst the mourners.

Fascinated, Jenna drew closer, shining her torch on every poignant detail. The people were tiny and cartoon-like and yet each possessed a three-dimensional humanity that shone from their expressions and stances. Who had done this work? Was it old? It didn't look in the least faded or timeworn. And the anti-Harville sentiment was an odd thing to find in Harville Hall itself.

'This is crazy,' she murmured to herself, shining her phone on the next panel, which showed the general strike of 1926. It was unfinished, and in front of it stood a legion of paint tins and a bucket of white spirit with brushes in it.

Her throat tightened with sudden fright and she wheeled around, shining the torch behind her.

'Oh fuck,' she whispered.

An indeterminate bundle under the opposite eave proved to be a sleeping bag and lying in the sleeping bag was a person.

Chapter Two

She could see it was a man, and she could see that his eyes were shut, scrunched up against the torchlight, but they didn't open. She moved the beam swiftly aside and went closer, to investigate. An open backpack lay next to his head, which was covered in a dishevelled mop of dark hair. He looked as if he'd never seen the sun, his blue-tinged pallor making his dark stubble stand out all the more. He had full, sensual lips that made him look sulky in sleep. Long eyelashes fluttered and shadowed his high cheekbones.

He could be very attractive with a bit of a makeover, Jenna thought. But what the hell was he doing here? And what would he do if he knew she'd found him?

She stepped back again, intent on finding her phone, but a peripheral glimpse of one of the paintings stopped her in her tracks. If this was her artist – and it surely must be, judging by the paint streaks on his fingers – then she wanted to know more about him.

She wanted to wake him, but she sensed that to shock him into consciousness might well be dangerous. She would go down, get her phone, and if he gave her any trouble at all she'd call 999. But with luck he would take it well and tell her about his painting. Already, a nebulous vision of sponsoring his first gallery show was developing in her brain. She was a professional talent-spotter, after all. OK, her field of expertise was music, but why not diversify into art? And such art! A hazy feeling of being in the presence of greatness had quickened her spirits and awakened that intangible sense of excitement she got when something special came to her notice. She'd had it with Warp and Weft, with Crew Two, with Sophie Cator. This could be her next big thing.

She went downstairs, got her phone and, in a flash of inspiration, picked up the cat, who was standing on a windowsill, howling at the birds in the garden. He could be deployed to wake up her mystery artist.

The cat seemed quite happy to be picked up and cradled in her arms, purring away as she ascended the stairs. At the door to the attic rooms, she popped him on to the floor and let him run up the stairs ahead of her. Whilst she made her way up, he padded over to the artist, as she had hoped he would, and sat down by his head to commence a volley of miaows.

She watched the artist's face move from one expression to another, then he spluttered as the cat waved his tail beneath his nose.

'Bo,' he muttered, still not quite awake. 'Fuck off, I'll feed you in a minute.' The stranger had a strong local accent so that 'Fuck off' sounded more like 'Fook off'. The richness of his accent made the swearing sound almost affectionate rather than hostile, the vowel luxuriously elongated.

The cat put its front paws on his shoulder and started to climb all over the sleeping bag. The man groaned, shifted position then reluctantly opened his eyes.

'What?' The light coming in from the open attic door was evidently a shock to him. He sat bolt upright and stared at Jenna, who stood by the open square, ready to make a speedy getaway if needed.

'Don't panic,' she said, quickly. 'It's OK.'

'Fuck!' he said forcefully, fighting his way out of the sleeping bag. He reached for the backpack, repeating the expletive. For someone who was clearly sleeping rough, his clothes were relatively clean and Jenna could see that there was plenty of power in the body beneath his cheap tracksuit.

'Fucking hell, Bowyer, leave it!' he scolded the cat, who was trying to leap inside the bag as he rummaged through it.

'Your cat's called Bowyer?' said Jenna, grasping at anything that might calm him down and make him think.

Stan Bowyer had been the leader of the local chapter of the mineworkers' union during the strike. Still a hero to many, he had thrown himself in front of a bus taking hired labour over the picket line and been killed.

The man looked up, his hand still in the bag.

'What about it?' he said, then he went back to rummaging.

He pulled out a penknife and a packet of chicken tikka pieces with a past-the-sell-by-date sticker on. He peeled the chicken packet open, flung it on the floor for the cat, then stood up, brandishing the penknife in front of him.

'I'm warning you,' he said. 'Don't come near. Don't get your phone out.'

'My dad worked with Stan Bowyer,' said Jenna. 'He used to come round our house when I was little.'

The man just stared, then said, 'Who the fuck are you?'

'Well, I might as well ask, who the fuck are you? And what the fuck are you doing in my house?'

For a moment, Jenna's native accent made a surprise reappearance.

'Your house?' The man narrowed his eyes. 'Are you a Harville?'

'No. Far from it. But this *is* my house. I bought it, fair and square. Nobody told me about the sitting tenant, though.'

'You've . . . He sold it? Shit!'

The man looked so utterly crestfallen that Jenna really couldn't be afraid of him. His eyes were enormous and a deep, velvet brown, like an orphan child in a sentimental Victorian painting.

'Yes. Harville Hall is mine, as of yesterday.'

'I never thought he'd sell up. The bastard. You're from round here then? Funny, I don't recognise you.'

'You've never watched *Talent Team* then?'

He laughed, not in mirth but in head-scratching bemusement.

'*Talent Team*? I've only been camping out up here a few weeks, not years. I've heard of that show all right. Everyone has. Christ, are you the girl that left town and became one of them judges on it? You're not—?'

'Jenna Myatt Diamond. At your service. Though I'm losing the Diamond.'

'Fucking hell, now I come to look at you – but you've always got ten tons of slap, and some blinging dress on, in that. Fuck me. Is this a dream, or what?'

'I've pinched myself more than a few times this morning, let me tell you. I buy an empty house, and what do I find in it but a resident artist? Did you paint all this?'

He nodded.

'It's amazing,' said Jenna. 'Look, would you mind putting down the knife? I'm no threat to you, I promise. But I'm very interested in your work.'

'Are you taking the piss?'

He sounded fierce, but he put the knife down, all the same.

'No, seriously. This is incredible. You've been to art college, I take it?'

'Have I fuck!'

'You were never taught?'

'I did GCSE art, but I never handed in my coursework folder, so I failed.'

'So how did you learn this technique?'

'Technique? I used to decorate the youth club walls. That's about it. Kept me out of trouble. For all of about five minutes.'

'Look. Do you want to come down? I haven't got anything in the way of food but I could take you out for brunch if you like. I've got toothpaste, and—'

'So have I. I'm not some kind of wild man. But I don't think so,' he said. 'I can't leave here.'

'Why not?'

'Because if I leave this house, I'm as good as dead.'

Jenna, who had been growing in confidence in her dealings with this unexpected guest, was reduced once more to heart-fluttering anxiety.

'What? Why?'

'People out to get me. Bad people, you dig?'

'People . . .are trying to *kill* you?'

'Yeah, if it comes to it. I'm in hiding.'

'But . . . well . . . surely, the police? Or someone ought to be dealing with these people?'

He laughed bitterly. 'You've been out of Bledburn a long time, haven't you? It isn't the police in charge of things round here. No jobs, no futures – everyone's a dopehead or a dope dealer and most are both. If I go to the police, I'm deader than dead and, besides, they'll have an easy arrest in me. They won't go looking for the real bad boys. They're scared to.'

'Surely not. It's their job.'

'I told you, love. This is Bledburn.'

'You make it sound like the wild frontier. And don't call me "love".'

'Look, it's rough around here. I know. And I haven't exactly been an angel myself, but I've tried to keep my head down and steer clear of the really bad stuff. Sometimes the really bad stuff comes and finds you, though. And that's what's happened to me.'

'I see.'

'You're going to call the Feds, aren't you?'

He bent again, as if about to retrieve his knife.

'No,' she said hurriedly. 'No, I'm not. Unless you persist in calling them "Feds", because it really irritates me. This is England, you know. Call them what they are. And I'd like to call you by your name. What is it?'

'I'm not telling you my name. But everyone calls me Leonardo.'

'How fitting.'

'Yeah, well, most people ask me if it's after the Ninja Turtle. Or DiCaprio. But it's after the artist.'

'I thought it might be. You have such a talent. You could make a name for yourself. Your own name, not someone else's.'

'In another life,' he said bleakly.

'Oh, there must be a way.'

'Trust me. There isn't.'

'How have you been living here? What have you been living on?' She looked around her. There were no signs of cooking apparatus, or supplies.

'I go out late at night to the supermarket, down the road, and bin-dive.'

'Bin-dive?'

'Yeah, you know. Look in the hoppers, for food that's been chucked. There's stacks of it. All still good. It's fucking criminal, really. People are going to food banks because they can't afford to eat.'

'Aren't you afraid you'll be seen?'

'I'm careful. Supermarket's got CCTV, but I know the blind spots. Anyway, I don't care for myself but Bowyer's got to eat. He's a good mouser, mind. This place was infested before we came on the scene.'

'He sounds like a handy housemate to have around.'

'He is. You should let him stay.'

'I should.'

There was a silence. Leonardo sat back down on his sleeping bag and buried his face in his drawn-up knees. He looked lost and hopeless and tired.

Jenna wanted to give him a hug.

He looked up.

'I could be out tonight,' he said. 'If you don't mind waiting till dark. I don't know where I'll go, but I'll have to think of something. Just please don't call the F . . . the cops.'

Before she could think, Jenna had said, 'Or you could stay here.'

He looked wary, as if he suspected a trap. 'Why would you offer that?'

'Because I want you to finish this.' She indicated the wall paintings. 'Because, whatever's happened in your life, you don't seem so bad to me. Because you've done nothing to harm me. Because this house is big, and it's years since I was in Bledburn, and I could do with the company. All sorts of reasons.'

He looked her over, quietly but intently.

'Give you one thing,' he said, 'you've got balls.'

'I'm not afraid of you.'

'I think I might be, a bit, of you,' he said, and the sudden smile was a glorious reward, lifting Jenna's heart.

'Good,' she said. 'Now I'm going to town to get breakfast for us. You stay put – I'm expecting a heating engineer in an hour or so. Get another hour's sleep – you look done in.'

'It's the high life does it,' he said deadpan.

When she came back an hour later, with coffee and pastries for him, green tea and miso soup for her, he was back in his sleeping bag, curled up like his cat, who lay with his head on Leonardo's chest.

Jenna had given the situation a lot of thought while she was out, and the blank, grey faces of Bledburn had seemed to endorse her decision. She couldn't throw this talented young man back out into the featureless, hopeless sprawl. It would consume him, devour him, and the world would never benefit from his undoubted talent.

She'd done the same for Deano.

Why couldn't this man be just as big, in his way?

Of course, whatever hot water he was in would have to be sorted out first, but with her legal team on his side, she was sure it could be arranged.

She was in an optimistic frame of mind as she set the paper bag down by his feet and patted his shoulder.

He kicked out and his hand went automatically for his knife.

She sprang back, rattled.

'It's me,' she cried. 'It's OK. Just me.'

He sat up, blinking into life, his expression haunted.

'Jesus,' he said. 'Don't do that. I could've killed you.'

'You're really scared, aren't you? Of being found?'

'So would you be,' he muttered, picking up the paper bag and peering in. 'What's this?'

'Coffee and a *pain au chocolat*.'

'A panner-what?'

'Try it. It's delicious.'

He looked suspicious but bit into the pastry, dropping flakes all over the sleeping bag.

'Thanks,' he said. 'Been a while since I had anything fresh-baked, like.'

'I've been thinking,' she said, and he grimaced as he chewed, as if he expected only bad news could come from thought.

'Don't look like that,' she said with a laugh. 'No, what it is, is that I've got this house, in serious need of repair, and you're knocking around here like a spare part, so . . .'

He swallowed. 'You're after a handyman?'

'A bit more than that. This is as much a creative project as it is a practical one.' She had a feeling she'd need to appeal to his artistic sensibility to get any honest work from him.

'A whatsit then? Interior designer?'

'Yes, that's it. A designer. I mean, I have ideas, but I'd really value your input.'

'You sound like the youth workers at the club,' he said. 'They were always *valuing my contribution*, trying to get me on community projects. Unpaid work, more like.'

'It wouldn't be unpaid,' said Jenna. 'I'll feed you and give you free lodging. And I'll put some capital behind your artistic career, if you'll commit to this.'

'You'll what?'

'I'm very excited by your work. I want to represent you.'

'Well,' he said dubiously, 'I could do with some new brushes, like. And that paint's almost done for. I can hardly pop down to Hobbycraft for more.'

'How long have you been here?'

''Bout six weeks,' he said, popping the lid off the coffee and taking a draught.

'Six weeks, shut up in here? I'd go mad.'

'Perhaps I have,' he said, with a disconcerting little smile. 'I'm your madman in the attic.'

'Do you know *Jane Eyre*?' asked Jenna, charmed by the reference.

'No. Friend of yours?'

She couldn't tell if he was joking or not, and something made her think he was teasing her, making her feel hot, and a bit cross.

'Six weeks ago was when I bought this place,' she remarked. 'Did you know it was up for sale?'

'No. Thought it was going to be left to rot. I was hoping I could stay here and become the town ghost.

Somebody would find my skeleton years later when they came to knock the place down, and perhaps a Harville might get done for my murder. That'd give my ghost a good laugh.'

'They wouldn't do that, would they? Knock it down, I mean. It's listed.'

'Who in their right mind would want to take on Harville Hall? You're from round here. You must know what they are.'

'I'm not interested in the Harvilles,' she said after a moment's pause, during which she thought how like Deano he sounded when he talked about them. A guilty memory of her fantasy about Lawrence Harville made her skin prickle. 'This house is my house now. I can do what I like with it. And you can help me turn it into something different. You can help me kick the Harvilles out, lock, stock and barrel.'

This had been the right tack to take, she saw. Leonardo brightened straight away, liking the idea.

'They must be sick as pigs about having to sell up,' he said, cheerfully, sitting up and running his hands through his overlong, unkempt hair.

Jenna shrugged. 'How did you manage to avoid the surveyor?' she asked.

'I know this place inside out. Kept a step ahead of him while he was poking about. Went into the garden for a bit. Came back in when he left.'

'You must have known somebody was interested in buying, then?'

'Didn't think it'd go through. There must be a hundred things wrong with this place. Like I said, who in their right mind?'

'Perhaps I'm not in my right mind,' said Jenna.

Leonardo drank his coffee, his brown eyes fixed upon her.

'You look all right to me,' he said, once he'd swallowed, and she felt that heat and prickle again.

Leonardo, for all his show of wilful ignorance, was clearly bright and articulate, and there was something of swagger about him, something of charisma. The same things Deano had had, and squandered.

It made him strangely dangerous. Not in the knife-wielding, killing way, but in another way she didn't really want to think about. Dangerous to her defences.

The moment was interrupted by a hammering on the door.

'Fuck,' said Leonardo, reflexively curling his fingers around his knife.

'It'll be the heating engineer,' said Jenna, after an heroic effort to return her thoughts to the earthbound and practical. 'Don't worry. I'll let him in. And just think – you'll be able to have a bath. You must be desperate for one. I know I am.'

She let herself out of the attic, leaving Leonardo to restore the hatch.

She became so engrossed in watching the engineer at work and listening to his verdict on what else needed to be done and how much it would cost that she quite forgot she had arranged to meet Lawrence Harville for lunch.

His knock at the door almost made her react as Leonardo had done – with fear and hostility.

'Oh,' she exclaimed to the boiler man. 'I forgot. I have to go out for an hour or so. Are you OK here on your own?'

'Fine,' he said. 'I've got another couple of hours' work at least. I should think I'll still be here when you get back.'

'Good. See you later.'

She opened the door to Lawrence Harville, ashamed of her unprimped state. Jeans, cashmere hoody, messy topknot, flipflops. Still, it would save her being recognised by too many rubberneckers.

'The state of me,' she said apologetically, looking a suited and booted Lawrence up and down. 'I've been playing heating engineer's mate this morning. Got carried away with it all and forgot we were going out. If you'll give me a minute I can change . . .'

'Not necessary. You look lovely,' he said gallantly. She noticed he held a tissue-wrapped bouquet in one hand, which he now proffered. 'I thought these might go nicely in your living room. Or wherever.'

'Oh, peonies and sweet peas, that's kind of you. I'll put them in water. Now I've got some.'

She stuck them in a bucket, which was the nearest thing she currently had to a vase, decided against putting on her raincoat since the skies were looking clear, and dashed out of the house.

What would Harville think if he knew the Hall had had a house guest for the last six weeks? Of course, he hadn't been living there, so he would never have noticed. All the same, it might give him the creeps, especially if he knew that his attic-dweller was no great fan of the Harvilles.

'How's it going?' asked Lawrence, steering his expensive car out of its parking space and towards the outskirts of the town. 'I hope the thunder didn't keep you awake. Not the ideal place to spend that kind of night, I must admit.'

'I was in two minds about keeping it on,' Jenna confessed. 'It's so huge and dark and lonely. I was considering putting it back on the market at three this morning.'

'Really?' His quizzical look emphasised the crinkles in the corner of his bright blue eyes. 'And now?'

'Oh, you can't make decisions like that at 3 a.m.,' she said. 'Everything looks different in daylight.'

'It does, of course. So what are your plans for the place?'

Along the ring road, then the highway out of town, they talked of stripping walls, knocking through, exposing floorboards, replastering and architraves, until they arrived in an outlying village in the foothills of the Peaks, where there was an attractive half-timbered pub.

'I don't mean to sound rude,' said Lawrence, once they had ordered, 'but you can't possibly run your career out of Bledburn, can you? It's a London/LA/New York kind of thing, surely.'

'I'm taking a year off,' she said. 'For personal reasons.'

'Ah,' he said delicately. 'Personal reasons. Must be awful to have your business broadcast in all the media. Of course, as a Harville, I'm no stranger to scandal, but this seems much too invasive somehow.'

'If you want the inside track on why Deano I and split up . . .' said Jenna.

'God, no. Of course not. What do you take me for?'

'No, I wasn't going to bite your head off. I don't think you're trying to pry at all. I was actually going to say that in some ways it might be a relief to talk about it, a bit. But I don't want to bore you.'

'Well, I'm told I'm a good listener,' said Harville, leaning forward.

Jenna had thought she wanted to unburden – just a

little, not a big emotional splurge, but suddenly the look in Harville's eyes silenced her.

I can't trust you, she thought.

'Oh, no,' she said with an embarrassed laugh. 'I'm sorry. It's all very boring and I mustn't. I've promised myself I'll look to the future. Let's drink to it, shall we?'

They clinked glasses of sparkling water.

'The future,' said Harville. 'Is it wrong of me to mention that I've always been a huge fan of Deano Diamond? His first album knocked my socks off.'

'It's a great album,' acknowledged Jenna.

'And it would never have been made without you. You're something of a national treasure, to my mind.'

'Oh God, what a thing to be accused of.' Jenna laughed, slightly appalled. 'I'm no more than a talent-spotter, honestly.'

'Of course, the old man disapproved. I had to listen with earphones on, or there was a risk the CD would find its way into the rubbish. He didn't like some of the songs he wrote that touched upon, well, Bledburn affairs.'

'Deano was a firebrand in those days. He's much less political now. Contributes a lot to the Colombian economy, though.' She couldn't help the bitchy remark, which caused Lawrence to raise his eyebrows high.

'Ah,' he said. 'Yes, he does seem to have mellowed. Musically speaking, I mean. That last album . . .'

Jenna shook her head. 'I advised him against all that grand operatic stuff. So self-indulgent. But he's not half the force he used to be.'

'Creativity can't always be commercial,' said Lawrence, an insight she had not expected from him.

'No, you're quite right,' she said, examining him more

closely. He was so well kept, so impeccable, so perfectly suave. That fantasy she had had seemed out of place, now. He was too perfect for passion. 'But it wasn't that. I know all artists need to explore and experiment. But he's getting stale. And bombastic.'

'I suppose you won't be working with him now?'

'I'm not ruling it out. I'll see how I feel in a year. Of course, it will depend on him, too.'

'Can a business like yours survive a sabbatical? I mean, it all rather depends on your being in touch with what's hot and what's not, doesn't it?'

He was perceptive, she'd give him that. And he sounded genuinely interested in her. Jenna began to warm to him again.

'Yes,' she agreed. 'You know, I'm perfectly prepared to go back to the office in a year from now and be told that all my clients have defected and someone younger and fiercer and more fashionable has taken my seat on *Talent Team*. It would happen sooner or later anyway – that's the way of this world. I've got a great guy covering my role, but he doesn't have my name . . .' She turned up her palms. 'Oh well. A part of me thinks that it would be good for me to move on from all that. There's more to life, I think. I just need to get used to the real world and I might find out what it is.'

'You're tired of living your life in the public eye?'

'Perhaps.'

'Well, Bledburn's the place to be in that case,' he said, with a smile. 'The public eye rarely comes to visit.'

'And so you're moving to Nottingham. Is that for work? What do you do?'

'Property,' he said, but he didn't seem keen to elaborate

and his face relaxed when the waiter appeared with large plates of seafood salad for them both. 'So, tell me about LA. You must have a few tales up your sleeve about life in the city of angels.'

She did indeed, and she told them with relish, so that two hours slipped by easily and without any further thought of the sexy stranger in her attic.

She remembered him, though, on the drive back when they passed a retail park just off the ring road.

'Oh. Would it be a real pain if I asked you to drop me off at this shopping centre? I want to go to Hobbycraft.'

'Hobbycraft?'

'For paints and crafty bits and pieces,' she said, as Lawrence turned on to the slip road.

'Wouldn't a DIY store be more appropriate?'

'For the house, yes. I just thought I might get into painting. I've never had time for that kind of thing, till now.'

'Of course. Perhaps you can quit showbiz and become a famous artist instead.'

She laughed. 'It's that easy, isn't it?'

He accompanied her round the store as she filled her trolley with artists' materials. Going shopping in non-designer shops was something Jenna hadn't done in years. She had assistants to do all that kind of thing for her, usually. She enjoyed the novelty of pushing the trolley and choosing all the different pots and tins. But it was a little nerve-racking to be doing something for Leonardo while Lawrence stood by and watched her. It was as if she was giving him away.

She almost asked him if he could take her to the super-market too, but then thought that might be stretching a first date too far. She'd run into town herself later on and get some food in. The new range would be delivered tomorrow and she'd be able to cook properly. When had she last done that? Until then, it would be cold cuts from the deli counter and perhaps a bottle of wine. Wine glasses.

Her mental shopping list took her all the way back home.

'You're quiet,' commented Lawrence, parking outside the house.

'Sorry. Got a lot of planning to do and it's on my mind – about the renovation. Thank you for a lovely lunch.'

'It was a pleasure. I don't suppose there's any chance of a coffee?'

Jenna laughed, but she had no intention of inviting Lawrence inside, not while Leonardo lurked in the attic. Thank goodness for watertight excuses.

'No chance at all – I don't even have a kettle. I'm afraid the boiler man is still working on the hot water so the mains is probably off. Another time, perhaps.'

He nodded gravely. 'Another time. Yes. Well, thank you for the best company I've had in ages. We must do it again, soon.'

'Yes, we must.'

He was leaning over towards her. A waft of his expensive aftershave drifted up her nose, delighting her olfactory nerves. She reciprocated, bending towards him until their lips brushed, just lightly enough to be polite, just firmly enough to mean business.

She got out before he could make another move, which seemed very likely.

'I'll call you,' she said.

'You do that.'

He didn't drive away immediately but sat in the car while she hurried up the steps and into the house. From the drawing room window she saw him, still there. He was texting somebody, by the looks of things.

The heating engineer came out to get something from his van, and this seemed to spur Lawrence into action. He pulled away, waving a hand out of the window before he turned out of the driveway.

'All done,' chirped the engineer from the hallway.

'Oh, really? We have hot water, then?'

'Hot, cold, as much as you can handle,' he said.

'Fantastic. Thank you. I've got your invoice – I'll have the money transferred this afternoon.'

'That's what I like to hear. Good luck with this place.' He looked around as if he didn't envy her her new home. 'I can recommend a good firm of builders if you aren't fixed up yet.'

'Oh, thank you, but I think I'll be fine. I'll give you a call if I change my mind, though.'

The engineer hefted his toolbox through the front door and left Jenna alone in the house.

Except she wasn't.

She wanted a bath, but the idea of having one with Leonardo treading the boards above her was too weird. She decided to go up and give him the painting materials and take things from there.

He was painting when she entered the attic, Bowyer the cat curled up on the sleeping bag at his feet.

'I've been to Hobbycraft,' she said, putting the bag down before hauling herself up through the hatch.

'No shit?' he said, turning round and pouncing on the offerings as if he had been Bowyer with a mouse. 'Fucking

A,' he said, peering inside. 'I'm right down to my last few drops.'

'Well, now you're restocked,' she said.

'I'm starving,' he said. 'You didn't go to Tesco on your travels, did you?'

'Sorry, not yet. I'm going to have a bath then head into town to get some food. Don't you have anything to eat?'

'Some stale custard creams and a tin of cold baked beans,' he said. 'It'll do. I was hoping for some fruit and veg, though, before I get scurvy.'

'I'll bring you fruit,' she promised. 'And, once I'm out of the bath, it's all yours.'

'Right. Can I borrow your shampoo?'

She held her breath for a moment. She bought the most expensive beauty products available and she never shared.

'OK,' she said, after a beat. 'I'll leave you to it, then, shall I? You look as if you've got the muse for company anyway.'

'And the mews,' he said, looking down at Bowyer.

Hot water was bliss, and so was feeling properly clean after a day of roughing it. She dressed, casually again, and left for town, shouting up to Leonardo before she went.

The Bledburn branch of Marks and Spencer was small, but probably the only 'nice' shop in town: one of very few that didn't have windows either blacked out or plastered in massive sale signs.

She thought, as she walked around the grocery aisles looking for picnicky yet healthy foods, about Lawrence and Leonardo. Lawrence Harville was personable, good company, handsome and wealthy but there was something about him that made her keep her distance. What was it? She simply couldn't put her finger on it.

On the other hand, Leonardo was terrible on paper – a foul-mouthed fugitive from the wrong side of the tracks, and yet she felt a faith in him, and a trust. She very much wanted him to succeed, and she wanted to be a part of his success. Life had dealt him a bad hand and she was in a position to slip him a few aces. These were strong feelings to be having about a man she had only just met.

Was it a post-traumatic thing? Stress-related?

As much as she told herself to step back, to keep him at arm's length, she found herself all too soon in the menswear section, buying him underwear and socks and some T-shirts and two pairs of jeans. She had to guess his size but he was about six feet tall and, somewhere inside that baggy, scraggy tracksuit, quite well built. It would be nice to see him clean and scrubbed and – oh, razors – shaved, in decent clothes. In fact, something at the back of her mind told her it would be more than nice.

Ugh, don't be a cougar! He's younger than you, late twenties at most.

There was no harm in aesthetic appreciation of a good-looking man, she told herself. As long as she didn't embarrass herself by blatantly ogling him.

'Is it Jenna Diamond?' An elderly lady in a headscarf touched her on the arm.

'Myatt. I don't go by Diamond any more.'

'Oh, no, sorry. It's a treat to see you back here in Bledburn. How's your mum?'

Jenna focused properly on the woman and saw a face that had often appeared over her garden fence when she was a girl.

'Auntie Jean!' she exclaimed. 'I didn't realise it was you. How are you?'

'Mustn't grumble,' she said. 'Mind, I'm not getting any younger and me arthritis has taken a turn. Got a new hip just last year.'

'Oh dear, I hope it's a good one.'

'Marvellous what they can do these days. Made of rubber, it is.'

'Mum's fine. And Dad. Enjoying the Spanish sunshine all year round.' She raised her voice a little; Auntie Jean (her long-time next-door neighbour, not her real aunt) struck her as a trifle hard of hearing. 'Are you still at Shelley Road?'

'I am. Got new windows and doors put in last month. The council are doing up the whole estate. Well, it's that or knock it down, isn't it? Ooh, the state of it now, love. You'd shake your head. You must come round for a cup of tea.'

'Yes, I will. And you'll have to come and visit me in my new house, once I've got it done up.'

'Where's that then? That new development out of town? Proper nice, those houses are. I've seen inside 'em. Our Michaela's husband did the electrics.'

'No, not there. Harville Hall.'

There was a silence.

'Say, what, dear? I'm a bit deaf, these days.'

Jenna said it more clearly, conscious of curious nudges and murmurs of recognition going on around her.

'What on earth are you living there for? You aren't one of them, are you?'

'I bought it.'

Auntie Jean shook her head. 'I don't know what the world's come to sometimes. Well, don't forget that cuppa. I must get on.'

And with that she moved away as fast as her arthritic knees could take her.

Jean's husband had left her, when he couldn't find work after the pit shut. He went to Manchester, looking for something, anything. He didn't find work, but he did find another woman. Jenna remembered endless cups of very sweet tea in the back kitchen, Jean sobbing all over her mother then putting on lippy and going up the Mecca for bingo.

She hadn't told her parents about buying Harville Hall because at the back of her mind she knew that it made her, in some obscure fashion, a traitor. As for lunching with Lawrence of that ilk, it would be considered completely beyond the pale.

What was she thinking?

She went to the counter, so lost in thought that she had to be told twice how much she owed. The checkout operator clearly recognised her, but didn't say anything, to her relief.

Back at the Hall, Leonardo was still in the bath. She could hear the splosh of water and him singing, rather well, an old Robbie Williams number. Good old Robbie, she thought. Perhaps she should look him up?

She put the bags of clothes down and knocked on the door.

'I've been shopping,' she said. 'There are some new clothes for you in the hall, if you want to change.'

Silence followed, then the thumping plunge of a substantially sized man standing up in the bath.

'What the fuck are you buying me clothes for?' he said.

'That tracksuit was hurting my eyes,' she replied primly. 'Up to you. But they're there if you want them. I'll be downstairs. I've got a bottle of wine if you fancy a glass.'

She ran downstairs before he could object to anything else. She knew the local men were prickly buggers when you tried to offer them anything they might construe as charity. It seemed Leonardo had inherited that tendency. But how the hell was he going to buy anything for himself? He would just have to wear it. Literally.

She poured herself a glass of Merlot and she was sitting on the broad windowsill, sipping it and looking out into the weedy front garden, when Leonardo came into the room.

She almost double-took.

Jesus, he scrubbed up well. He scrubbed up a lot more than well.

His hair shone like polished conkers, matching his melting eyes. She wanted to go over and bury her nose in it, knowing it would smell divinely of her expensive shampoo. But that wasn't all she wanted to do. His face, now clean and shaved, seemed to actually *shine*. It was pale but as full-lipped and high-cheekboned as some exotic, angelic creature painted by a Renaissance master. He reminded her of a portrait she'd seen by Pietro Perugino – an older version of that melancholy-eyed young man.

But he was taller, and broader, and undoubtedly fully developed, and she found herself transfixed by his forearms, sinewy and powerful – one of them sporting an amateurish tattoo that she couldn't quite make out from this distance.

The clothes fitted well, having that tell-tale recently unfolded look such new garments always did. He had not put any socks on, though, and stood in the doorway barefoot, gripping the top of the splintering frame so that she could see his long, surprisingly delicate fingers splayed across the peeled paintwork. His nails still bore little crescents of black deep down – paint, she supposed.

His stance was almost aggressively masculine, and she had to remember to breathe before saying, 'Help yourself to wine.'

'I'll do, then, will I?' he said, staying put for another moment.

She thought that he was displaying himself to her, but then she dismissed it. He was young and unearthly beautiful. What would he want with her?

'The clothes fit well,' was all she could come up with.

'Yeah. Not sure they're my style but . . .'

'What is your style?'

She smiled and he walked over to where the wine bottle stood on the floor with an empty glass beside it.

'Ghetto,' he said shortly, picking up the bottle. 'Not so fabulous.'

I don't know about that.

'I'm not sure if I like wine,' he said, sniffing at the bottle neck. 'Never had it before.'

'Never? Seriously?'

'Nope. I'm a superstrength lager man, myself. As long as it's on special.' He poured himself a glass. 'Gets you the most pissed for the cheapest price,' he elaborated, with a combative look in her direction.

He was trying to tell her who he was, she realised. He was giving her a get-out clause. *I am who I am. Take it or leave it.*

'Wine is nice. I don't usually indulge, but I can call this a housewarming, I suppose. Try it. Go on.'

'Why don't you?' he asked, filling his glass to the brim.

'Don't you like drinking?' He had to sip a bit off the top to prevent spilling it.

'I like it. I just try not to like it too much.'

She came over and sat on the mattress, hoping he would do the same.

He did.

'Oh yeah, you're into all that Hollywood shit, I suppose?' he said. 'Stupid diets and all that. Mountains of speed so you're never hungry.'

'I don't take drugs,' she said, primly. 'You see a lot of what they can do in my line.'

'My line too. Funny, that.' He sounded angry, but he mellowed a little in continuing. 'I'm with you, mind. Can't be arsed with 'em. They've got half the lads round here walking about like zombies. We don't need zombies round here. We're fucked enough as it is.'

He looked sad and haunted, more like the renaissance picture than ever.

'So, do you like it?' she asked, nodding at the wine glass.

'What? Oh. Yeah, it's all right. Reminds me of Purple Rain Mad Dog.'

'God, it's years since I tasted that!' Jenna laughed. 'Takes me back to my teenage days, sitting on the wall outside Boozemasters.'

'You used to do that, too? Half the lads from school still do. Fucking wasters.'

'It was the place to be. God knows why. A crappy old concrete shopping precinct that howled with wind in the winter and baked in the summer. We thought we were it, sitting there with our cider and cigs and a big old boombox playing The Prodigy.'

Leonardo laughed, genuinely rather than sarcastically for the first time, and the sound warmed Jenna all over.

'Seriously, you? I can't see it.'

'Why not? Am I so old and past it?'

'Not at all,' he said, and there was something in the way he said it that made Jenna look away so he couldn't see the heat rising to her cheeks.

'It was twenty years ago,' she said. 'A lot of water under that bridge since then.'

'I just meant that – you know – you're a TV personality and all that. You've got stylists and PAs and whatnot. But you used to pose around the shops just like the girls I were at school with. None of them went to Hollywood. A few in Holloway, though.'

'What about Mia?' She was looking at the bad tattoo on his forearm. 'Where did she go?'

He turned his arm inward, shielding the ink from her eyes.

She wished she hadn't said it. He was tense now, and defensive.

'If I knew that,' he said, his voice jagged, 'I wouldn't be here now.'

He downed the glass in one and started coughing.

'Fuck, it's stronger than you think, isn't it?'

She waited for him to catch a breath, then changed the subject.

'Someone must have taught you to paint.'

'I told you. I dropped out of GCSE Art. I taught myself. Bit of spray-can work at the youth club, some stuff I was made to do after I got into trouble with the law. There's a mural at one of the old people's homes that I did. Got in the local rag for that. But they had to mention I was doing it as community service.'

'What sort of trouble were you in?'

'Stupid stuff. Angry stupid. Getting into fights and whatnot. I've calmed down a lot now. Was thinking of going to night school, doing an arts foundation course. Oh well. Mind if I have another?'

'Help yourself. What sort of trouble are you in now?'

'I was fitted up. Walked into a house, bang, police raid, I'm found with drugs worth fifty thousand pounds in my backpack.'

'What?'

'It wasn't even my backpack.'

'Whose was it?'

'Mia's.'

'Oh.'

'But I got away, just legged it before they could cuff me. No way am I doing time for some other bastard.'

'If you didn't do it, can't you go to the police and tell them?'

'No way, they'll bang me up before I can say what's what. I've got form. That's why I was set up. I'm easy. I've got a guilty face as far as everyone round here's concerned. No questions asked.'

'But if you didn't—'

'Jenna,' he said, loudly and emphatically, and her name on his lips blew all her words out of her brain. 'I was caught with the stuff. That's what they call evidence. I've got a bad record and no fixed abode. I can say I wasn't there and I didn't know anything about it till my face turns blue. They'll still have me for it.'

'What about Mia?' she whispered.

'She didn't know any more than I did. She was looking after the backpack for a friend. Asked me to take it back to this bloke's flat while she went to the shops because it was too heavy to lug around.'

'Seems to me that Mia holds the key to all this. But you say she's gone missing?'

'I don't know where she is and I wouldn't have her dragged into it if I did. It's not her fault. Best we can all do is lie low and wait for the truth to come out.'

'If it ever does.'

'Someone stood to make a lot of money there, and they'll want to collect. With any luck they'll come out of the woodwork, make a mistake, get caught.'

'I want to look into it. It seems wrong that you're stuck in hiding while the real culprits are at large.'

'Jen, I really wouldn't. There are people in Bledburn now . . . Well, it's not like it were when you lived here, that's all. You don't want to know these people.'

'Don't worry, I'm not going to do anything risky. But I might ask a few questions, you know, discreetly.'

'You can't mention me. You can't draw attention. I'm not fuckin' joking.'

'All right.' He was shaking a little, and it made her want to touch him, soothe him. 'I'm sorry. I'll leave it. For now.'

'Look, thanks, all right,' he said, turning haunted eyes to her.

'It's OK,' she said.

'No, I really owe you, big time. Anyone else would have had the police in by now.'

'Well, I don't need the extra publicity. And besides, I believe you when you say you were set up. I believe you because I want to believe you, because it would hurt me to see your stunning talent taken away from the world and shut in prison.'

'Well, I do owe you, and I'll work on your house, do whatever you want, until it's paid off.'

'Whatever I want, eh?' Jenna topped up his glass, feeling that the wine was going to her head much too quickly. Why had she said that? It sounded as if she was propositioning him in a terribly sleazy way.

He didn't seem to take offence, though – in fact, he played along.

'Hmm, whatever you want,' he repeated. 'And I think you're a demanding woman.'

This was far too close to blatant flirtation for safety, and yet she couldn't stop herself.

'I'm not demanding,' she said. 'But I do have very high standards.'

'I don't get what I'm doing here then,' he said, but he held her eyes and she felt pinned down by him, the space between them thick with attraction.

If she wasn't careful she was going to . . .

'Mia is your girlfriend, then?' she said. Phew. Disaster averted.

He bit that pouty lower lip of his.

'Yeah,' he said. 'But we were going through a rocky patch. We were this close to calling it a day. She changed a lot over this past year. Keeping secrets from me. Going out all night and saying she'd passed out on a mate's couch. But I know she didn't.'

'Are you sure she wasn't involved with this drug thing?'

'She wouldn't stoop that low. I know her, Jen, she wouldn't.'

He looked down at his hands for a moment, and Jenna watched his expression travel through stages from dark to light until he met her eye with a cheeky glint and said,

'Anyway, as the smooth bastards in the flicks always say, enough about me. Let's talk about you.'

Jenna was still processing the fact that he'd called her *Jen*, something nobody had done in a long time. For years now it had been Jenna or Ms Diamond or Ma'am. Deano's pet name for her had been Dyno, short for Dynamo Diamond. It had pleased him – Deano and Dyno: the dream team. But lately it had been Jenna. Or 'you hard-faced bitch'.

'There's nothing to say about me,' she said nervously. 'It's all in the tabloids anyway.'

'I don't read that shit. And how can you say that? Fuck me. You and Deano Diamond are the only interesting people to come out of Bledburn, ever. You were held up to us at school as examples – the reasons why we should work hard and get our exams.'

'Deano dropped out at fifteen,' said Jenna, with a laugh. 'How ironic.'

'Ah, see, they never told us that. Propaganda.' Leonardo shook his head in disgust.

'Was Psycho Sanderson still teaching there when you went?'

Leonardo clapped his hands, accompanying the gesture with a long, low chuckle.

'Bullying knob that he is, yeah.'

'He was the reason Deano walked out. Called him a shirtlifter for coming into school with an earring.'

'Once a wanker,' said Leonardo, philosophically. 'He's part of the reason I left, too. Just couldn't stand the thought of looking at his face for one more day. But you did your GCSEs, yeah?'

'Yes, I stayed on. Went into the sixth form too, but

left when Deano's band started getting attention in the music press. Became their agent slash manager. The rest is history, yadda yadda.'

'So you were a kid, really. You must've been tough as nails, going into that business at that age.'

'I don't know. I had so much faith in Deano, I'd have fought lions to get him the recognition he deserved. I didn't really think about needing to be strong. I just did what I had to do.'

Leonardo nodded, looking impressed. 'You're a good person to have in a bloke's corner,' he said, then his smile took on a devilish hint. 'Are you in my corner? Nice and tight.'

It was the second time he'd given Jenna a frisson of excitement that came from low down between her thighs. *Dirty boy, you're trying it on with me.*

'I'm more than willing to represent you,' she said, trying to sound prim, but her mouth wouldn't harden enough and she knew she was breathing too fast. What the hell was wrong with her? This was worse than the time she'd met Madonna and her mind had gone a giddy blank.

'You can't exactly put my name in lights,' he pointed out. 'There's a warrant out for me. Hey, perhaps I can be like Banksy. Faceless ninja artist, putting my stamp on the world. I reckon I'd be good at that.'

'I reckon you would, too. Actually, that's a really good idea. I mean, a bit derivative, but I don't think Banksy has a copyright on anonymity. We'll have to give it some thought.'

'What I don't get,' he said, putting down his wine glass after a long swallow, 'is why you've come back here at all. I mean, you got out. Last I heard, you were on TV, every

Saturday night, making pots of dough. Who the fuck comes back to Bledburn? And why?'

'You know I'm divorcing Deano?'

Leonardo shook his head.

'Like I said, I'm not up with that kind of thing. And I've spent the last six weeks holed up here. So, what, broken heart? You're going to let some bloke ruin everything you've worked for?'

Jenna laughed sharply to hear Deano Diamond, the triple Grammy winner, described as 'some bloke', then she sobered.

'It isn't like that. I don't have a broken heart. Me and Deano – it hadn't been working for a while.'

Leonardo gave her a long look.

'Someone else?' he asked gently.

'For him. Someone – some*thing* too. Coke, mainly. Staying up all night, wanting to party, while I went to bed with a book and a couple of Advil. The writing was on the wall, really.'

Leonardo exhaled, never breaking eye contact with her.

'What a wanker,' he said, almost prayerfully. 'Leaving you to go to bed alone. He wants to see a fucking shrink.'

'Oh, he's got several of those,' said Jenna, but her cheerful tone was forced, and a huge, red danger alarm pulsed all over body.

'I'll bet. So you didn't have anyone else, then?'

Jenna shook her head. 'No time for any of that. Plenty of opportunity, but you know people are only trying to get you to bed so you'll give them something. A contract, a newspaper exclusive, a spot on the show. Fuck it, Leo, I'm so tired of it all. So, so tired.'

She put her glass down at her feet and laid her head on

her arms, which were crossed over her knees.

Saying the words had made her realise it, made her finally see that she couldn't carry on with the LA life.

'Hey.' His voice was a little breath, but so heavy with concern that she made no objection when he put his hand on her shoulder.

When she stayed put, the hand crept around the base of her neck, so his arm was around her. He was close, clean and fresh-smelling, warm and strong. She felt protected. How mad. How could she feel protected by this feral fugitive, years younger than her? Yet she did.

His fingers were firm on her shoulder while his thumb lightly stroked the base of her neck. It was very soothing, and very tender, and it made her see how long it was since anyone had performed a really caring gesture towards her.

'So you're a runaway, too,' he said.

She still sat slumped, head down.

'I guess I am,' she said, muffled but clear enough.

He bent and she felt his lips at her ear. He could do what he wanted. She had no strength to fight him off, even if she had wanted to.

'I think,' he said, 'it's time you were in bed.'

Oh God. Here it was. The seduction scene.

'Leonardo, I don't know . . .'

His hand tightened on her shoulder, fingertips digging in to her soft flesh.

'Fuck off!' he said. 'Do you think I'm trying to . . .? Jen, I'm thinking of you. You're knackered and you need to sleep. That wine's good stuff for insomnia. Even I might get a few hours kip tonight.'

She raised her head and cast bleary eyes in Leonardo's direction.

'I'm sorry,' she said. 'Of course I didn't think that. Why would I? You're young and good-looking, I'm a shrivelled old bag. I'm sorry.'

He looked so furious at that that she shrank away from him, but he reached out and held her face in his hands, his darkest of dark eyes boring down on her.

'Shut. Up,' he said fiercely. 'Don't you dare talk about yourself like that. D'you hear me?'

She swallowed and tried to nod. He dropped her face and stood up.

'Get to bed,' he said, and he stalked out of the room, stopping only to pick up an unopened pack of sausage rolls from the table.

Jenna did as she was told, but all the while she was undressing and brushing her teeth and taking out her contact lenses she felt this odd, hot, weak feeling, as if she were coming down with a virus.

'Perhaps I am,' she murmured, slipping under the covers. 'Perhaps I've caught something.'

Chapter Three

'Feeling better this morning?'

Leonardo looked over his shoulder at her. He was wearing the old hoodie, but only because he was painting and didn't care too much about ruining it, presumably.

'I've brought you breakfast,' she said, putting the Starbucks paper bag down beside him. 'Hopefully in a couple of days I won't have to do takeaways any more. They're starting to fit the kitchen today. So you'd best lie low till they're gone.'

'That's what I'm good at,' he said, leaning over to make the tiniest alteration to a brick red terrace of houses he was in the middle of depicting.

He put his brush in a jar and picked up the paper bag, taking it over to his sleeping bag.

'You didn't answer my question,' he said, looking hard at her. There was a smudge of blue paint on his cheekbone and his hair was mussed again, stubble dotting the lower portions of his face.

Jenna tried to banish the flip-flopping feeling she

got from looking at him. *Aesthetic appreciation is fine, Jen. Ogling is not.*

'I'm good, thanks. Slept well. You need an old shirt or something.'

He uncapped his coffee and gave it an appreciative sniff.

'Why?'

'To paint in a tracksuit seems all wrong somehow. You should have a great big smock and a floppy beret.'

Leonardo laughed. 'When I want to look like a tosser, I'll let you know.'

She walked over to the painting and inspected the progress he had made.

'This is just stunning,' she said. 'Their faces – each one of them is a person, not a lumpen crowd. All human life is here. You're very observant.'

'I watch people,' he admitted, blowing at the steam on his coffee. 'Always have done, since I were a scrap. People's faces are interesting, aren't they? They say a lot more than words do, half the time.'

'Yes,' said Jenna. 'You know, before I started work on *Talent Team*, we had a briefing on how to stay poker-faced during the acts. How not to give away what we were thinking. It's extraordinarily difficult.'

'I bet you got it, though.'

'I can do it when I'm watching a new act. Not so much in other circumstances, really. What made you such a watchful child?'

Leonardo had to put down his coffee, fearful of spilling it on Bowyer's fur and scalding him. He stroked the cat on his lap as he spoke.

'My mother. She said one thing and meant the other.

She did that a lot. It worried me, so I had to learn to watch her face, then I'd know what she meant.'

'How odd. Why was she like that?'

'Survival, I think. She had a rough life. I used to watch her telling the latest boyfriend what a big man he was, when really she meant he was a handy bastard and she was afraid of him. And she'd tell me off, in front of them, but she never meant it. She only did it because they wanted her to. Once I got that, I was less worried. I knew she still loved me, after all.'

A wave of sympathetic tenderness almost bowled Jenna over. She wanted to rush over to him and hold him, seeing the anxious child he must have been behind the swaggering young man.

'Oh,' she said. 'That must have been hard.'

He shrugged, tipped the cat off his lap and took a mouthful of coffee.

'Is she still around?' asked Jenna. 'Your mother?'

'She's still alive,' he said. 'I don't know about around. She's in and out of hospital a lot. Depression.'

'I'm sorry.'

He shrugged again. 'Not your fault,' he said shortly, rummaging in the paper bag for the egg muffin she'd brought. 'What about your folks? They left town, didn't they?'

'They're in Spain. Marbella.'

'Nice. You should go out there and pay them a visit.'

'Nah, I'm sick of the sun.'

He smiled crookedly. 'You came to the right place, then.'

They locked eyes for slightly too long, until Jenna's lips began to ache from holding the complicit smirk they shared.

'Right. Kitchen. I wish you could have helped me design it, but it's the one room I had to sort out before I moved in, so it's all ready to go. I'll be in all day, pretty much. I'll come up and make sure you're OK every couple of hours. By the way . . .'

'What?'

'What did you do about, you know, personal functions? While you were in hiding?'

'I can get in and out, you know. I used the lav, of course. What do you take me for?'

'Sorry. I just wondered . . .'

'Bowyer's a different matter, mind. Don't worry, I clean up after him.'

'Shall I take him down with me? Let him into the garden?'

'I don't know.' Leonardo tickled the cat's neck. 'He likes it up here with me. Probably a good thing to give him a bit of freedom, though. Let him see how he likes it out there and, if he doesn't get on with it, I'll have him back.'

Jenna let the cat out into the wilderness, which he seemed interested in exploring, then let the kitchen fitters in. She made tea for them in the drawing room, using a cheap kettle and mugs she'd picked up in the supermarket the day before, and watched them strip the old walls down and rip out the ancient pipes. The floor, with its original granite tiles, was staying, but everything else was leaky, broken or rotten and had to be replaced.

She took a quick break to go to the nearest corner shop and buy packaged sandwiches and bottles of water for herself and Leonardo, plus a tin of tuna for Bowyer. Bowyer, however, seemed more interested in self-catering: on her return, she found a dead mouse on the doorstep.

'He's a survivor,' said Leonardo, proudly, when she told him. 'Like me. How's your posh kitchen getting on?'

'Who said it was posh?'

'What, so you're getting a Baby Belling and some knock-off cupboards with doors that don't shut properly? Come off it, Jen. I bet it's all *Grand Designs*.'

'What's *Grand Designs*?'

'TV programme. You've been away a long time, haven't you?' He adopted a faux-plummy voice and said, 'Jenna is now the proud owner of a space that can be used for so much more than cooking. And this is how good design can influence good living.'

She laughed. 'Well, it's probably a bit posh. But I wanted it to be in keeping with the original, a proper old country house kitchen. Not in an over-styled way – just a big, warm, comfortable, working room.'

'So are you getting people in to do every room?'

She thought about this.

'To be honest, I was wondering if we could do it ourselves. Once the kitchen's in, we're fine. There's an electrician down there sorting out new wiring for the downstairs rooms. Upstairs can come when we get to it. It's just a case of some sanding, painting, plastering. Have you ever done anything like that?'

'No,' said Leonardo. 'Well, except painting.' He bent his head towards his fresco.

'I think we could do it, though. I've been looking forward to it. Getting my hands dirty – honest, hard work. Doing something real.'

'Hey, my painting's real.'

'Of course. It's my line of business I'm not sure about.' He smiled.

'Yeah, why not?' he said. 'Let's work up a sweat.' He tore into his chicken sandwich and she felt that weak, virusy thing again. Suddenly her tuna on granary didn't hold much appeal.

Once the fitters had left for the evening, leaving a room stripped bare and thick with choking dust, she alerted Leonardo and dialled up a takeaway. Bledburn was not like LA, where you could have perfectly balanced, body-respecting meals delivered from a different place every day. No, here the choice was: pizza, curry, Thai. At Leonardo's request, she ordered curry.

'I don't know if I dare eat this,' said Jenna, looking bleakly at the array of foil trays oozing brightly coloured oils from between the edges of their cardboard lids. 'My system might go into shock. I've lived on alfalfa sprouts and tofu for the last five years.'

'Get it down your neck,' said Leonardo with scorn. 'I don't even know what Alf whatsisname is. A decent biryani never did anyone any harm.'

She watched with some admiration as he tore into a doughy pouch of naan bread. He had an unabashed appetite for life that made her wonder if she'd ever had anything similar. She had, of course, she had. She remembered the nights in that tiny little Italian restaurant in the early days of her relationship with Deano – garlic bread, pasta of the day, tricoloured ice-cream sundaes. What a glamorous treat it had all seemed; real grown-up, adult living. Was it still there? She tried to remember what it was called – Semifreddo's. That was it.

'How long since you had a curry?' she asked him.

'Too fucking long,' he replied through a mouthful of chicken madras. 'Did you order any beer?'

'No, they wouldn't deliver alcohol. I did buy you a couple of bottles at the shop earlier, though. They're not very cold, I'm afraid. Once the kitchen's done . . .'

She reached into the box of provisions in the corner of the room and handed him a beer to go with his bottle of water.

'Not having one yourself?'

'Beer? Oh no. I couldn't.'

'Of course you could. Have the other one. I don't like drinking alone. One must follow the rules of etiquette, you know.' He was speaking in his fakey posh voice again.

Jenna had misgivings about letting such a gaseous liquid into her body, but she comforted herself that it was just the one, just this once. In future she'd remember not to buy the stuff.

'So, what are you thinking of doing in this room?' he asked, looking around at the peeling plaster and general air of mildewed woe that surrounded them.

They talked easily and with enthusiasm of different furnishing styles, floorings, paint versus wallpaper, lighting options, until the last grain of spice-drenched rice was disposed of. They had laughed at each other's jokes, mirrored each other's body language, and Jenna had found herself twirling strands of her hair far more often than she was accustomed to.

'Where are you going to sleep?' he asked, once the topic was exhausted. 'Upstairs, I suppose?'

'Eventually. I think I'll just camp out in whichever room is warmest until I get round to the upper storey. It's almost midsummer.'

'The nights will be drawing in,' said Leonardo, giving

her a strange look. 'Long, lonely nights. Don't you miss him?'

'Who?'

'Diamond.'

That was the sixty-million-dollar question. Did she?

'I miss what we once had,' she said, putting aside her empty beer can.

'And what was that?'

She had to think.

'When it was just us. When we could just spend time fooling around, and laughing, and talking about rubbish. When we used to spend whole days in bed. When we thought we were soulmates and nothing would ever come between us.'

'And when was that?'

She exhaled heavily.

'Fifteen years ago. Then our careers started to take off and nothing was ever the same again. We were pulled in every direction, every waking minute of our lives. It changed us. We became different people.'

Leonardo grimaced. 'Life'll do that to you. So, how are you different now, compared to what you were like at twenty-odd?'

'I've lost my starry eyes. I've seen what's in the stars, and it isn't that great.'

'Wow, that's poetic.' Leonardo nodded sagely. 'So you used to be romantic, and now you're not?'

'I don't know. Perhaps I could be again . . .' She floundered. 'This is why I'm here, Leo. I'm trying to find what I am, what I want, after it's been worn away by all the glitter.'

'Terrible stuff, glitter,' said Leonardo. 'Gets everywhere.'

She laughed.

'It's corrosive,' she said, suddenly serious. 'Nobody gets that, until it's too late. But don't listen to me. I'm rambling.'

There was a silence, strangely awkward.

'You're lonely,' said Leonardo.

'Yes. But I'm used to it now.'

'You shouldn't have to be. Someone like you.'

He had a look in his eyes that liquefied her.

'Someone like me?' she whispered. 'What's that?'

He cupped her cheek in one hand and she let out a breath, almost of relief. Yes, he was touching her. Yes, now she realised she had wanted him to all day.

'Gorgeous,' he said. 'And amazing.'

'Oh, don't,' she said with a laugh of terror. This had to stop, didn't it? This couldn't happen, could it?

'I mean it,' he said. 'You've made something of your life. You're special. If I were Deano Diamond . . .' He looked away, as if he could scarcely believe what he knew of that individual.

'Leo . . .'

'Hush. When was the last time you were kissed? Properly, I mean.'

'I can't remember.'

'That's a fucking disgrace.'

There was a moment that seemed to stretch forever, when his pupils were giant in his eyes and all Jenna could think was *Go on, then, if you're going to. Kiss me!*

He tightened his hold on her face and tilted it up to him before ducking down to meet her lips with his.

How can it hurt? It's just a kiss. It's all right to kiss.

It was more than all right. Leonardo knew how to do it. Just the touch of his skin was electric, and when he brought his mouth to bear on her she thought she might swoon away into a froth of desire on the mattress. How had she forgotten the elemental pleasure of a warm, male, human body close to hers? She pushed her lips to his and gave him tacit permission to keep the pressure up, to increase it if need be.

She placed her hand on his upper arm, making it clear that she wanted this togetherness. Her fingers curled tightly against his solid muscle, just about where his bad tattoo was. He, in his turn, circled her waist, keeping her pressed into him.

His lips were fuller and more satisfying that Deano's, which were thin and hard. There was a luscious softness to them that made the firmness of his kiss paradoxical and perfect. She could never tire of this feeling. It was better than wine and better than money and better than fame. If he carried on kissing her, she could be made to agree to anything.

What kind of woman did that make her?

She was slightly horrified with herself, but it still didn't induce her to give up this glorious much-missed feeling, which was now spreading through her body like liquid flame.

And why not? Her inner voice still tormented her with apprehensions of how wrong this was. *Don't I deserve a little human comfort, a little pleasure? After everything I've been through?*

The kisses were feverish now, hungry and all-consuming. Leo's fingers raked through her hair, pulled at it, setting off little sparks in her scalp. He pressed and pinched and gripped her until they fell, sideways on, flat to the mattress.

Now their legs rubbed and wrapped around each other and they were close as could be, no space between them for so much as a sliver of card. Jenna felt her chin and lower face grow slippery and a little raw from his evening stubble. His tongue broke through and she accepted the surrender with enthusiasm, pushing her own back at him.

The more they took from each other, it seemed, the more they wanted. Each new act of wantonness opened up the possibility of more, an endless vista of sensual pleasures. She wanted him in her, her in him. While they were locked together like this, nothing else mattered.

His hands travelled hungrily over her upper body, and when they found her breasts she did nothing to repel them. Instead she let him cup her sweater-clad curves, enjoying the slight but delicious friction of the soft wool against her nipples.

She, for her part, tried to slip her hands inside his T-shirt, loving the flat firm warmth of what she found inside. His muscles moved against her palm and she felt them directing their efforts towards her, towards getting her and having her.

His denim-covered knee slid up between her thighs and nudged them apart.

They were panting now, heavy with lust and beginning to sweat.

Snogging like a pair of teenagers at the school disco. He'll give me a love bite next. Oh, but how could I have forgotten how good it feels?

And now a hand inside her jumper, reaching for her bra, pulling down the cup on one side. Her nipple seemed to bloom against his touch, engorging itself to fill the space between his finger and thumb. Her knickers were freshly soaked, her sex alive and vibrating with sensation.

Her phone rang.

'Leave it,' gasped Leonardo.

But the years had conditioned Jenna to be on alert for every call, because the next call could change the game again. Reflexively, she slid out from underneath Leonardo and snatched up her phone in shaking fingers.

It was Lawrence Harville.

'Jenna, hi, I was just passing. Wondered if you'd fancy a drink?'

'Just passing? Where are you?'

'I'm parked at the end of your street. What do you say? There's a decent place about five minutes walk from the house. Nothing fancy, but it's snug and serves good beer, with minimal tracksuited rowdies.'

She glanced over at Leonardo. Her tracksuited rowdy, albeit minus the tracksuit this evening.

He looked immortally pissed off.

Immortally pissed off and at least half a dozen years *younger than her.*

This was madness. She should get her wits together and act her age. Her head was all over the place, what with the divorce and the sabbatical. Now was hardly the time to go leaping into intense flings with artistic fugitives from the wrong side of the tracks.

But I want to, whispered her disloyal desires.

Well, you can't, retorted what she thought of as her rationality.

'I don't know,' she said to Lawrence. 'I've had a takeaway curry and it's made me rather sleepy.'

'Well, how about I come in for a snifter? Then you don't have to make an effort.'

'No, no.' *God, no.* Looking at Leonardo with an apologetic expression she hoped might be interpreted as 'Sorry, business, can't get out of it', she spoke into the phone. 'It's fine. I'll just get my bag and put on a bit of lippy and I'll be with you.'

'Excellent! Ciao.'

'Hot date?' enquired Leonardo with hostile sarcasm, as she took out her mirror compact and began applying lipstick.

'I'm sorry. I've got to go out. I won't be long. You might as well go up to bed.'

'Up to my sleeping bag in the attic, out of your way.'

She tried to sound soothing. 'It's not forever. Look, I'm sorry. I shouldn't have . . .'

'Right. Of course. Moment of madness, eh?'

He looked as if he might smoulder into a pile of ashes.

'No, not that – it was lovely, you're lovely, but . . . The timing, it's all wrong. Look, I'm sorry, I have to go.'

She virtually ran out into the hall.

'I'll wait up for you,' Leonardo called. 'I'm not going anywhere.'

Shit, she thought, crunching along the gravel to the front gates, her head apparently broken into tiny pieces. *What the hell am I going to do? Should I throw him out? But I can't throw him out. Back to London, then. Sell the house. But where will he go? Why should it be my problem? It wasn't me that got myself mixed up in a load of estate gangland rubbish. But I can't just throw him to the wolves! I care about him.*

These thoughts carried her up the street to the corner where Lawrence was parked.

'Goodness, penny for them,' he said, opening the car door and offering his arm.

He looked very eye-catching tonight, in a low-key pair of jeans, tweed jacket and open-necked blue linen shirt. Casually expensive and impeccably groomed. He smelled quite intoxicating too.

'Sorry?' She took his arm.

'I was watching you in the rear view mirror. Your face was like thunder. Are you all right?'

'Oh. Yes. Fine. Bit tired, you know. It's been a dusty day.'

'Dusty?'

'The kitchen fitters. Stripped everything down and left clouds and clouds of dust.'

'Ah. You'll be thirsty, then. Here we are.'

It was a street corner pub, left in quaint pre-war condition, with an old-fashioned snug and an old-fashioned clientele, some of whom still wore flat caps in a non-ironic manner.

'Ah, there used to be one of these on nearly every street,' remarked Jenna, accompanying Lawrence to the bar.

'Yes, I remember. Twenty years ago. Now they're all converted into flats while big flat-roofed bunkers serve the estates with Sky football and cheap cider.'

'Oh, they were there all along,' reminisced Jenna. 'The Lord Harville got vandalised, and boarded up though. Is that still there?'

'I think it may have changed its name,' said Lawrence uncomfortably. 'What are you having?'

'Best stick to still water, thank you. My head feels thick as treacle.'

Not just her head, either. Between her legs she still felt

a kind of erotic hangover, a heaviness that wouldn't lift. She could be lying on her mattress with Leonardo on top of her right now.

She shivered. It was a lucky escape, but it certainly didn't feel like one. It felt like a wrench.

She escaped to sit at a high-backed bench, attempting to get herself in the frame of mind for light chat with added flirtation.

Lawrence was a good-looking man. She watched his back and shoulders as he exchanged pleasantries with the barman, then her gaze drifted down to his bottom, half-covered by the tweed jacket, but not entirely. It was certainly squeezable.

God, Jenna, stop it! It's as if you've gone man-crazy after years of keeping this kind of thing down. You'll get yourself arrested.

He came and sat beside her, placing her mineral water on the beer mat while he took a sip of his own whisky and soda.

'Barman recognised you,' he said. 'Asked me what you were doing here.'

'And what did you tell him?'

'Told him I was your new business partner and we were starting a venture – Bledburn's very own Talent Team. Turns out he's a very skilled juggler and he wants to know if we'll put him on our books.'

'Oh, you rotten liar.'

'OK, I didn't tell him that. It's a fair question, though.'

'You know the answer. I'm on sabbatical. I need space. I can get it here.'

'Jenna, the only way you'll get space is if you take yourself to Cape Canaveral and buy yourself a rocket trip. Wherever you go, people will be curious. You're a household name, here and abroad.'

'People forget that kind of thing quickly enough, if they're allowed to. Otherwise those *Whatever Happened To . . .?* shows would never get made.'

'You really want to end up on one of those?'

Jenna shook her head. 'I don't know. That's the point, Lawrence. I don't know what I want.'

'Let me help you find out. I have a dozen sure-fire business ideas – all they need to get off the ground is a savvy partner and some capital. Why don't we put our heads together and see what we can come up with?'

Jenna stared at him.

'I don't believe it. You want to get your hands on my money. You've had what I paid for the house, but that wasn't good enough for you. Classy, Lawrence. Real classy.'

She pushed aside her glass and stormed out of the pub, Lawrence chasing her down the road with pleas for her to listen and not to misunderstand him.

But she left him behind and hailed the first taxi she saw, switching off her phone as she clambered into the passenger seat.

Back home, in the drawing room, Leonardo lay where she had left him, on his back on the mattress staring gloomily up at the ceiling.

He sat up when she came fully into the room and made to rise to his feet.

'You weren't long,' he said.

'No. Meeting wasn't worth going to,' she said briskly, letting her bag fall with a jink on to the floor. 'Yet another chancer after my money.'

There was a pause while Leonardo decided against standing and sat back on the mattress.

'Is that what you think of me?' he said.

She frowned in incomprehension.

'Of course not.'

'Right. Just you said "yet another". Thought you might include me in those.'

'Well, I don't. I've met a lot in my time, that's all.'

They held each other's eyes, neither one of them knowing how to break down the invisible wall that lay between them.

'Listen, Leo, I'm tired,' muttered Jenna, but there was no conviction in it.

'Do you want me to go?' asked Leonardo.

She couldn't answer, and so he did it for her.

'You don't want me to go,' he said. 'When we kissed, it was like unlocking the door of our old broom cupboard. Everything always fell out on top of you, all at once. That's what it was like, kissing you. Like you'd had all your . . . Fuck, this sounds stupid, but all your *passion* . . . shut up behind that door and when it was opened, blam! Drowned me in it.'

She looked away, burningly embarrassed. She had overwhelmed him. She imagined him in his tracksuit sitting on the wall by the supermarket, bragging to his mates. *She fucking couldn't get enough of it. She was desperate for it.*

'It's been a while,' she said coldly.

'Hey,' he said, holding out a hand that she didn't take. 'Don't be like that. Don't push me away. I felt the same, Jen. It was exactly the same for me. I've held so much back, these last few years. It was a relief, you know, to get some of it out. Come and sit down.'

'It's getting late—'

'Come. And sit. Down.'

She was startled by his commanding manner, just as she had been on the previous evening. It allowed her to stop resisting, to be docile and to do what he said – which was what she wanted anyway.

'Bossy bastard,' she grumped, but she was half-smiling as she gave him the corner of her eye.

'When I have to be,' he said. 'Which is quite a lot, with you, I think.'

She laughed at his pure effrontery.

'I'll have you know that *nobody* bosses me about, mister! Not if they want to keep their careers.'

'Yeah, well, that's your problem, isn't it? Used to being in control. Can't let go.'

'What are you *on* about?'

'Jen, you want to let go. You want to let the sexual woman out from behind the sharp business player. But you're scared. You've kept her behind bars for too long and you might find something out about yourself, something that might break up your perfect little image of yourself.'

'Oh, shut up! Are you some kind of bogus counsellor?'

'No, but I can offer you sex therapy.'

'Leo! This isn't funny.'

'I'm serious. Deadly fucking serious. You want space, you want peace, you want quiet, yeah, I can dig all that. But if you try telling me you don't also fancy a bloody good shag, you're a liar.'

His words, together with the lazy, low-toned, arrogant way in which he spoke them, were a shot right between the thighs.

He was uncannily right. She wanted nothing more

than to get him on top of her and have him ride her into the night until the sun came up and her body fell to pieces.

But if she was going to involve herself in his career, it couldn't work, could it?

'Think of it as a holiday fling,' he said, closer to her now. 'You've been lying in the sun all day and a sexy Spanish *hombre* has just turned up to slap on the suncream and show you what a good time really is, *señorita*.'

She laughed. 'Don't be ridiculous.' But his gravelly tones, combined with the heavy hand on her thigh weakened her conviction.

'Be honest, then,' he said. 'Admit you could do with it. Why is it so hard for you to be honest?'

'I am. I'm honest . . .' She floundered, all at sea, and every wave was Leonardo, coming for her, tilting her this way and that, capsizing her. 'I do want to. I just don't know if I should . . .'

'If you want to,' he said, 'you should.'

And that was that. Her token resistance was shot to shrapnel.

She let him wind her up in wiry arms and lay her down on the mattress while he planted his pelvis on top of hers and stopped up her mouth. It was something she couldn't resist, and that knowledge gave her mind permission not to fret or couch objections through the writhing and grabbing, the biting and sucking.

Sex could be this way – hungry, urgent, needy. Her hands got tangled in his clothes and she parted her thighs to let the unyielding rock of his erection sit comfortably in her apex. Elsewhere, their bodies bumped and crashed into each other, graceless in their lusty rush to have what they must.

Leonardo let her flail for a few minutes before taking both wrists and pinning them above her head, looking down at her from the greatest height he could achieve in a horizontal position.

'You're fighting me,' he said. 'Keep still. We don't need to tear each other to pieces.'

Jenna tried to catch her breath and work out what had come over her. She had been like a polecat, wild with need.

'You're stronger than me,' she said. 'It makes me want to try and overpower you.'

'Well, you can't. So don't try. Have you always been in control in bed?'

'Mostly.'

'Try something different. Lie back. Let me do the work.'

Let me do the work. What a blissfully calming concept.

Immediately she felt the worst of her tension dissolve and she knew that, if he let go of her wrists, she would keep them there. No need for pinning any more.

'All right,' she whispered. 'I'll try.'

'Good girl.'

The words made her bristle as much as they melted her. When had anyone called her a good girl, since her parents, years ago? If anyone had dared they would have been blasted out of her presence with a whole circus of fleas in their ear.

But when Leonardo said it, that was different.

He released her wrists and lowered himself gently to her face, kissing it all over, from her hairline to her jawbone, then moving down to her throat. The kisses were soft, butterfly rain, gentle teases. She almost wanted to snap at him to get on with it, but she stopped herself. She was going to let him do the work.

When he pushed his tongue, slowly and luxuriously, into her mouth, it was worth the wait. A moan filled the empty spaces between their oral duellists and she raised her spine, without knowing she was doing it, inviting him further in.

He pushed his hips down, keeping her in position – an unspoken rebuke. His tongue made its mastery clear at the same time, pushing further. He moved one hand back up to her wrists in warning whilst his other lifted her top clear of her breasts.

Her moans continued and she had to work very hard not to make a move of her own when he began running his finger along the scalloped lacy edge of her bra. It was such an obviously teasing gesture she felt he was testing her. But what was the test? Did he want her to react, to try and force him to go further? Or did he want her to submit and allow him to torment her in this way?

She felt that the latter was what he really wanted, but she was not at all sure her passivity could last much longer if he kept it up.

He carried on the stroking, one fingertip thrilling along the lace, never digging deeper, never uncovering her nipple. It felt huge now, straining at its restraining cup, bursting through the patterned fabric – as did its twin on the other side.

If only he'd let her mouth free, she might beg. She wanted to beg. She thought that what he really wanted was to know that she ached to disobey him and yet continued to obey. That was the payoff for him.

It was perverted and strange but, by God, it was turning

her on in a way she had never before experienced. She shimmied her hips in mute entreaty. He understood and chuckled into her helpless mouth. He plucked at the bra cup and brought his other hand down to deal with the other side.

He raised his head only to whisper, 'Don't you dare move,' before plunging his tongue back into the place it seemed to consider home – inside her mouth, silencing her.

Now both his thumbs had breached the border of the brassiere and they rubbed at her soft slopes underneath the lace. They wouldn't get close to her nipples, though, and she made a strangulated sound of frustration and tried to force them lower.

He removed his thumbs immediately and went back to pinning her wrists.

It was a punishment. She knew it, and she burned to protest, to demand of him whom he thought he was playing with, but still she kept herself in check.

She was more interested in what might happen next than in asserting herself. If this was a game, it was the most compelling – and arousing – one she had ever played.

He made her surrender to minutes more kissing whilst immobilised before he rewarded her with the return of his hands to her breasts.

'Are you going to behave yourself now?' he asked, his lips a millimetre from hers, his voice smoky as sin.

She didn't want to answer but, to her shame, she nodded and made a little 'hm' of acquiescence.

'Didn't catch that,' he taunted, letting his thumbs hover close enough to her bra for the fabric to catch against his skin.

Oh God, just rip it in half and do what you want.

'Yes,' she mewled, turning her face from him.

He pushed his lips into the hollow under her ear, kissing and licking it, then took the lobe into his mouth and sucked. 'Look at me,' he whispered, once she was good and wriggly, and sure that her knickers couldn't be any more soaked.

She could hardly bear to meet his eyes but somehow she did it.

'I know you,' he said. 'I know what you want. Is it this?'

Very gently, he lowered the cups of her bra until her fat, ripe nipples were exposed to the room.

'Um hmm,' she said. His eyes scorched her. He was in absolute seventh heaven, she could tell.

'Are you sure?'

'Please.' It was a whimper.

He smiled like the Cheshire Cat and dropped a smacking kiss on her lips.

'That's nice,' he said. 'I like to be asked properly.'

His thumb pads brushed the undersides of her breasts, massaging the tender skin, just close enough to her nipples to make them tingle with every sweep.

Again, the urge to get hold of him and make him hurry up, make him pinch her nipples, put them in his mouth, anything, was almost too strong to resist. She made fists with her hands and pushed them hard into the mattress. Her belly was flipping over and over and her sex was throbbing so hard she expected it to break into buzzing at any moment. Had it ever been like this with Deano? She couldn't remember. Surely she'd remember something like this?

But there was no room in her mind for anything but

the immediacy of her desire, and the way Leonardo was stoking it and stoking it until its flames practically licked the sky.

Speaking of licking . . . At last, at long and shuddering last, he bent his head and deposited a little steamy breath at the peak of each nipple.

Now, finally, she would get some satisfaction. Now it was coming. She squirmed in anticipation.

'You want it bad, don't you?' he growled. 'I almost want to make you wait longer.'

'Oh no, please.'

He grinned crookedly. 'You're going to be so much fun to tie up.'

Filthy, evil, delicious, dirty pervert. Oh God, why does the idea of that make me want to explode with excitement? Nobody ever tied me up before.

His inquisitive thumbs arrived at the southern side of her nipples and touched them, lightly but enough to make her wail again.

'I'd keep this up for hours if I could,' he said. 'But I can't, not tonight. I'll be able to control myself better once I've had you a few times, I think.'

A few times. Ah, now here was the advantage of a younger lover, what Deano had had in the early days. Stamina.

Oh, the glorious melting mess she was now that he had his hands fully cupping her breasts and his thumbs stroking her nipples with skilled precision. The fact that she still wore her bra, cups wrenched down, added something to the whole feeling – something shaming but ferally hot. Teenagers in the disco car park, against the wall. That was how it felt.

He stroked her until she couldn't keep still and she

jolted this way and that, bumping his erection into her groin.

He took her wrists yet again and breathed on her poor abandoned nipples until they were damp with steam.

'Oh, I can't!' she begged. 'I can't.'

'Keep. Still,' he commanded. 'Or somebody's asking for a spanking.'

She actually squealed.

'You wouldn't dare,' she exclaimed, knowing as soon as she said it that it was the absolutely wrong thing to say.

He braced himself above her, eyebrows high, hands tight at her wrists.

'That wasn't very clever, now, was it?' he said.

'I'm sorry,' she back-pedalled. 'I know you would. But please! I'll keep still.'

'I'll let you off, just this once,' he said. 'Just this once. Have you settled down? Can I get back to work?'

'Yes. I promise. Oh, God.'

This last was her response to his tongue, darting out and performing an elegant circling of her right nipple. He followed up by taking it fully into his mouth and giving it a long and fulsome sucking. His left hand plied her left breast, while his right was laid flat on her stomach, as if holding her in position.

She needed it. She was in a constant fight with her spine, trying not to arch it high in an effort to fit Leo's erection tightly between her thighs and engage in a spot of illicit friction.

She was starting to feel the need to come, quite badly.

'Gorgeous,' he said, releasing her nipple from his mouth with a smacking sound. 'You're proper gorgeous. I can't count the ways I want to have you. So many men want to have you, and it's me who gets to do it. Thank you, God.'

With this heartfelt prayer, he moved on to her left nipple. This time, the hand at her belly crept lower, to stroke her hips and fit itself underneath her coccyx, testing the stretch of her waistband.

Her heart bumped at this promise of what was to come.

She had only to lie still and enjoy what he did to her, and she would get a huge orgasm, she was sure. Probably more than one. And, if she was honest with herself, the whole spanking thing had ratcheted her up more than a few notches. What if he actually did it? What on earth would that be like?

She tried to picture herself on all fours, getting her bottom smacked over and over until it was hot pink. Another gush dampened her knickers. Surely they would have to be thrown away?

'Too many clothes,' was his verdict, and he made her sit up while he pulled off her top and unclipped her bra. Then she had to lie back down and raise her hips so he could pull off her jeans. Her knickers followed them halfway down her thighs, but Leonardo held them in position.

'Not yet,' he said, to Jenna's frustration.

'Oh, why not?'

'Because I don't want to rush,' he said, maddeningly. 'You don't go to fancy restaurants and bolt the food down like it was a Maccy D's, do you?'

'Years since I had a McDonald's, so I can't answer that one.'

'Tell you what,' said Leonardo, disposing of the jeans, and the socks, once and for all. 'One day I'll treat you to the works. Quarterpounder with cheese, fries, large Coke and a McFlurry. That's living it up, that is. In Bledburn.'

'I can't wait,' said Jenna sardonically. She hadn't replaced her wrists in position after sitting up, and her hands were available to prod Leonardo in the chest once he had taken off his own T-shirt.

'Get them back over your head,' he ordered, standing up to remove his own jeans and socks. 'Cross them, yeah, like that. Now you look ready for me.'

Stripped to his boxers, which bulged with promise, he did a few limbering up moves and pushed his hand through his hair.

'Warming up?' asked Jenna.

'Too right. Got quite a workout ahead of me. OK. As they say on the cop shows – spread 'em.'

Jenna parted her thighs, filled with wonder at this man's astonishing sexual confidence. He didn't doubt for a moment that she wanted him, and would do anything to have him. It must be quite a gift, to be able to know that. Even at the peak of her fame, with her clothes, hair and make-up dissected and fawned over in every celebrity magazine, she had never felt that the men who chased after her really desired her. They wanted something else, something that was nothing to do with who she was and what she had to give. They wanted a trophy.

They had never given her what Leonardo was giving her now – genuine, eyes-on-stalks, salivating lust for her. Being bared to his gaze was almost frightening – he looked as if he might eat her up. She consoled herself with the knowledge that she was the tasting menu at one of Heston Blumenthal's restaurants rather than the two-gulps-and-gone burger. If he was going to devour her, at least he would take his time.

He shuffled himself, on his knees, between her legs and took hold of her hips.

'Nice and slow,' he said, nudging his hardness against her softness, the double layer of cloth doing little to soften its impact. She gasped at the contact, then he lowered his upper body over her so he was crouching, ready to pounce, his palms flat on either side of her head. 'I want to feel your skin.' He let himself down little by little. When her bare nipples were brushed by the hair on his chest, it was electric and she squirmed into his erection, longing for friction.

He held himself just there for the duration of a dirty, animal kiss, tickling her nipples with his dark, wiry hairs while she tried to rub her legs up and down and clamp them over his thighs.

'You're hungry,' he said, breaking off, and giving her that first glorious taste of skin against skin. He had the kind of body she most liked – a spare frame, not over-muscled but certainly not flabby either. Heavy enough to cause a crushing feeling behind her ribs, which she found oddly comforting. Trapped underneath his pinion weight, she was secure and endangered at the same time.

He soon rose again, before her breath became too short, kissed her ears and neck and moved his mouth back down to her breasts. One hand held her still at her hip while the other slid underneath her, to take a handful of her bottom.

The stroking and squeezing drove her to gasps – this part of her had always been sensitive. When he snapped her knicker elastic against the top of her thigh, it didn't hurt, but it did make her desperate for him to get them off.

'It's all happening down here, isn't it?' he said, cupping

her aching, soaking sex. He held his palm there and watched her push herself into it. 'Someone wants to come.'

'Oh, please,' she said, her eyes shut, all her pride having leaked away or been transformed into need.

'Let's take a look at you, then.'

He peeled the silky knickers down, so slowly that she could imagine him unveiling his own works of art in a similar fashion.

'Mm,' he said. 'Oh, you're bare.'

'Kind of compulsory in LA,' she said. 'Not really by choice.'

'Let's have a proper look, then.' He tossed the briefs aside and made a dive for Jenna's lower lips. She kept her eyes shut and her fists clenched, finding this mortifying in the extreme. If only it weren't also so exciting.

'Get those legs properly wide,' he ordered, his voice harsh and thick. He pushed her thighs apart until they strained. She felt her lips split and expose the juicy pink folds to his eye. Her clit, plump and full to bursting, was warmed by his breath. How could he just *look* at it for so long?

'I want to paint you like this,' he said, his hands still holding her thighs wide. 'I want to paint you inside and out.'

'God, who'd want to look at that?' she said with a hysterical little laugh.

'Who wouldn't?' he said, quite reverently.

He moved his fingers to her outer lips and prised them further apart.

'It's gorgeous,' he said. 'I love how it's all made for pleasure. You've got to give it to Mother Nature, haven't you? A man mightn't have thought to make this.' His thumb drifted, very lightly, over her clitoris, causing her to jolt upwards.

'You'd like a bit more of that, I take it?'

She still had her eyes shut, but she knew he was smiling.

He gave her inner thigh a gentle pat.

'Don't I get an answer? Open your eyes, Jen.'

Oh no, don't make me look at you. It's easier if I can pretend you're making me do and feel these things.

'Jen.' His voice was stern now and, almost involuntarily, her eyelids flew open.

'What?' she said sulkily.

Obviously I want you to touch me there. Obviously! For fuck's sake!

But she knew he was going to make her say it.

'Do you want my fingers on your clit?' he said, his eyes like hard, black buttons.

'Yeah,' she breathed.

'Are you sure?'

The effort of keeping her eyes on him was making her face crumple. Her lips were wobbling. She thought she might even start to cry. This felt too huge for her emotions to deal with. It was worse than declaring love, it was worse than confessing to anything else. It was utterly soul-baring for her.

'Sure,' she whispered.

He nodded and, without taking his eyes from her, he began to rub her clitoris with the gentlest pressure at first. Somehow she couldn't break their eye contact. It was as if he held it with a laser beam, keeping her utterly focused on him.

His touch grew firmer and she lay back and let it, giving herself up to him.

This is surrender, she thought foggily. *Why does it feel better than victory?*

Her body, thrumming all over, began to pool all its sensations at the pit of her stomach until she was aware of no other part of her but what was between her legs and its immediate area.

'Do you want my fingers inside you?' asked Leonardo, just at the point where everything was starting to turn molten inside her.

'God, yes,' she whimpered, not having to think about it any more.

'Say please,' he taunted, pushing one fingertip into the shallow dent.

'Oh, please, please, yes, please.'

'I like that,' he said, then one of his fingers slid inside her, so easily it was shocking. 'Christ, you're wet. I hardly felt that. You need something bigger, thicker.'

Two, then three fingers were inserted and now Jenna felt them probing inside her, stretching her without pain. In the meantime, Leonardo's other hand kept upping the ante on her clitoris. She felt quite invaded and beaten, completely at his mercy now.

He thrust with his right hand and stroked with his left until she began to quiver, everything standing on end, a wild, fast unfurling moving from bottom to belly to all over her body.

'Yes, yes, I've made you come,' crowed Leonardo. 'Good girl, nice one. Oh, your face. What a picture.'

He withdrew his fingers with a sucking sound and shimmied over her to capture her mouth in a delighted kiss. She felt like water, flowing around him, having no substance of her own. He had done for her. He had conquered. He could put her in his pocket and keep her there.

'Didn't you need that?' he made her admit, between kisses. 'You came so hard. You must have needed it really bad.'

'Mmm,' was all she could say.

'I wasn't going to let you come yet,' he said. 'Not until I was in you. But just because you've done it once doesn't mean you can't do it again. Benefits of being born a girl – not fair, if you ask me. Besides, I think you've earned a treat.'

'You're so bloody cocky,' said Jenna, half-affectionately.

He laughed. 'You don't know the half of it yet, sweetheart.' He tutted sympathetically. 'You look wiped out. Ready for more yet?'

'More,' she repeated weakly.

'I want to fuck you,' he said. 'I want to be in you. Do you need a break, or . . .?'

She shook her head.

'I've got condoms in my handbag,' she said, reaching blindly over the side of the mattress. But Leonardo was already on the case, fishing inside for the packet of three.

'You were prepared for this, then?' he said. He opened the cardboard carton and removed one of the little foil packets.

'I always carry them. Well, ever since things with Deano . . . Not because I expected to have sex. Just in case. Precaution.'

'You're a smart cookie,' said Leonardo.

He pulled down his boxers, displaying a very impressive erection.

Jenna looked swiftly away. It felt rude, somehow, to stare at it.

How silly. The rudest night of your life and you're worried about staring.

'Don't be frightened,' said Leonardo, evidently pleased by her reaction. 'I won't hurt you.'

'You might, you know.'

'You can take it. You're more than wet enough, that's for sure.'

He held its length in his hand, as if priming it, then he ripped open the foil condom package and made a slow performance of putting it on.

Jenna wondered if it felt horribly tight. She hadn't slept with anyone using a condom since the very early days with Deano. The days of cringing at the check-out of Boots and deciding against buying lube because that would be *too embarrassing*.

She sensed that it wouldn't be too embarrassing for Leonardo, though. He would pile up his multipack of Extra Large and his lube and God knows what else on the counter with a swagger and a glint for the cashier. *You want some of what my girlfriend's getting?* She betted all the girls had been wild for him, showing off their teeny miniskirts and highest heels in the supermarket car park. And it wouldn't hurt that he was one of the few lads capable of talking in more than monosyllables. Oh yes, he would have been a heartbreaker all right.

And now, here he was, wanting her.

'You've heard of kissing it better,' he whispered, looming over her, shifting his hips to achieve optimum positioning. 'Well, this is my version. Ready?'

'Mmm.' She was more than ready, as her leg brushing up and down his thigh signified.

He pushed forwards and she was lost in a dark place of half-memory, half-new experience. It had never felt like this before. She hadn't felt so stretched, so filled, so raw, so vulnerable before. He had a gold chain round his neck with a ring attached, and the ring swung over her breasts then brushed its cold metal traces over her face while Leonardo eased in, inch by inch.

She was reminded of the early times with Deano – the heady aroma of that body spray that had been so popular with the teenage boys back then. Leonardo didn't smell of that but there was something else, so familiar and so instantly transporting to those days of innocence that her heart contracted. A natural scent, a musky animal thing. Desire. Sex. Youth.

Lately, with Deano, a sour chemical smell had accompanied him everywhere, even to bed. Jenna didn't miss it one little bit.

Here, with Leonardo, she was suddenly aware of an opportunity – to have everything she had with Deano, but to take a different, better path. She could find out what she could have had, if they hadn't been consumed by a whirlwind of fame.

Lying here, while Leonardo entered her with considerate deliberation, watching every flicker of expression on her face for signs of pain or discomfort, she was aware of a clarity that had eluded her before. Sex was trying to teach her something. She needed to make sure she understood what it was.

'Jesus, you feel sweet,' he whispered, his dark eyes huge above her. 'So tight. God.' His voice gave out.

She reached up and touched his cheek.

'I'd forgotten,' she said, and then she had to shut her eyes in case he saw the glisten.

As if prompted to remind her, Leonardo began to thrust.

She felt the passion in every move he made and was swept along with it, wrapping her legs and arms around him and clinging on for dear life.

He kept his eyes upon her and she watched them grow rounder and darker and darker and rounder while the rest of his face remained pale and immobile. When his chest pressed against hers she felt the hectic bumping behind his ribs. He was hot against her, and their skin stuck together in places.

Between her legs, he was inside her, drawing all her consciousness down to that place until the rest of her body floated off beyond the periphery. Everything was concentrated there, in that central nexus of sensation, while a white noise of panting and scents and the gold ring knocking against her teeth misted around it.

'You've needed this,' he said.

He reached down between her legs and pushed the pads of two fingers against her clitoris. Together with the slick invasion of her sex, this drove her towards a rapid and violent climax, and she tensed against him, sure her whole frame would seize up, before pouring it all out.

'Yes,' he growled, 'yes, yes, I can make you feel it.'

He held her tightly and pushed, pushed, pushed, taking her so hard it almost hurt, and then he was there. His eyes had done too much work, and the rest of his face joined in at last, screwing itself up into configurations of agony and bliss that made Jenna want to kiss it all over.

They lay all corkscrewed up in each other for a long time. Jenna felt her body loosen, little by little, whilst she breathed in her lover.

Some people, she reflected, described certain relationships as 'just sex'.

How odd that 'just' seemed, when sex, after all, was such a huge thing. So huge that she quickly moved from satiated to terrified, before Leonardo had time to yawn. What had she done? What had she given of herself? Could she afford it?

She disengaged from him and sat up, pushing her fingers through her hair.

'You all right?' he asked. His hand on her thigh felt heavy, almost like a dead weight.

'Yeah,' she said, but she couldn't look at him. She stared at a damp patch at the top of the wall, where the old paper was peeling. She couldn't take her eyes off it.

She heard Leonardo shift, and felt him prop himself on his elbow.

'No, you aren't,' he said quietly. 'Come here. Look at me.'

He nudged her back down, strong fingers at her arm. She couldn't face him and hid her nose in his shoulder. He stroked her hair silently for a while, which made it all worse. It was too lovely, much too addictive. If she started to *need* human warmth and all that, where would it all end?

'Look at me,' he said again, more softly still, but there was real intent behind the whispery tone and she knew he wouldn't put up with much more of her evasion.

She lifted unwilling eyes to his. She seemed to be accusing him of something, but she wasn't sure what.

'I'm pretty sure you enjoyed that as much as I did,' he said, his head on one side. 'Hmm?'

'Yes. God. Yes.'

'So . . .?'

She shook her head. 'Nothing.' As ever, it came out unconvincingly.

'Bollocks,' he said. 'I haven't known you long, Jen, but I know when you're not being straight with me. What's up?'

'Perhaps I enjoyed it too much,' she said after a pause.

'What's that mean?'

'It means . . . I'm not in a good place for this kind of thing.'

'You're not in a good place? Why did you leave LA then? You know what it's like round here.'

He misunderstood her deliberately, she realised. He was telling her that he wouldn't accept any Californian psychobabble.

He bent his head to hers until their brows touched.

'Listen, sweets,' he said, and the endearment made her curl her toes with guilty pleasure. 'You've had a rough time. You've ditched the selfish bastard you were saddled with. You've run away from your life. I get that you've got a lot on your plate.'

'Thanks. Good.'

'But I don't think that's your problem with me, is it?'

'What do you mean?'

'I mean, look at me, love. Compared to my fuck-up of a life, yours is the Garden of bastard Eden. But do you see me trying to fob you off with what a "bad place" I'm in?'

'I . . . Well, people are different, Leo, aren't they?'

'When everything else in your life sucks, you grab

anything that doesn't with both hands, and hold it close. I like you. You like me. We've got something a bit like electricity going on between us. Why push it away? Why?'

'All right, all right. I'll tell you why. All my life, I've made it my business never to bite off more than I can chew. When you swim with the sharks, you have to keep a clear head. I let everyone else around me ruin themselves with drugs and illicit affairs and over-ambitious projects – they crashed and burned and I came up smelling of roses every time. It's the secret of my success. But now, with you, with what we just did, I feel like I've broken my own rule.'

She looked away.

'Jen,' he said. The touch of his hand was like a static shock. She thought her hair might be standing on end.

'You were right about the electricity,' she said haltingly. 'I feel like I've been switched on and now I can't switch off.'

'You're scared,' he said flatly.

She nodded.

She was scared. She wanted him to keep touching her, to keep holding her. She wanted him again. She thought she might want him all night.

And the next night.

And the next.

She wanted it too much.

'I don't know why you're scared,' he said. 'But I know how it feels. I know how it felt when I went into that house to look for Mia and she wasn't there, but a whole vanload of Feds were. Sorry. Did I use the F word again? Cops, then. I was scared. I did what I've never done in my life before, and I ran.'

'You got away from them?'

'Pure luck. The pub was doing a firework display for someone's birthday do and I'd got a couple of bargain boxes off the back of a lorry for them. Set a couple off in the back kitchen and legged it.'

'So – you went to a house that was raided by the police? Wrong place, wrong time?'

'Well, a bit more to it than that. I was set up. Everyone knew I had Mia's backpack, and she'd told me to drop it off at that bloke's address. Hey presto, police raid. Somebody wanted a fall guy. House was full of gear, nothing to do with me.'

'Gear?'

'You name it. Stolen shit, drugs. I didn't really have time for a good look round but I got the picture. I mean, there's always been crime around the estate. People with spare rooms full of Xboxes and whatnot. But this was on a way bigger scale than anything I've seen before.'

'Who would do that to you?'

'I've got my theories. Can't prove any of them though.'

'That's so awful. Leo, you must let me help you. See if I can find anything out.'

He laid her back down and leant over her, playing with her hair.

'You're sweet, Jen,' he said. His breath tickled her skin. She wanted to pull him down in a bear hug and snog him to death. 'But there's nothing you can do. Except what you're doing. Hide me here until . . . I dunno.' He shut his eyes for a few seconds. 'Just hide me here. And let me have my wicked way with you.'

'You aren't wicked,' she said.

'Oh, you ain't seen nothing yet, babe,' he said. 'Nothing at all. But I'm looking forward to showing you.'

She swallowed, overcome by her horrible tenderness towards him again.

'This is a mess,' she said.

'And a half,' he agreed. 'But we can make it go away. I can make it all go away for you, Jen. I can make you feel all right.'

Chapter Four

He had made her feel more than all right, all night.

Now, in the car, on the way to visit Auntie Jean while the kitchen fitters fitted on, she was feeling the after-effects.

Her eyes were scratchy, her head was light, every tug on the gearstick was painful and she was sore. But God, it was worth it. Every twinge and wince brought back a flood of luxurious memory, of some dirty, delicious thing Leonardo had done to her. *I've been seduced*, she thought, and the words made her squirm with pleasure.

She tried to imagine what Deano would think if he knew she had let some Bledburn estate hood do all those things to her. God, what would the papers say? What a field day they could have.

Shuddering, she turned off the main arterial road heading eastwards out of town and found herself swiftly in a dense maze of red brick. This was where she had grown up.

The estate had never been a glamorous place, but it had gone even further to seed since she had walked

these streets. Far more abandoned shopping trolleys
and mattresses than she remembered, fewer neatly kept
front gardens. Curtains and blinds were almost uniformly
drawn against the surrounding gloom. People here were
under siege, she thought.

Boozemasters was still popular, though. In the little
concrete precinct where it stood, people with dogs and
cans of strong cider sat waiting to be moved on by the
local PCSOs. If they dared.

The only cheering feature of the whole place was the
kids, everywhere, on scooters, on bikes, on skateboards, in
pushchairs, all hell-bent on squeezing some joyful juice
out of their grim environment.

Fair play to them, thought Jenna. *I was one of them, once.*
And so was Leonardo.

He would have been one of the skaters, or perhaps he
would have had a BMX bike. He would have hightailed
around the streets in a back-to-front baseball cap listening
to Blink 182 on his headphones, hand-drawn 'tattoos' all
the way up his arms, swigging from a bottle of some blue
energy drink.

Exactly the kind of boy she used to wrinkle her nose at.

Auntie Jean's house was just as she remembered it.
The sloping front garden had a row of gnomes at the
top, fronting an array of flowering tubs. The door and
window frames were smartly painted, almost in defiance
of the drab, splintering versions on either side. Her old
house, next door had electricity and water meter boxes
on the wall now, their doors hanging off the hinges. An
abandoned pink scooter lay on the front lawn and the
wheelie bin had fallen on its side, disgorging bursting
black plastic bags.

Another child in her old bedroom.

The thought made her shiver.

She parked the car and hurried up the steps to Auntie Jean's front door. Next door, the front window blind twitched.

It took a long time for Auntie Jean to make it out to the passage from her kitchen and, by the time she opened up, a small knot of children had gathered by the front wall.

'Is that 'er, like?'

'She don't look like she does on TV.'

'Are you sure it's 'er?'

'Yeah, that's her old house.'

Auntie Jean came to the rescue, ushering her into her little front room. She still had the same gas fire on the wall, the same wallpaper, the same dark carpet. The flatscreen TV and a fishtank seemed to be the only new features.

'Sit down, love, I'll get you a cup of tea,' said Jean, but Jenna didn't take a place on the plastic-covered chintz sofa.

'Oh, let me do it,' said Jenna, realising too late that she had made the cardinal mistake of offending a Bledburner's sense of independence.

'No, no, no. I might be ancient but I can manage a kettle, love. Go on with you.'

'I didn't mean . . .' said Jenna, but Jean flapped a hand and shuffled out to the kitchen, returning minutes later with a tea tray.

'Two for one at the supermarket, these biscuits,' she remarked, offering a plate of pink wafers. 'Your favourite, they were, do you remember?'

Jenna laughed. 'Jean, I was six.'

'Ah, you never grow out of pink wafers.'

She took one, mentally crossing that evening's treat of

Greek yogurt with berries off her list. These would cancel them out.

'So, how are you?' she asked, pouring her milk. 'Do you get out much these days?'

'Down the club for bingo on a Saturday night. There ain't much else going off. I don't like to be out after dark these days.'

'Do you still see your old mates down there? What were they called? Di? And Lynda?'

'Oh yes, they're still about. Do you remember Sheila Tarbuck, though? She died, couple of years back.' Jean leant forward. 'Suicide,' she whispered.

'Oh God, how awful. She had kids, didn't she? A little bit younger than me?'

'Little girl, Mia, broke her heart.'

Jenna took a sharp breath and gripped her teacup tight. 'Mia Tarbuck?'

'That's right.' Jean looked curious. 'You wouldn't have known her. She was still a nipper when you went off to London.'

'No. Sad, though. Does she still live around here? Mia?'

'Here, there and everywhere. Into the drugs, ooh, terrible. What a shame, she's a lovely girl. Used to be so pretty. Now she's into all kinds, got a boyfriend on the run from the police.' Jean lapsed into tutting.

'Sounds like it's all been going off here. Who's the boyfriend?'

Jean pursed her lips.

'Kathy Watson's boy. Bad blood there, mark my words. She weren't no good, either.'

Jenna racked her brains, trying to recall who Kathy Watson might have been.

'Was Kathy Watson the one—?'

'Ooh, you'd know her if you saw her, love. Used to be down the club every night in that silver dress, hardly anything to it. Slow-dancing with all the married men.'

God, yes, I remember.

'Nobody knows who the lad's father is. Could be one of any number of fellas. Hardly surprising he turned out the way he did.'

'What's his name, then?'

'Jason Watson. Bad lot. He was in all the papers. Caught red-handed but got away from the coppers. A few weeks back, it were. A wanted man.'

'Is there a reward?'

Jean shrugged.

'Nobody's got the money round here, love. I expect he's long gone by now, anyway.'

'But the girl, Mia, is still on the estate?'

'I don't know. I try to keep out of it all.' Jean sighed. 'Almost makes me glad I was never able to have kids of me own, seeing what they've all come to. Why can't they look to people like you and Deano instead of all these bloody drug dealers? I don't know.'

'They've no hope,' Jenna suggested. 'Nothing to aim for but pipe dreams and cartoon bling.'

'Eh? Cartoon bling? What's that, then, love?'

'Oh, nothing.'

'This place has lost its heart,' said Jean. 'It were so different, once. Do you remember?'

The rest of the visit was taken up with nostalgia about the thriving social scene of thirty years ago and more, the days before Leonardo – before *Jason* – was even born.

Jenna didn't dare refer back to the subject for fear

of being seen to take too deep an interest, but she kept the names deep in her heart, ready to be brought out later. Jason Watson. Mia Tarbuck. Ready for the Google treatment, as soon as she could get on to her phone.

By the time she left Auntie Jean's, there was a large-ish mob swelling on the pavement and sitting on the wall.

'Jenna Diamond,' shouted one child, leading to a general repetition of her name that rang around the street. They massed around her, an unkempt swarm, smelling of bubble gum and dirt.

'Why ain't you in America no more?' asked one little girl. ''Ave you left *Talent Team*?'

'Why?'

'Where's Deano Diamond?'

'Are you living back here now?'

She blocked all the questions with an upraised palm and a shake of her head.

'Let me past, please,' she said. 'Let me pass and I promise I'll come and do a talk at your school.'

'Cool!'

'Lame!'

Opinion seemed to be divided here, the girls being keener on this suggestion than the boys in general. Jenna made a slow but steady progress through the jostle, but when she got to her car, the wing mirrors were bent and there was a crack on the windscreen as if a piece of gravel had flown up from the road and hit it.

'Who did this?' she demanded, but laughter and shrugs were her only reply. A couple of older boys smirked over the handlebars of their bikes. She thought, vividly and suddenly, of Leonardo. He would have been one of them, once.

'You want to watch yourselves,' she said. 'Keep out of trouble. Once you're in, you're in and it gets harder and harder to stop.'

'What are you, a Fed?' asked one in disgust.

She climbed inside the car and turned the key in the ignition. Even then, it was some time before the kids would get out of the way enough for her to drive off.

Jenna didn't want to admit it to herself, but she was a bit shaken.

Don't be daft. It's just kids. You were one, once. You aren't going to let a bunch of snotty kids scare you off the streets where you grew up, are you?

Back at the house, the kitchen fitters were piling back into their van, ready to leave for the day.

'Are you almost done?' she asked, bumping into the last at the gate.

'Another day should do it,' he said. 'Got the worktops fitted now – it's looking good.'

She went straight up to the attic, where she found a shirtless Leonardo crouching down to brush in the street level detail of his latest work.

He didn't turn around, though he must have heard the attic door creak and slap down on the boards. She watched him, his dark hair brushing his bare shoulders, his spare, strong frame, the little gap in his jeans she could put a finger in and tug to tighten them over his abdomen. He was barefoot and the soles of his feet were filthy.

'Evening, Jason,' she said, once he had put the brush in his jam jar of water.

He still didn't turn but she saw his shoulders tense.

'Who've you been talking to?'

'My old next-door neighbour. Went round for tea.'

He stood up and turned, facing her down.

'So, did you find out what you wanted to know?' he asked tonelessly.

'Only what I already knew. Except your name. I didn't know that.'

'You didn't need to know.'

'But, Jason,' she said, liking the name as she spoke it, thinking it more suitable than the ridiculous Leonardo. 'Why shouldn't I know it?'

'I liked being who I am here. I liked having no past and no future, just my art and my woman. Now it's spoiled.'

'Oh, don't be silly. How could that have lasted anyway? We have to live in the world.' She felt a flutter at the pit of her stomach, all the same, at being described as his woman.

'I don't see why,' he said, stubborn and grim-faced. 'What's the fucking world got to do with us?'

'What,' she said tentatively, 'if I were to find Mia? If I were to find out what really happened and who was really responsible for what went on in that house?'

'Oh, no, leave it,' he said, shaking his head and striding towards her. He caught her arms in his hands and held them to her sides. 'You can't get involved, Jen. Don't go near this.'

'But if you could be vindicated—'

'It won't happen. All that will happen is that you'll put yourself at risk. Stay away from those people, Jen. Even Mia. It's too late for her. It's not too late for you.'

'But it's not right!'

'That's life.'

'But . . .'

He put a heavily paint-stained finger to her lips.

'I'm serious, Jen. Leave it.'

She shook her head, her mouth rubbing his finger so that dried paint flaked onto her lips.

'You're filthy,' she said.

He smiled at last. 'You only just worked that out?'

'I'm going to run you a bath.'

'I'm only getting in if you come with me.'

'Deal.'

Jenna watched the paint flecks melt in the warm water and lose themselves in the foamy depths. She sat opposite Jason, gazing at his face through the steam, her ankles pressing into his hips.

'You could do with a hair cut,' she said.

'What for? Disguise?'

She smiled. 'Maybe. If you're going to take the art world by storm, you need to be able to leave the house without getting arrested. What if we dyed it peroxide blond and cropped it really short?'

'Fuck off. I'd look like Miley Cyrus.'

Jenna burst out laughing. 'Hardly. Seriously, it was one of Deano's best looks. The fashion press went mad over it.'

'It's not for me.'

'No,' she agreed. 'No, it wouldn't really suit you. Your carpet and curtains wouldn't match, would they?'

He smirked at that.

'I could go for an all-over body wax,' he said.

'Oh, you could. Back, sac and crack. That was all the rage in LA.'

'Yeah, well, I don't think I'll be moving there any time soon. I'll keep the hair, thanks.'

'You're probably better off that way. But what am I

going to do, then? How am I going to bring your brilliance to a world that wants to arrest you?'

'When did I ever say I wanted to be a star?'

'Come on. You do.'

He concentrated on cupping her foot in his hands, lathering it up, heel, instep, toes, before answering.

'It's a daydream, though. It's never going to happen for real.'

'I believe it could. I believe in you. You're talented – more than talented.'

'So says the art critic.'

'All right, I don't know that much about art. But I have friends who do.'

'Invite 'em round for cocktails, darling.' He moved soapy hands up Jenna's calf.

'I'm not joking. I know I can't exactly show *you* off, but I can take your work to be evaluated at a top London gallery.'

'Ooh, a top London gallery. Fancy.' There was a hostile edge to his words, mixed in with the mockery.

'What's the matter with that? Why are you so chippy with me?'

'Forget about my artistic career, Jen. Leave it. Let's do up the house and then think about what's next after that.'

'Well. All right. If that's what you want. I'm not going to leave it, though, not completely. I want you to get the recognition you deserve.'

'Yeah, well, as far as some people are concerned that's a front page spot in the court report.'

'But—'

'Shut up.'

The abrupt and commanding tone silenced her. She tried to withdraw her leg but he held it tight.

'Shut up,' he said, more gently, 'and listen to me. We're strangers, Jen. We met a few days back. Why don't we get to know each other properly first?'

'I feel I know you.'

'Trust me, you don't. I want to show you exactly what you don't know.'

There was a look in his eye that convinced Jenna he was talking about sex.

'I have been married,' she said with a nervous laugh.

'Exactly,' he said. 'To a man who was more interested in what he put up his nose than what he put up you.'

'Jason!'

'It's true, isn't it? You told me yourself.'

'There's no need to be crude.'

'Yes there is. I'm crude because I'm real, doll. Nothing tinsel-town about me. I know what you need and I can give it to you, simple as.'

'You're an arrogant prick.'

'And? What's your point?'

She pretended to kick at him, but he held firm. He knew, damn him, that she wanted him right now, wanted him to pin her down there in the bath and surge into her, joining their respective energies until they were one. But her pride always made her fight it, even when her desire for him poured through her like liquid light.

'You know, you've disappointed me about LA,' he said.

'What do you mean?'

'I thought it'd all be wild, kinky porno sex out there. Threesomes and orgies and shit. Turns out Bledburn's got more of that going on.'

'Has it really?' She laughed.

'Oh yes. Really. You'd be shocked, my lady.'

'I don't remember anything like that.'

'Well, you're a bit older than me. But what do kids do when there's no work and no nothing in their lives? They shag, that's what.'

'That's what you did.'

'Of course. I was about the worst, cos I didn't drink a lot or smoke weed, which were the other popular hobbies round my way. I preferred the other, and so did the girls I knew, mostly.'

'So you've spent the best years of your life in bed?'

'I hope the best years of my life haven't ended yet,' he said. 'But yeah, basically. In bed, in sleeping bags, on floors, in fields, in alleyways, in the backs of vans. Threesomes, foursomes, moresomes. Then, when I got with Mia, she had a friend who did those parties – y'know, sexy knickers and vibrators and what not. We got into bondage. I'm good at bondage.'

'Surprise, surprise.'

'I'm good at the kinky stuff, me. I think it's because I like to be in control – that's why I never got into the booze or the weed, thinking about it. I hate the feeling of being out of control.'

'And was Mia into it too?' Jenna could barely speak her name without a sharp pain in her abdomen. Was it jealousy? Or anger at how she had abandoned Jason to his fate?

'Yeah, big time. At first.' He frowned. 'Before she started going AWOL.'

There was a silence. Jason dropped her leg and reached for the shampoo bottle.

'Anyway, that's not what I wanted to talk about,' he said. 'Come here. I'll wash your hair.'

She twisted around and settled herself between his thighs with her back to him so he could apply the shampoo with strong, sure fingers. Little shivers of pleasure ran from her scalp to the rest of her body.

'I'm going to give you all the attention you've been missing,' he whispered into her ear. 'I'm going to show you what you've never had.' He took her earlobe between his lips and sucked it like a lemon drop before letting it slip back out.

His hands clasped beneath her breasts, he began kissing and nipping at her neck while creamy suds slid down her forehead, forcing her to shut her eyes. His palms closed over her nipples, squeezing. She wriggled back against his stomach, inclining her head to encourage him further, showing him that she was his to do with as he pleased. God, he was just so good at it, why deny him?

He clamped her thighs between his, locking her in his clutches. Behind her, between her bottom cheeks, she could feel the slow inflation and hardening of his erection. That wasn't going to go down until it had had its way with her, she thought with a thrill.

She tilted her head to meet his lips and fall into a warm, wet, steamy kiss.

He stroked her nipples through it, then broke off and grabbed the cup on the side of the bath, plunged it in the water and poured it over her head.

'Lather, rinse, repeat,' he said laconically. 'But I think I'll pass on the repeat.'

He stood unsteadily, climbed out of the bath, grabbed the nearest towel and wrapped it around his waist. Still dripping all over the ancient lino, he pulled Jenna up and lifted her into his arms, not even bothering to cover her streaming skin.

Instead, he carried her down to their drawing room campsite and dropped her on the mattress.

'I'll get it wet,' she complained, but he didn't seem to care at all, although he removed the towel from his waist and laid it down on the bed before putting his back and soaking head on top of it.

He reached down beside the bed for the condom packet and put one on while Jenna was still groping around for a comb or a bathrobe or anything to take off the sudden chill of being removed from the hot water.

'Never mind that,' said Jason, pulling her over him. 'Get on me. Get me up inside you. I want you now.'

The gravelly urgency of his voice banished all thoughts of damp patches and goose pimples from her mind. He was there, next to her and underneath her, his hot skin against hers, and nothing else mattered.

She lay on top of him and held him around his neck, kissing him for dear life while he shifted and jolted beneath her, seeking the little slick niche in which to fit himself.

When he found it, he took hold of her hips and made sure she couldn't swerve or shy away from his bold ingress. He slid up inside her, lightning swift, filling her until she cried out with satisfied surprise.

'That's it,' he growled. 'That's what you need.'

She couldn't argue. Already she was bearing down, as if she wanted more of that thick root, enough to stretch her to splitting point. She ground herself over his pelvis, feeling him touch every limit of her tight passage and grant the promise of enough friction to drive her, and her g-spot, over the edge.

'Hot for it, babe,' he said, moving his hands around to cup her buttocks in a tight grip. 'So hot for it.'

She leant down to kiss him again, enjoying the way her nipples brushed his chest hair and his own little nubs. The tickling was exquisite – he should never wax.

He nipped down on her lower lip and pushed her bum forwards, urging her into the ride. She began a slow back and forth, interspersing with side to side moves, relishing the sense of having every inch of his stalk deep inside her. How good and thick it was, a truly substantial tool. The thought that it had pleasured half the lasses of Bledburn flitted through her mind, giving her momentary pause, but then she drove it out of her consciousness. It was in her, now. She was its quarry and its destination. No other. And besides, there was a lot to be said for experience. A hell of a lot.

As she bore down on him, he spread her bottom cheeks apart, making her feel wide open and whorish. It bucked her up, spurred her on to greater equestrian heights, making her dizzy with the dirtiness of what he did to her.

What he had said about threesomes gatecrashed her imagination and she pictured him holding her open for another man, another lover from the dirty streets of the estate, low-voiced and foul-mouthed, knowing her for what she was, knowing what she wanted . . .

'Get down on me,' he whispered, but his eyes were glazing now, taking on a faraway look. 'Work harder. Really work.'

She was sure she couldn't work any harder; her abdominal muscles were starting to tighten and ache and she knew she'd be sore inside afterwards. But Jason put the tip of one finger inside her bottom cheeks and she jolted so hard she thought she might crush him. Instead, she came, gripping his shoulders and gasping into his face, her thighs weak and trembling.

This made him triumphant and ready to release his own climax. He bucked and bucked inside her and she felt sorry that she wouldn't have his semen to show for it. For a moment, she longed to feel it, wet and creamy on her lips, the proof of the taking.

'Dirty girl,' he crooned in her ear when she had collapsed on top of him. 'You liked my finger there.'

She wanted to deny it but she couldn't.

'It was novel,' she whispered.

'You've never done anything of that kind, I take it?'

'I suppose you have.'

'You suppose right. I'm an arse man, always have been, always will be.'

'You're a manwhore.'

He laughed at that, stroking her damp coils of hair.

'An arsemanwhore,' he corrected. 'Phone the Oxford dictionary. A new word for 'em.'

'You're pure filth,' she said with happy sigh.

'You're not so squeaky clean yourself.' He kissed the top of her head and rolled her gently off him and on to her side. Forehead to forehead, they locked eyes for a while, until his dark gaze seemed to laser through her. 'I could fall for you,' he said.

'What about . . .?' She couldn't say the name.

'Hush. That was over anyway. You've made me see it. I owe you one.'

'You owe me more than one.'

'Yeah, don't worry, you'll be paid in full. In orgasms. Does that sound like a deal?'

'Mmm.'

She must be mad. This was madness. She couldn't get embroiled with this no-hope low-life, brilliant, sexy . . . She yawned. He was asleep already.

'You're going to have to lay off me for a day or so. I can barely move.'

Jenna winced her way over to her suitcase to pull out a pair of clean knickers. She and Jason had ignored their sore bits and pieces to have each other again in the dead of night, and after that there had been copious lashings of oral sex until the sun came up and they drifted off again.

'Shit,' she said, peeking through the window. 'They're here already. I'll have to keep the door shut and make sure they go straight into the kitchen. Do you think you can creep very quietly up the front stairs once they're hammering away?'

'Hammering away,' repeated Jason in a slow, sticky voice. 'I could do that job.'

'You already do.'

'Can't you just throw a blanket over me and I can stay down here?'

'It's only for one more day. Besides, you're so close to finishing that panel you're working on. Once it's done, we can make a start on gutting this place.'

He grunted and wrapped the duvet tighter around him. Jenna left him to it and went to greet her kitchen fitters.

Once they were fully furnished with mugs of tea and Radio 2, she crept up to the attic, expecting to find Jason there. He wasn't, and his cat was less than pleased with the situation, miaowing loudly from his corner bed of old dust sheets and the abandoned tracksuit.

'Why didn't you come downstairs, silly?' scolded Jenna. 'The door was open.'

But Bowyer retained stubborn loyalty to his dwelling, it seemed, and Jenna had to go back downstairs for a tin of tuna before he would be pacified.

'Where's your dad, then, eh?' muttered Jenna, watching him dive nose-first into the compacted fish. 'Lazy so-and-so. Bet he sleeps all morning.'

She looked around her at the surrounding frieze, now depicting the town's history right up to the middle of the last century. A happy era of 1960s full employment was the latest panel: the workers enjoying their leisure time in the music clubs and coffee bars that had opened in the town. The swinging, Bohemian element of that decade had passed Bledburn by, but Beatle moptops and huge beehives could be seen on the little figures darting up and down the prosperous high street.

On the hill, this very house, Harville Hall, stood, decked out with bunting, hosting the annual gala. She had forgotten about that but now childhood memories came back: listening to the colliery band in tears because her balloon had flown out of her hand. It had all ended when she was about five, after the strike, though. Jason was too young to have ever attended one. Perhaps he had learned about them from his mother.

Bowyer, the tuna can empty, sauntered away from his bed to the attic stairs, intent, it seemed, on stretching his legs outside. Jenna bent down to pick up the tin, noticing as she did so that the old tracksuit comprising Bowyer's bed rested on top of a big threadbare canvas backpack.

All of Jason's worldly goods.

She cast a swift, nervous glance at the trapdoor. There was no sound but the clanking and banging of the kitchen fitters. Jason was apparently still glued to the mattress.

She knelt and unclipped the front flap of the bag. In the smallest pocket was a provisional driving licence with a photograph of him looking very young and very cocky, staring the photobooth camera in the eye as if challenging it to a fight. A number of old birthday and Christmas cards were held together with an elastic band, but Jenna didn't investigate those any further. She was more interested in the little square notebook full of sketches.

In the main body of the bag she found more pads, large ones, filled with watercolour paintings of different local landscapes and people.

She held her breath, her heart thumping. Was he really this good? She had the feeling she was looking at an urban Constable, his bucolic scenes replaced by blackened bricks and boarded-up shops. There was an urgent quality to the pictures that prevented her looking away, once seen. They demanded close examination, and they evoked emotion. Unexpectedly, she found herself on the verge of tears, looking at a picture of an overgrown front garden with an armless doll and a broken pushchair lying in it. On the page after this still life was a picture that could only have come from Jason's imagination, with grotesque demonic figures grouping beneath a huge chimney for some kind of ritual. Some of it was teen experimentation, but a lot of it was far more than that.

It was inconceivable that this wealth of incredible work should remain invisible. Without thinking, Jenna took the pictures from the backpack and slipped back down the ladder with them, hiding them in one of the upstairs bedroom cupboards. As soon as she could, she would take them to London to show Tabitha. This week, if possible.

She flitted back up to the attic, shoved the backpack under the old tracksuit again and took Jason's water jar down for replenishment in the bathroom.

While she swilled it out under the tap he shambled in, half-naked and yawning.

'Ta for that,' he said, quirking an eyebrow at the jar.

'Did they see you?' she asked, trying not to be too winded by the sight of him in his masculine, unshaven glory, still warm and dishevelled from sleep.

'The fuck do you take me for? Of course not.' He reached for his toothbrush, now kept by the sink despite his misgivings. ('What if someone sees it?' 'I'm not about to invite anyone into my private bathroom.') 'Where's Bowyer?'

'I've fed him. He's outside.'

Jason brushed his teeth while Jenna watched his broad back bend and flex over the sink. The hollow in it, just above the belt of his jeans, cried out to be touched, but she kept off, mindful of her sore and overused condition.

'What are you up to today then?' he asked. 'More detective work?'

'No,' she said, feeling a little guilty for in fact she was thinking of trying to smoke Mia out of hiding.

'I hope not. The quicker people forget about me, the better. Don't mention my name, whatever you do.'

'I wouldn't. Anyway, I'm only going shopping for technology. Need a decent computer. It's killing me, only having my phone.'

'Poor princess,' he said, making a comedy sad face at the mirror.

'Oh, come on. The information age has made it as far as Bledburn, surely.'

'Yeah. But, you know, people have to choose between broadband and breakfast round here.'

'Not this person,' said Jenna briskly. She stepped forward and kissed his bristly cheek. 'Shave and hide yourself. I'm off to Web World. See you later.'

But Web World was only reached after a diversion to the estate, specifically the low, flat-roofed, extravagantly graffitied building that hosted the local youth club. These days it was surrounded by a barbed wire fence, and accessible only through a triple-padlocked gate. It looked as forlorn as Jenna felt, and she was about to turn away, when a youngish woman in a parka hurried across the car park of the neighbouring pub, waving to her.

'Hullo. Did you want me?'

'Sorry, I just dropped in on the off-chance . . . Kayley!'

'Oh my God, Jenna! Oh my God. I heard you were back but . . . Oh my God!'

They laughed at each other for a few moments, then Kayley unlocked the gate and led Jenna to the bunker, unlocking several more padlocks on the way.

'I'm gasping for a cuppa – do you want one? So, what brings you here?' Kayley set about boiling a kettle in a little kitchen corner of a room full of pool tables, gaming machines, computers and bookshelves.

'Just a thought that I might start giving something back to the place that made me,' said Jenna. 'I want to make a donation to the youth club, maybe you'd like me to come in and give a talk, that kind of thing. Perhaps pay for recording equipment.'

Kayley turned around, beaming. 'Seriously? Give us your hand, love. So I can bite it off.'

They laughed again.

'This is like a dream,' said Kayley. 'We've been drained dry by successive local council budget cuts. We can only keep going because people volunteer their time and donate their old gear now and again. Seriously, hand to mouth stuff. A recording studio, wow! I can't tell you how much that would mean to the kids we serve here.'

'I want to help. I used to come here, when it first opened. It didn't have all that amazing artwork on the walls then, though.'

Jenna looked around her, detecting the hand of Jason in at least some of it.

'Yeah, we've got some talented artists.'

'That one there – of the big foot coming down on the little antlike people . . .'

'It's brilliant, isn't it? Lad who used to come here a few years back. Jason. He could've gone all the way, if he hadn't got sucked into estate low life.' She sighed and reached into a cupboard for a box of teabags.

'Serious talent,' said Jenna, almost to herself. 'It can't go to waste.'

'Tell me about it. Crying shame. We've got a girl who comes here now, could be a professional dancer if she wanted, but she's met some lad and she's started going round to his place to smoke puff all night instead of coming here to rehearse like she used to. I don't know. What can we do? We do our best. That's about all we can.'

She brightened.

'But hey, now you're here, perhaps you'll inspire her.'

'I hope so. God, Kayley, I haven't seen you in, what, seventeen years?'

'Must be about that. Shit, shut up. I sound really old.'

'If you're old, what does that make me? I used to babysit you.'

'You'd think working in a youth club would keep me young, wouldn't you? The opposite. Look at this.' She plucked at a silver hair growing amongst the brown.

'Oh, I couldn't even guess what colour my hair is now. It's so long since I saw its natural colour. How's your mum? And your crazy brothers? Thanks.'

She took the cup of tea and they sat down to discuss possible donations and projects for the club.

'You know, those paintings are really brilliant,' she said, looking around her at the evidence of Jason's talent all over the walls. 'It's a real shame about that bloke you mentioned,' she said, as casually as she could muster once the talk had lapsed a while. 'Jason, was it? Isn't there any way he could get back to his painting?'

'Not now,' said Kayley, briefly. 'Unless they do art classes in prison. I think they do, actually.'

'He's inside?'

'No, but if they get hold of him he will be.'

Jenna sighed. 'Sad.'

'Yeah.'

'He's AWOL, then?'

'Uh huh. Nobody knows where.'

'Somebody must know. His mum? His girlfriend?'

'Mum neither knows nor cares. Girlfriend, ditto. Actually, nobody's seen her in a while, but one of the kids

said she was supposed to have moved to Manchester. I
don't know if it's true.'

'Right. Nobody's in touch with her, then?'

Jenna sensed from Kayley's slight hesitation that she
was digging too deep. She needed to keep things more
casual.

'Not that I know of. You haven't changed career and
turned private eye, have you?'

Jenna laughed, hoping fiercely that she wasn't caught
in a blush.

'Sorry. Just trying to get my head around Bledburn. It's
changed, you know. It was never this . . .'

'Hopeless?' suggested Kayley.

'I hate to say it, but . . .'

'Yeah. I hate to say it too.'

Jenna drained the last of her tea.

'Listen, Kay, it's been so good to see you again, but I
have to get going. I'll be in touch about that talk and I'll
call the council about that money for the recording studio,
too. You know I've bought Harville Hall?'

Kayley put her mug down with a thump.

'No. I didn't know that.'

'I've been thinking. Maybe I'll start the Gala up again.
Bledburn needs something like that – a celebration.'

'Ah, the Gala. That used to be highlight of the year,
didn't it? Proper funfair, great music, like a festival. And
you're not wrong – we could all do with a celebration.
Listen, thanks. This means a lot. So you're sticking around
then? Not hopping off to LA any time soon?'

'Definitely not.'

'You must have a screw loose.'

Kayley's laughter echoed after Jenna as she left the club

to cross the basketball court to where she had parked the car.

But there was a problem. The wheels were on bricks, and minus tyres.

'Oh *shit*,' she moaned, banging the bonnet and clutching her forehead. She had believed Kayley and Auntie Jean when they told her the estate had gone downhill, but not to this extent. She would need an emergency tyre fitter, but where the hell she would find one, she hadn't a clue. She was about to turn around, and go back to ask Kayley's advice, when a figure emerged from the back door of the pub over the road and crossed the forecourt, waving at her.

'Fancy bumping into you here.'

'I could say the same thing.'

It was Lawrence Harville, in a pinstriped suit, carrying a briefcase.

'Business,' he said briefly. 'Listen, about the other night . . .'

'You do look rather businesslike. And yes, you owe me an apology, a massive one.'

'I'm sorry. I behaved inexcusably. I don't expect you can forgive me, but I'd like the chance to make amends.'

'Well, I'll have to think about it. No promises, though. Are you really involved with that pub?'

They both looked over their shoulders at the unlovely single-storey building with two of its windows boarded over.

'It used to be called the Lord Harville, you know,' he said with a weak grin.

'Not any more.' The faded sign swinging from a post in the car park proclaimed it to be the Stan Bowyer.

'No, but I have some interest in the land, so I still have a foothold in the area. Just about.' His smile had a fixed quality. 'But we must do something about your car. Let me ring a chap I know.'

'Oh, would you? That would save my life.'

'I wouldn't go that far,' he said, but he seemed pleased with the idea, flipping out his phone and putting it to his ear.

'I can't believe you got all dressed up to go to the Accident and Emergency,' said Jenna, using the old nickname for the pub that had prevailed in her schooldays.

Lawrence winked and was about to reply, but somebody answered his phone and he fell instead into a curt description of Jenna's plight.

'He should be here within twenty minutes,' he said, snapping his phone case shut. 'Perhaps we might wait in the bar?'

'Are you sure?' Jenna looked dubiously at the pub.

'Oh, it's not open yet. It'll just be us and Tommy. He'll sort us out with coffee.'

'OK.'

The interior of the pub didn't seem to have changed much since Jenna's days of sitting in the 'family room' with a bag of crisps and bottle of Coke. The carpet was still sticky and, despite a smoking ban of many years' standing, it still reeked of wet cigarette butts.

'Tommy,' hailed Lawrence, and Jenna recognised the landlord as Tommy Ross, who had joined the army at sixteen and come home from Bosnia with a bald head and arms full of tattoos. He was only a few years older than her, but you wouldn't have known it.

'Thought we were sorted?' said Tommy with a frown.

'I bumped into this young lady and rendered her a service,' said Lawrence, smoothly. 'Would you mind making us a coffee while we wait for somebody to come and fix her tyres?'

Tommy put down the bar towel he had been folding and disappeared without a word.

'Perhaps he might have an idea who did it?' suggested Jenna, but Lawrence shook his head.

'I doubt it's pub regulars – it'll be kids.'

'Kids of people who come here, though. When I used to live here, everybody knew everybody. You couldn't get away with anything.'

'Times change,' said Lawrence lightly.

'Not for the better, around here.' She gave him a curious look. 'I really *am* surprised to see you here. I thought your business interests were all in Nottingham these days.'

'I still own property in Bledburn. Anyway, what are *you* doing here?'

Jenna almost replied that it was her home. The shock of it made her catch her breath.

'Do you know, I was about to say, "I live here." How quickly the years fall away when you come back to your childhood haunts. It's extraordinary.'

Tommy came in with the tray, set it on the table in front of them, and went back to cleaning up the bar area.

'Actually, I was visiting the youth club. Thought I'd like to get involved with it, you know, as a patron or something.'

'Very public-spirited of you,' said Lawrence, pouring cream into his cup. When he offered it to Jenna she declined.

'Not really. I was one of these kids, running wild around the estate, once. Though I never stole anyone's tyres! I suppose I'm doing it to help children like me, which isn't that noble really.'

'I think it is,' said Lawrence, and he laid a hand on her forearm. 'I think you're amazing.'

A prickle of discomfort made her want to pull her arm away, but she was mindful of causing offence, and kept it there against her will.

'Thanks, but I'm not. Where is this man? I hope he isn't caught in traffic?'

She looked anxiously through the thick, not very clean, net curtains.

'Is there somewhere you need to be? I can give you a ride, if you like. Leave the tyre man to tow your car to the garage.'

'No, no. I was only going to the retail park to look at computers.'

'Ah, well, I'm glad we met again. I've been meaning to call.'

'Have you?'

'I have a friend opening a new restaurant in town. I thought you might like to come to the Grand Opening with me. I know it's hardly the Grammys or the kind of thing you're used to but . . .'

'Oh, I don't know.'

'Well, I expect you're used to personal five-star chefs and valet parking. It was just a thought.'

'No, that's not what I'm saying. Do you think I'm a snob? You do, don't you?'

'Of course not. It's just hardly surprising that the opening of a tuppenny-ha'penny restaurant in a grim little English town doesn't exactly fire you up. Don't worry about it. I'm sure I can find a cheaper date.'

'Lawrence, stop it. I'll go. I'd love to support local business.'

His smile over the rim of his coffee cup was wide and toothy.

'I like the way you make me work for you, Jenna,' he said. 'You must know that.'

'I don't know what you mean.' But she did and she couldn't help smiling along with the flirtation.

'I just hope my hard work pays off. I think it will.'

Oh God, if you only knew, somebody else has been working harder . . .

Her guilty reflections were interrupted by the arrival of the tow truck.

Jenna banged down her coffee cup and ran outside.

'It's tomorrow night,' Lawrence called after her. 'I'll pick you up at seven.'

The tyres were replaced, the new computer ordered and Jenna returned to the house with groceries and a large cheque for the kitchen fitters.

They left with all their equipment, leaving Jenna with a brand new but rather dusty kitchen. She was wiping down the Corian surfaces, marvelling at how the sparkle emerged from beneath the reddish patina of brick dust, when Jason emerged, half-naked and wrapped in the duvet.

'Have you been in bed all day?' Jenna was appalled.

'Seemed like the best plan. You've drained all my creative juices, woman. Put the kettle on, eh?'

'Put it on yourself. I've had a long day.'

She began emptying the grocery bags into the brand new, stainless steel American-style fridge, but she had only unpacked a few items before Jason wrapped her in the duvet from behind, resting his chin on her shoulder.

'Get off,' she said, laughing, trying to push him back, but this only resulted in a tumble on to the granite tiles. They scrambled and squirmed against each other until Jenna was on the floor, pinned beneath an exultant, still unshaven Jason.

'Brand, spanking new kitchen, eh?' he said. 'You know what this means?'

'I think *I* know but I daresay you've got some weird idea of your own.' Jenna tried to push him off but he was impossible to dislodge.

'Needs christening,' he said. 'Doesn't it?'

'Go and cook something then,' she said, pushing her knee into his thigh. It was solid as rock.

'You want me to heat something up, love? That can be done.'

He moved one of her wrists carefully beside the other so he could hold both in the pinion of one hand then, with his other, reached over to fumble in the nearest shopping bag.

'Oh, strawberries,' he guessed, fingering a package. 'Yeah?'

'Well, it is nearly time for Wimbledon.'

'Seasonal. Did you get cream?'

He drew out the punnet of strawberries and broke the seal with his teeth.

'What the hell are you doing?'

'You wanted me to sort out some dinner,' he defended himself, putting the strawberries down beside him. 'And I'm thinking of killing two birds with one stone. Well, not killing. Unless the massive orgasms I give you turn out to be fatal.'

'Jason. I can't. I'm so sore all over . . .'

'So am I. I'm not going to fuck you. But a man needs to eat.'

He reached back into the bag and identified a carton of double cream.

'Now are you going to lie there nice and quiet while I get this tea ready?' he asked.

'The duvet . . .'

'Got a nice new washer, haven't you? The duvet can be its first load. Are you going to, Jen? Or do I have to tie you up?'

She felt a twinge of delight at the thought and almost said 'no' to test this resolve, but there was time enough, in more comfortable circumstances, to take her first steps towards bondage, so she nodded acquiescence.

'Good girl.' He released her wrists and unsealed the lid of the cream.

He unbuttoned her shirt dress with sure fingers, then reached underneath to unclip and remove her bra. Her knickers soon disappeared too, leaving only her sandals, but he left them on. He slipped a hand between her thighs, easing them apart, then he took the carton, held it high over her ribs and began to pour.

It was cold and she gasped as the thick white liquid splashed on and between her breasts. Jason poured a trail down her belly, then angled her hips up so he could deposit the rest of the cream in and around her lower lips, coating them thickly. The chill of it felt deliciously soothing to the mild burn that had affected that area all day and Jenna lay back and let it all happen, caught in the luxuriant lasciviousness of it all.

'You're making me hungry,' he said.

She felt the drips running down the curve of her bottom, pooling in all her creases and cracks.

Her nipples stood up, emerging from the cream-slick like pink lifebuoys.

'When I look at you like that,' he said, breathing heavily, 'I'm imagining that cream didn't come from a carton. You look too fucking hot to take.'

He sat back, panting and looking her up and down with a starved eye.

She really thought he might bend down and bite a chunk out of her.

Instead, he grabbed at the strawberries, took a handful and scattered them across her torso. He picked the tops off two and mashed them down on her nipples until they stuck there, like mad, scarlet caricatures of what they covered. The rest were pushed between her lower lips, into a jumble that might eventually become a purée. How soft and firm and cold they felt, added to the thick cream and her own streaming juices. Jason kept the heel of his hand at her pussy, holding the fruit in position, while he lowered himself over her and began to lick and lap at her belly and breasts.

His heat coupled with the cold collation brought the pitch of sensuality high. She twisted and gasped and tried to push her pussy, full of strawberries, further into him, to crush them and turn everything to pink mush.

'Mm,' he said, raising his head. 'Getting it ready for me, babe?'

His tongue drew lines and swirls in her warm cream coating, sucking it from her skin until it was bare again, but shiny from his attentions.

He made her wait, kissing every inch of her upper body, before lowering his face between her thighs. He took his hand away from the crushed strawberries and flicked his glance towards her face.

'Time for my just desserts, then, eh? Sorry.'

Her groan at the joke was soon transformed into another kind of outpouring. The workings of his tongue and lips on her sweet, fruity centre melted her until she was pure juice, gushing into his mouth. He devoured her, feasting off her clit, her lips, her widespread inner core, until she was dizzy with it and her orgasm began to circle wildly into being.

The climax pushed her bottom off the floor into his greedy face, making him laugh on her pussy and lick harder.

'Oh *God*,' she cried. 'What *are* you? Oh God, oh, God, oh *God*!'

When he finally knelt up, sometime after her third orgasm, and set her free from the tyranny of her own body and sex, he had a glow of feral victory in his eye that made her pulse race, despite her ragged state.

'Never been licked like that before, eh?' he panted.

She could only shake her head.

'Those big Hollywood dicks can't do it like this Bledburn boy, eh?'

Again, a shake of the head.

'You're something else,' she managed to say.

It took some effort of will, but she propped herself up on her elbows and looked down at her ravaged body, sticky and patterned here and there with drying pink fruit pulp. Then she looked up at Jason, kneeling in only his boxers, which were significantly tented.

Fair was fair.

She dragged herself to her knees and rummaged in the shopping bags.

'What you looking for?' he asked, amused, guessing her intent.

'Just . . . Hmm, Madras curry paste, probably not.'

'Fuck, no!'

'Peanut butter?'

He shook his head rapidly. 'I'm allergic.'

'What about Marmite?'

He laughed loudly.

'Whatever turns you on, darlin'.'

'Not Marmite. Ah. Now.'

She smiled radiantly at him, drawing from the bag a jar of lemon curd.

'I haven't had that in years,' he said. 'Used to love it in a sarnie.'

'A sarnie isn't what I have in mind. More like a breadstick.'

'Breadstick? Don't take the piss. This ain't no breadstick.'

He lowered the waistband of his boxers over the straining lump, unveiling the rampant beast within.

'Well, something you can dip then,' she said with a giggle. 'Maybe a crudité.'

'I'll take your word for it.'

'Celery. Or cucumber.'

'You're making me hungry. Get to it.'

As invitations go, it might not have been the most romantic, but Jenna needed no further encouragement. She unscrewed the cap and scooped up some of the sweet viscous substance on to a finger. She stroked it on to his twitching erection, slowly and smoothly, as if plastering a wall, until it bore a sheeny, lemon-smelling coat of the stuff.

Then she cupped his sacs in one hand and wrapped her lips around his shaft.

Oh, lemon curd was more delicious than she remembered. She lapped and sucked it with such hunger that she barely noticed each inch of him, slipping further and further into her mouth. She rarely allowed herself anything sweet and this was a treat of treats. Once it was all licked off, she reapplied it, rather to Jason's tormented impatience.

He got hold of her hair when she took him back into her mouth, growling that this would be her last helping.

Undaunted, she polished off every last drop of the preserve, until her tongue ached and her jaw was slack, then she sucked extra hard just to make sure no tinge of sugary citrus flavour remained on his tumescent skin.

It was a different kind of taste in her mouth once the lemon curd was all gone – a quick burst of bitter salt, spurted to the back of her throat by the thick length that gagged her.

She swallowed with grace and aplomb, then removed Jason's softening cock from her mouth and licked her lips like a cat.

'My compliments to the chef,' she said, and the pair of them cackled with laughter then kissed and wriggled together on the now-filthy duvet until they were too tired, hungry and sticky to resist the seductive ideas of bath, dinner, bed.

She spent much of the next day trying to get her computer up and running while Jason painted. He declined to help with the technological headache, protesting that 'me mind's not built that way' and she let him off on the grounds that he was an artist.

She had almost forgotten about the restaurant opening, until Lawrence texted her a reminder, and she hurried to compose herself into something that was recognisably the Jenna Diamond they would all know from the TV.

'Where you going?' asked Jason, coming down from the attic, with paint all over his face and hair.

'A restaurant opening thing I was invited to. Honestly, since I've arrived here I've been plagued with these invitations. Opening here, reception there.'

It was true. Jenna's PA had been texting her a steady stream of invitations for every event in the Bledburn social calendar, however tiny. She had advised the woman to return polite refusals. This one was her only engagement, and only because Lawrence had personally railroaded her into it. She had come here seeking peace and quiet, and peace and quiet was what she would damn well have.

In between all the detective work, that was. And the sex. So much sex.

Jason, at the bottom of the stairs, made a grab for her in her cocktail dress and costume jewellery.

'Don't!' She put her hands up, laughing but a little alarmed at the prospect of paint on her pristine silk.

'You look so perfect,' he said. 'I want to mess you up.'

'When I get home,' she said, looking into a flyblown old mirror on the hall wall, a relic of years past. 'If you want to wait up, that is.'

'You aren't going to be late, are you?'

'Oh, no. I'll eat whatever they shove in front of me and leave, I expect. It's just a photo opportunity for the restaurateur, basically.'

All the same, she was nervous of Jason seeing her get into Lawrence's car, and silently thanked the previous owners for the high box hedge that hid the house from view of the street.

'Don't eat too much garlic,' he advised.

She tiptoed up to give him a light kiss on his stubbly, white-spirit-smelling cheek.

'I won't. See you later.'

Stepping out into a warm summer evening, she wished everything could be different. If only she could be taking Jason as her guest, instead of being Lawrence's arm-candy. She pictured herself introducing him to everyone as the up-and-coming young artist, he in a smart suit, she in her silk. Or perhaps he ought to dress more hipster-ish. She smiled, imagining Jason faced with a fringed scarf and pair of snakeprint skinny jeans.

'Fuck off!'

She mouthed the words in his accent, smiling to herself as she click-clacked along the pavement to Lawrence's waiting car.

'Something's funny?' he asked as she climbed in.

'Oh? No. Just thinking. You look nice.'

He was groomed to within an inch of his life but he'd overdone it on the aftershave, she thought, straining not to cough.

'Thank you. You're stunning. A face made for television, Ms Diamond.'

'I don't go by Diamond any more.'

'Sorry. I forgot. It so suits you, though.'

He gave her a long look and she had to fidget with her bag and check her phone before a blush crept forth.

'So, what kind of food did you say this place specialised in?'

Lawrence, denied a flirtation, reached for the gearstick, clearly resigned to polite chit-chat all the way to the restaurant.

The food was gastropub fare, the restaurant averagely pleasant and stylish, the company a gaggle of town councillors, local paper journalists and small business proprietors. Most of them were visibly and staggeringly starstruck by Jenna, but she caught the owner of a dog grooming parlour telling her friend she 'looked older than on TV, and those pictures in *Glamour* were obviously airbrushed', which made her smile. Comments like these were par for the course in showbusiness; she had long ago learned to shrug them off.

Lawrence was barely able to exchange a word with her, so monopolised was she by curious local politicians wanting to know if Colin Samson, *Talent Team*'s Mr Nasty, was like that in real life, or if she'd ever partied with the show's winners.

It wasn't until the pudding course – which she eschewed in favour of a black coffee – that he was able to direct a little of her attention towards him.

'Sorry they're all such nosy bores,' he muttered. 'The highlight of their year is usually some dispute about a conservatory roof. You can't blame them for going a bit crazy, I suppose.'

'I don't, at all,' said Jenna. 'Honestly, I expect it. I'm used to it. I don't mind.'

'You're very professional, which is wonderful, my

dear. But you must long to go out somewhere you won't be recognised, and besieged by questioners, sometimes.'

'I used to,' she said. 'Especially when it all started. That was insane. From obscure nobody to huge star – Deano, I mean, I was still in the background then. It was all too quick, really. But that seems to be the way in this business. Your career changes on a hair's breadth. One photo in the right magazine, one line of a song that touches hearts, one off-the-cuff remark at an awards ceremony. It can be anything, really. I mean, my career is built on making it happen, but I still get the mix wrong sometimes. If the mix is wrong, the magic doesn't work.'

'How poetic. You deal in magic, Jenna, in dreams.'

He spoke the words with a smoky intensity that made her respond to him despite herself. He was smooth, she caught herself thinking. Too smooth. She shouldn't be drawn in.

'Don't be fooled. There's cold hard strategising behind that magic and a lot of those dreams fall flat. Remember The Gold Standards? No. Well, there you go. I put a lot of time and effort into them, but I couldn't make it work in the end.'

'Everyone fails sometimes. Your successes far outweigh the flops.'

'Yes, that's true. But I can't take all the credit for it. I'm not the talent.'

'You're an alchemist. You take base metal and turn it into gold.'

'Or the Gold Standards.' She laughed briefly. 'Lawrence, you have a very exaggerated idea of my skills. A lot of people could do what I do. I've just been lucky.

And worked bloody hard. Luck and hard work. It's what most success is down to.'

Lawrence looked away from her at that, taking a sip of his coffee and brushing off a question from a councillor's wife at his other side.

'I have an idea,' he said, turning back to her. 'I've been thinking of it ever since I saw you outside that youth club yesterday. A little project we could do together.'

'Oh, Lawrence, you know my thoughts on that.'

'I don't mean business. This is for the good of the town.'

'Really?' She was slightly alarmed at the prospect of getting more intimately bound up with this attractive but slippery-seeming man. 'I've got a lot on my hands with the house renovation and—'

'It wouldn't take an enormous amount of input from you, I promise. I'd do all the preparation and publicity, if you like. You just need to lend your name to it and come along on the night.'

'On what night?'

'Talent show night. A very special Bledburn *Talent Team*. It'll be good for the youth club, for the kids, for your profile, for the local paper . . . Well, come on. It would be fun, don't you think?'

'Well, I don't know. It's a bit more than I was planning for . . .'

'Jenna, you could find the next Madonna, the next Michael Jackson – here in Bledburn.'

'You know, I think every town is capable of throwing up a Madonna or a Michael Jackson,' said Jenna. 'If talent is nurtured properly, it can turn into stardom. But I'm not here to do that, Lawrence.'

'Oh, look, it's just a bit of fun. A nice ego-boost for

some local kid with a nice voice. And it'll be good for Bledburn. How about it?'

'I had a plan of my own that I thought would be good for Bledburn.'

'Oh? What's that?'

'To restore the Miners' Gala. Obviously without the Miners' bit. But a big summer party for the whole town in the grounds of Harville Hall, just like I remember it. Bands, entertainment, stalls, free food, big beer tent, all of that. Wouldn't that be great? I was thinking, September time, once the house is done but the weather is still fine.'

But Lawrence didn't seem to share her enthusiasm one bit.

'There's a reason that ended,' he muttered.

'Because the mine shut, yes.'

'Because my family became pariahs. I don't want the town reminding of that, not now, after all this water under the bridge.'

Jenna considered this, but she was a bit cross that Lawrence's personal reluctance was more important to him than some pleasure for the town.

'Nobody bothers about all that Harville stuff any more,' she said. 'Like you said – water under the bridge.'

'Not for the older people round here,' he said. 'For them, Harville Hall is still a symbol. I wouldn't invite them in, seriously, Jen. It's asking for trouble.'

'I'm not a Harville. I'm Bledburn's best and brightest – well, me and Deano, I suppose. However they feel about you, they're OK with me. I don't think they'd cause me any bother.'

'You're naïve. Been in La-La-land too long.'

'And you're overstepping the mark of our friendship.'

She stood up, reaching for her purse and looking for the proprietor to thank and congratulate.

'Walking home, are you?' asked Lawrence with a sneer, standing along with her.

'There are such things as taxis.'

'I wouldn't go and hail one from the cab rank outside Wetherspoons if I were you. Gets rough this time of night.'

'You think I've existed in cotton wool all this time? Showbusiness is tough, Lawrence. I'm tough.'

'Look.' He grabbed her elbow and she tried to yank herself free without drawing attention, which proved impossible, so she let him stop her, for the time being. 'Jenna. I'm sorry. I've given you my opinion – I'm not going to force you to take it. Let's agree to disagree and change the subject, eh?'

She exhaled deeply in an attempt to dispel her irritation.

'Fine. But don't ever call me naïve.'

'I won't. Overly optimistic, perhaps . . .'

'Lawrence!'

'I'm sorry. Come on, I'll drive you home, if you've had enough.'

'I am tired,' she admitted, with a yawn. But the thought of Jason waiting for her, perhaps with all kinds of nefarious designs on her body, quickened her pulse and chased the beginnings of fatigue away.

They wished the chef all success in his venture, avoided the lone 'paparazzo' of the *Bledburn Gazette*, who was busy smoking by the bus stop anyway, and hurried to where Lawrence had parked before anyone could see them.

'Thanks, that was nice,' she said automatically, climbing into the passenger side.

'Yes, wasn't it? Look, Jen.' He looked as if he was

struggling to reach for the right words, and a sense of foreboding entered Jenna's soul. *Just turn the key in the ignition and drive, damn it.*

'I really am exhausted,' she hinted. 'Even that delicious coffee can't seem to perk me up.'

Lawrence gave up.

'Let's get you home then,' he sighed, revving up.

Outside Harville Hall, he turned off the engine, which Jenna thought was a bad sign. Did he expect to be invited inside?

'Thanks again for a lovely evening,' she said, her hand on the door handle.

She leant over and pecked him on the cheek.

He reached out and cupped her face, turning it so her lips were lined up with his.

'Lawrence, I'm sorry, I don't think this is . . .'

'Shh.' She tried to twist her neck away but he held her tight and close. His lips were hard and hot and that aftershave still threatened to overpower, even three hours later.

It only lasted a moment, Jenna making her reluctance absolutely clear by pushing against his chest.

'I see,' he said unpleasantly, then he took a deep breath and changed his tone. 'Too soon. I see that. I'm sorry.'

'I'm not in the market for a relationship,' said Jenna. 'If I didn't make that crystal clear, then I'm sorry, but you need to know it, so I'm telling you now.'

'On the Diamond rebound, I suppose,' said Lawrence, moodily.

'Exactly. I came here to make my life simpler, not more complicated.'

She felt her stomach lurch at the hypocrisy of her

words. After all, what could be more complicated than the situation with Jason?

'I'm not complicated,' said Lawrence. 'All I want is to treat you like a princess. Don't you feel you deserve that?'

'Please. I've said no. All I ask from you is that you respect that decision. If it means you feel you can't see me again, then I'll understand.'

'No, Jenna, please. Not that. Can't we be friends?'

'Of course we can.' Though it was against her better judgement. 'Friends. Yes?'

She opened the car door.

'At least let me walk you to the house,' pleaded Lawrence, also getting out.

Jenna shook her head, looking anxiously at the upper windows for signs of Jason. She couldn't see him, but then, it was dark now and there were no lights on.

Perhaps he's gone to bed.

'Honestly, I'm fine.'

'It's so dark now and there aren't streetlights. You ought to get a security light for your front porch, you know.'

'Hmm, maybe.'

Lawrence was determined not to leave her until the last possible moment. He opened the gate and ushered her through. The lower storey of the house was also unlit and the overgrown front garden was a place of strange shapes and dark masses.

'They say the place is haunted,' said Lawrence, halfway up the path.

'What? Why would you tell me that? Is that what you were about to say when you let me in the first time?'

'Yes. But I thought it wasn't a very friendly thing to tell a new resident. You're in now and settled, so I thought I'd tell you. You don't believe in ghosts, do you?'

He paused on the bottom step. Even in the dark, Jenna could see a kind of malevolent enjoyment in his eyes.

'Of course not,' she said briskly. 'Who's it supposed to be?'

'A young woman, lived here at the tail end of the nineteenth century, married to my great-great-grandfather. Or is there another great in there? I never can remember.'

'But wouldn't that make her your great-great-grandmother?'

'No. She was his first wife, but she died before they had any children.'

'Poor thing.'

'Suicide, or so they say.'

'God.'

'Well, on that note, I'd better leave you. Unless you want a bit of company?'

He lingered on the top step, clearly hopeful of being invited in.

'I bet you've made up all this ghost stuff to freak me out so I'll ask you in,' Jenna accused. Her tone was jokey, but she wasn't joking, not really.

'Would I?' Lawrence held his hands up and laughed a sheepish laugh.

'Yes, you would, you git. Now go on. I'm fine. Goodnight.'

She hurried through the door and shut it firmly behind her without looking back at him.

Go, she thought, listening for his footfall down the steps.

The hall was not quite in total darkness, a shaft of moonlight coming out from behind a cloud to cast a pale

bar across the grubby black and white tiles. The door of
the drawing room in which she had been living until now
was closed.

She made her way towards it, but her progress was
impeded by a sudden jolt beneath her ribcage, so sudden
that it was some moments before she realised it was an
arm, pulling her backwards until she was held against
something tall and solid and warm and human.

She screamed, her confused mind not yet having made
the right connections, thinking for a mad moment that it
was Lawrence. Then her sense of smell came to her rescue
and she knew her captor beyond doubt.

'Jason!'

He put his hand over her mouth.

'Hush,' he said. 'Fucking 'ell, who did you think it was?
You sounded like something out of a horror movie then.'

Her breath was gushing out of her at such a rate she
couldn't have spoken even with a free mouth.

He held her in a bear hug, waiting for her to calm, then
removed his hand.

'Sorry,' he said. 'I thought you'd know. I thought you'd
like it.'

'I would. I did. I mean, I wasn't thinking. I'm not good
with surprises.'

'I'll bear it in mind.' He kissed her hair in its chignon
and the exposed nape of her neck. 'You smell gorgeous. I
still want to jump you.'

The last breaths of panic wafted from her body. Now
a different kind of red alert was coming into being, and it
emanated from between her legs.

She rubbed her head into his shoulder, nuzzling like
a cat.

'Bad boy,' she said. 'Very bad.'

'D'you want me to be good?'

She shook her head and he laughed into her ear.

'I said I wanted to mess you up and I'm going to do it,' he vowed. His lips fastened to her neck and the white curve of her shoulder while the hand that wasn't engaged in holding her fast against him slid down to raise her skirt and massage the tender flesh of her inner thigh.

Thoughts broke up inside her head and rushed out of it. He hadn't seen or heard Lawrence, or he would be asking questions. Lawrence . . . She ought to do something about him, some kind of subtle discouragement, or would it take a more forceful approach? A forceful approach, like Jason's, now . . . Oh, it felt good . . .

Lawrence was banished, blanketed over with the urgent need for more of Jason's touch. Her lover's hands were all over her now, disregarding the boundaries of her cocktail dress as if they didn't exist. He touched her breasts, her bottom, and now he let his hands glide over its curve and into the valley below. His teeth nibbled at her neck and ears and the sensitive skin between them at will. All she could do was push herself further into him, silently begging for more.

He closed a fist in her hair, wrenching it out of its perfect style so that it tumbled all over her. The half-thought that it still needed cutting was swallowed up by his tongue in her mouth.

'I can't wait for you,' he growled, coming up for air. 'Get over there.'

He manhandled her to the wall and lifted her so she perched on a tall, long-legged antique table, one of many pieces left abandoned in the house.

The clink of belt buckle, the rasp of falling jeans, drew her eyes downwards and she was rather impressed to notice that he was already wearing a condom. Be prepared. What a boy scout.

'You were confident,' she whispered, reaching out to touch his rubbered erection.

He pushed her hand away and rummaged in her skirts, pushing them up and her knickers aside – he didn't even have time to pull them down first.

It was swift, it was sudden, it was almost painful, but so piercingly satisfying that she cried out on his sheathing within her.

She wrapped her knees around his hips and her arms around his neck, holding on for dear life while he took what he wanted. She laid her head back, feeling its rhythmic bump against the peeling old wallpaper, feeling much more the enormity of his energy and passion. And it was all directed at her. This force of nature had no other end in mind but the having and possessing of *her*.

It had never felt this urgent or primal, even in the early days with Deano. She had never felt so caught up in the centre of a huge forcefield.

It was over quickly, but not before he had wrenched an orgasm from her with impatient fingers, then slammed all the harder until she felt the moment of give, of buckling at the knees, the sudden expression of beautiful pain that meant it was done.

'Don't pretend you aren't mine,' he panted, letting her slither down around the sides of him until her shaky feet hit solid floor. 'Don't you fucking dare pretend that.'

'You're something else,' she told him.

'I know.' He helped her to the drawing room, smug as

all hell. 'You could maybe get me a gig as a porn star. I'd be good at that.'

'I'm sure you would, but no.'

She sat down heavily on the mattress, grimacing at the bump to her bottom.

'Bed shopping soon, I think,' she said.

'Oh yeah,' he agreed, sprawling himself out at her side. 'Most important piece of furniture in the house, the bed. Well, for me and you, anyway. Never mind your "state of the art" kitchen. The bed comes first, since it's what you were made for.'

At the 'you', he had propped himself up and pushed a fingertip beneath her chin.

It was extraordinary, how he made her feel like the sexiest, dirtiest, wildest woman alive. She had never had that sense of herself before, as a woman meant to be stripped down and spread open and pinned to the bed. It was almost alarming, but she couldn't stop worrying at the thought as if it were a loose tooth, pushing and pushing at it, getting the maximum mind-mileage from it.

Dirty, sexy Jenna Diamond. No, not Diamond. Just Jenna. Jenna 4 Jason 4 Ever. God, stop it. You aren't fourteen again.

It had all the hallmarks of that age, though, like a second rush of hormones raging through her. But without the spots, thank God.

'I can't sell your astonishing bedroom skills,' she said, snuggling closer into him. 'But you're welcome to give them away to me for free.'

He laughed then sobered, lying back down and staring at the ceiling.

'It's not for free, though, is it? It's for board and lodging. I'm your gigolo.'

'Don't be daft. I'd let you stay here regardless. You know what I think of your art. And – I don't know why, and I must be mad, but my instincts are usually good – I trust you.'

'You're the only fucker that does round here, then,' he said.

She lay down beside him and kissed his cheek.

'Perhaps I'm the only fucker round here with good instincts, then,' she said.

He brightened a little, stroking her face.

'Makes sense,' he said. 'Since you're the one that got away.'

'I'll get you out of here,' she whispered. 'I promise.'

He whispered back, 'Maybe I don't want to leave. Maybe I want to stay here, with you, in Never Never Land, forever.'

Chapter Five

Two days later, Jenna drove along Camden Road, feeling a kind of prickly sense of oppression she had never before experienced when entering London.

She remembered the very first time, on the train from Nottingham. As fields became streets and they slowed down, she and Deano had been glued to the window. The houses weren't like Bledburn houses, the roads weren't like Bledburn roads, the very air that surrounded them didn't seem like Bledburn air. There was something of glamour even in the terraces and high rises. Any cramped flat might house a famous future DJ or movie star, any one of those people in the street could have been on TV, never mind if it was only in an episode of *The Bill*.

'You can do anything here,' she'd said, but Deano had laughed.

'If you can afford it.'

That excitement, that hope that she might be able to pull herself and Deano up into the heights, was no longer with her. The streets outside her car window looked dirty and overcrowded, the funky bars and clubs of Camden

where she and Deano had spent their best – if poorest
– years just buildings. She had never seen the poverty,
desperation, crime and drug addiction that was woven
so seamlessly into the groovy fabric of London. She had
chosen to block it out, but now it seemed to thrust itself
in her face. Literally, when a gaunt-looking man, whose
age she couldn't have begun to guess, made an ill-advised
attempt to cross the road in front of her, forcing her to
slam on the brakes and make the taxi behind her honk in
fury.

He didn't even register her but staggered on across the
road, anxious to meet up with some guys outside a fried
chicken shop on the corner.

She got back into gear and drove on, but her hands
shook and she felt as if all this was a horrible mistake. She
should have stayed in Bledburn, in bed, with Jason.

Her eyes flicked to the bag on the passenger seat – a
portfolio in a clear plastic sheet. This *was* a good idea. It
was the right thing to do.

Doubts continued to assail her nonetheless, all the
way out of Camden, through the city streets and into the
expensively hushed environs of Mayfair, where her friend
Tabitha kept a gallery.

Tabitha's assistant, Petra, met her at the plate glass
door and showed her inside. Jenna found that she needed
showing – it had been some years since she had visited
Tabitha's gallery and it had had one of its periodic
makeovers. The blond wood floors and discreet spot
lighting she remembered had been replaced by shiny,
rubbery jet black tiling and lightbulbs in what looked like
inverted saucepans, fitted along long extendable rods from
the walls and ceiling. Bright white walls held an array of

works both representational and abstract, but all of it very, very good.

Jenna stood taking it in while Petra disappeared to the upstairs office to find Tabitha.

She was heralded by her clear, patrician tones from the back of the gallery, diverting Jenna's attention from the fascinating portrait made up of red and green dots she had been examining.

'Jen, darling, I can't believe it's you!'

'How are you? The gallery's looking stunning.'

'Thank you.'

Air kissing wafted an expensive scent, more Paris than London, into Jenna's nostrils.

'And how are you? Looking very well, I must say. I heard you were taking it easy.'

'Oh, no, I've just fitted a kitchen. That's real work. I was taking it easy before.'

Tabitha laughed, but there was a little indulgence in it, as if she understood that Jenna was going through the grinder and needed humouring.

'Do come up and have a drink. Coffee? Or is it too early for something a little stronger?'

'Oh, best not. I'm driving,' said Jenna, following Tabitha to the back of the gallery and the staircase.

'You? Are driving yourself? I'm not sure I'd remember how, but of course, I'm spoiled, living and working in London. No need for all that car rubbish.'

'I'm slowly getting used to it. LA was ridiculous, though. Chauffeurs, chefs, assistants, personal trainers. I could never go anywhere without an entourage. It's actually rather a relief to be just me again.'

'Well, then, that's good, isn't it?' said Tabitha, as if she needed convincing. 'Come into the pit. Sorry about the mess. I've got an opening in a couple of days and nowhere else to stash the sketches.'

Tabitha's office was pristine as ever, the only difference being a few large portfolio containers propped against one wall.

Petra came in with a coffee tray then left them to relax on the curved sofa set in one corner.

'Have you taken up painting, Jenna?' Tabitha had noticed the plastic wallet on her friend's lap.

'Oh, no, not me. I still can't draw a stick man to save my life. A friend. Rather a discovery, I think.'

'Really?'

Jenna reminded herself that Tabitha's look of professional scepticism was understandable. Of course she wasn't just going to take anyone's word that a brilliant new artist was about to burst on to the scene. She must hear this pitch a dozen times a week.

'Oh, I don't want to walk straight in and start thrusting these pictures on you,' she said, laughing and taking a sip of coffee. 'But I would like you to look at them sometime, if you don't mind.'

'Of course I don't mind.'

'I'm not expecting anything more than a quick "it has potential" or "it sucks". Just as a guide, that's all. I love art but you know as well as I do that it isn't my area of expertise.'

'Well, every time a really stunning piece comes to my gallery, it always seems to end up on your walls, darling, so I think I'd vouch for your taste. Let me drink my coffee and I'll have a look.'

They chatted about Tabitha's family and what was

happening on the London art scene until the coffee cups were dry.

Jenna could barely stand to look as Tabitha slid painting after painting from its transparent sheathing and frowned at each of them. She considered them all, looking from different angles, sometimes bringing an earlier one back to contrast and compare with the current focus, before putting them all back, carefully as if they were made of gold leaf, into the wallet.

'So?' said Jenna, and it came out as a whisper. 'What do you think?'

'Darling, I think if you were scared to tell me you'd painted these, you needn't be. They're wonderful.'

'No.' Jenna's laugh was near hysterical and she was surprised to find that she had tears in her eyes – of relief? 'Honestly, I didn't do any of them. But they *are* wonderful, aren't they? It isn't just me having a moment of madness?'

'Not in the least. They're remarkable. Who's the artist?' Tabitha's eyes were bright and Jenna realised, to her disappointment, that she was hoping it was one of Jenna's famous clients. Brilliant art plus a famous name would indeed be something close to the Holy Grail. But she was going to have to let her friend down gently.

'I'm afraid at this stage I can't tell you the name,' said Jenna, which only served to brighten Tabitha's eyes even more. 'Not that it would be one you'd have heard before.' The brightness dimmed.

'Oh? Then why ever not?'

'The artist wishes to remain anonymous. But they would like some, well, some recognition of their work. And to that end, they'd like your advice.'

'It *is* you, isn't it? Or is it Deano?'

'No, really, I faithfully promise you that you don't know, or know of, the artist. It's a private individual from my home town.'

'How intriguing.' Tabitha was clearly making an effort not to appear disgruntled. 'Well, it's certainly of displayable standard. If the artist were willing to step out of the shadows, I would be very happy to exhibit this. I think it would interest the arts media and might attract a buyer or two. And I'm not saying that as a favour to you. I think your mystery man or woman has exceptional talent. But exceptional talent is everywhere in this city, and often never finds its market.'

'Oh?'

'I'll be honest with you, if your man isn't willing to pound the pavement and do all the tedious publicity stuff, he won't get anywhere. I need a *person* to connect with.'

Jenna leant forwards, keen to sell her idea to Tabitha despite her misgivings.

'Yes, but can't we make anonymity work for us? You know – a touch of mystery, of enigma. I mean, look at Banksy.'

Tabitha paused. 'Well, we can't, can we? That's the whole point.'

'Quite. But do you get what I'm driving at?'

'There's only one Banksy,' said Tabitha firmly.

'Oh yes, but while the art is different, the publicity goal is the same. I think a mystery artist would interest the press and the public more than a few articles about his background and inspirations. And his work speaks for itself, surely.'

Tabitha shuffled through the pictures again.

'Well,' she said at length. 'I must admit, you've

intrigued me. I want to find out more about this person and see more of his work – it is a male, I take it, from what you've said?'

Jenna nodded. 'I'll tell you that much.'

'And if you're involved, we have an angle,' she continued. 'Because everybody's heard of you. If you act as his patron, for the purposes of our PR, that gives us a huge leg up from the start. Although it might also work against us – a lot of the art establishment is utterly dismissive of anything connected with popular culture. Modern popular culture, that is – they're mostly delighted to reference older versions of it. It might prevent his being taken seriously.'

'But we want to be popular, don't we?'

'I suppose we do. It's a risk. Everything's a risk in this game. We take a lot of chances.'

'So, will you take a chance on this?'

Jenna fought a strong urge to snatch Jason's pictures from Tabitha's hand. This could really happen, and it suddenly felt very dangerous indeed. His paintings couldn't now be unseen – nothing could be rewound. She almost wanted Tabitha to shake her head, to put them down, to say it was not for her.

'All right,' said Tabitha. 'For you, and because I really do think this work is rather wonderful, I'll get on board with you. I'll see about fitting in a private view – it might not be for some months, though, if you want to use the gallery. I'm fully booked until November.'

'November?' Jenna tried to compose her disappointed expression into one of mild understanding.

'I know it's a long time away.' Tabitha shrugged. 'We're doing well. What can I say?'

'I'm happy for you, but . . .'

'You're welcome to use the gallery's name if you want to hire a private venue.'

'Thank you. Perhaps I'll do that. Let me go away and think about it.'

'Yes, but—'

Tabitha put a hand on Jenna's arm, preventing her from reaching for the portfolio.

'Won't you tell me a little more about this man? I suppose he's some friend of yours?'

Jenna bit her lip. 'Really, I can't. It wouldn't be fair to him. I'm sure the day will come when he'll be happy to come into the public view, but it might be a while yet.'

'Goodness. I suppose he does know you're here?'

An unpleasant sensation of being hit in the solar plexus silenced Jenna before she could speak again.

'He . . . he doesn't like attention,' she stammered, fidgeting with her coffee cup.

'A recluse, perhaps?'

'Yes, that's it. He's a recluse. Never leaves the house.'

'How fascinating. May I keep the pictures?'

'Oh. Better not. Would you mind if, you know, perhaps you could take some photos of them?'

Tabitha sighed.

'This is all very cloak and dagger, I must say. All right then. Let's spread them out on the floor and I'll take a few snaps.'

They spent the rest of the morning trying to achieve the perfect photographic representation of each picture and sharing ideas about how to publicise Jason's work.

Jenna left with an unsettled feeling at the pit of her stomach that owed as much to fear as it did to excitement.

She was pleased to know that she was not alone in rating his paintings highly, but on the other hand, she had gone behind his back, and wished it could all be above board.

She called in at her company's London office after a solitary picnic lunch on its roof garden, then set straight back off on the long drive to Bledburn.

As mile after mile passed, she thought about all the offers her assistant had turned down on her behalf. Oodles of TV shows, adverts, voiceovers, appearances, free holidays had been offered and rejected. Every newspaper and celeb magazine wanted to know if there was a chance of reconciliation between her and Deano. He had made some veiled remarks in an interview, apparently, that made it seem as if it were on the cards. She would have to look that interview up, then send him an irritated email requesting him to keep her name out of his PR exercises.

These thoughts preoccupied her all the way home, so much so that they were still on her mind when she opened the front door. The sight of Jason, sitting on the bottom of the stairs reading yesterday's newspaper both startled and alarmed her.

'God,' she said. 'There you are.'

'Here I am,' he said, putting the paper down beside him and giving her a raised eyebrow of disapprobation. 'Did you forget about the bed?'

'What?'

'A delivery lorry turned up. Hammered at the door for ages before shoving this card through. I thought I'd best not answer it. You never know whether it's a trap.' He held it out.

'Shit, I totally forgot! I did order a bed to be delivered today. Damn. Oh, well, I'll just have to phone them . . .'

She trailed off.

Jason had spotted the portfolio under her arm. Why hadn't she left it in the car until the coast was clear?

'What are you doing with that?'

He reached out for it. With some reluctance, she handed it over.

His eyes were hard, black coals.

'Well? Are you going to answer me? Why have you taken my stuff out with you? What's going on, Jen?'

She sat down beside him on the stairs and took a deep breath.

'I took them to London with me.'

'What? Why?'

'Don't panic. Your name wasn't mentioned, nobody knows about you.'

'What,' he asked, very slowly and deliberately, and not a little menacingly, 'have you done?'

'I wanted a professional opinion on your work, so I showed them to a friend who runs an art gallery in London.'

'You did *what*?'

'Oh, don't. What's wrong with that? She loved them. She thinks you're brilliant. Jason!'

But he had shot to his feet and was storming upstairs, portfolio in hand.

By the time Jenna had gathered herself together to give chase, he stood on the landing. He withdrew one of his pictures – a dense landscape of terraces painted in a vertiginous, swirling pattern – held it up to her, then ripped it clean in half.

'Oh, Jason, no!'

She stopped, aghast, and could only watch as he

continued the process, tearing it to shreds which fluttered down the stairs towards her, settling all around like dark grey snow.

'Why?' she wailed.

'It's not mine,' he said. 'None of it's mine, any more.'

He flung the rest of the portfolio over the bannister, scattering pictures right and left, then stormed up to the attic, banging the door behind him.

'Jason!' she yelled, running upstairs in his wake. 'Jason, come down. Talk to me. Please.'

But no reply came from above, and he had weighted the trap door so she couldn't open it from below. After listening to the sounds of furious paint mixing and brushing, she decided to leave him to it and slouched downstairs, threw herself on her mattress and succumbed to the darkness, outside and in.

It was an hour, maybe two, before she moved. Her brain had run through every possibility, from leaving Bledburn tonight and never returning, to staying here forever and never re-engaging with the world outside. Somewhere, a workable balance had to be found. Jason's innocence had to be proved, so he could leave if he wanted or stay. If she hadn't thrown away that possibility for good.

She heard the creak of the trap door and stiffened, her nose still pressed firmly into the duvet. Soft steps whispered down the uncarpeted stairs – he wasn't wearing shoes, she thought – then crossed the hall.

She felt his presence in the doorway, even though she couldn't see him.

His voice, when it came, was a shock – rough and ragged at the edges.

'Sit up and look at me.'

It was a command, and she didn't dare disobey. She pulled her hot, rumpled face from the mattress and turned eyes, from which her defiance couldn't quite be extinguished, to him.

'I'm sorry,' she said. 'I should have asked first.'

'Aye,' he said quietly with an emphatic nod.

'But you'd have said no.'

His face, pale but set as firmly as that of a sergeant major about to give the battle signal, bore down on her, making her feel squeezed and a little breathless.

'I'd have said no,' he repeated after a pause. 'You knew that. But you went ahead.'

'I was doing it for you.'

'No you weren't,' he said, the anger flashing back. 'You were doing it for *you*. Your ego. Your satisfaction.'

She stared at him, open mouthed, wondering if he had a point.

'And why not?' he continued. 'Because look at you. Look at Lady Muck of Muck Hall, queen of all she surveys, including this poor bastard here.'

'Jason, no!'

But he spoke over her.

'I might be *on* your property, but it doesn't mean I *am* your property. You can't do what the fuck you like with me and mine, not without my consent, my permission.'

'I know that now, I'm sorry, please,' she gabbled, but still he went on.

'I know I'm only here to keep you happy in bed, and knock a few nails into walls, but you could at least *pretend* to have some respect for me.'

'But I do.' She rose from the mattress and stepped towards him, hands out, palms up. 'Jason, I promise you.'

He held up a hand of his own, establishing distance between them.

'What is it, Jen? Is it this place? Has it turned you into one of *them*? Made you think you can fuck the workers then sell them out? Is that it?'

She stared in horror.

'You can't think that of me. You can't. I'm one of *you*. I'm a worker.'

'Maybe you were once.'

'I still am.' She shouted it, desperate, wanting to grab him and shake him. 'Our lives are not a stupid metaphor for Bledburn, so you can shut up with that.'

'Right,' he said, breathing hard and fast. 'Right, I'll shut up. I'll clear off out of here. I'll go somewhere I'm respected, even it turns out to be prison.'

'No,' she cried, launching herself at him, in an effort to bodily restrain him from throwing himself to the wolves. She clung to his arms for dear life, refusing to be dislodged. 'I won't. You can't. You can't go to prison for something you didn't do. You can't go.'

She was crying now, the tears falling into her mouth and making her voice quiver and jolt, but she kept it up as forcefully as she could.

'I do respect you, I won't go behind your back again, I'm sorry, I won't. Please stay.'

She saw his eyes close, felt his resistance begin to ebb.

'Let go of me,' he whispered.

'Only if you stay. Only if you stay.' She kept repeating it until he grabbed her wrists and laid his head on her shoulder.

'All right,' he said. 'All right. For now.'

They held each other, tight enough to make their ribs

ache, feeling the other's chest rise and fall, feeling the heat, and the shaking, and the subsiding of rage.

'Why did you do it?' he asked, once they were calmer.

'It wasn't for glory. Please don't think that. I just thought that the world deserves to see your work.'

He shook his head on her shoulder.

'The world deserves fuck all from me,' he said. 'Sweet FA.'

Jenna didn't reply, but she understood what was at the heart of his objection and she could only sympathise.

'Call your mate,' he said, rocking back and forth now on his heels, taking her with him. 'Tell her it was a mistake. Tell her to forget it.'

'I will. I'm sorry.'

It had been too soon; she saw that now. She should have given him a little more time, waited until the legal nightmare was untangled. He would come round.

'You're a bit too free with me, Jen,' he said after a while, loosening his hold enough that he could look her in the eye. 'I'm not your toy. I think you need to learn that. I think you need to learn a lot of things.'

Jenna bristled at first, hating, as ever, to be told that she was not right and perfect in every way. After all, she'd grown so used to the sycophancy of the TV people in LA. It was a jolt to be seen as less than impeccable.

'And you're going to teach me, are you?' she said, slightly sulkily.

'Oh, don't tempt me,' he said with a hard little laugh. 'I could have you begging for mercy on this floor in three minutes flat. Don't think I couldn't.'

He was infuriating and yet his words inflamed her so much that she felt weak in his arms, ready to take anything from him. *Prove it*, beat her heart in an excitable tattoo.

'Look, I've said I'm sorry. I shouldn't have gone behind your back. *Mea culpa*. Can we move on from this? Please?'

'Yeah, because that'd suit you, wouldn't it?' he said. Hot breath in her ear. 'To get away with it.'

Her body was taut, knowing in advance that something was going to happen, preparing its defences. At the same time, her knickers were getting wetter and wetter.

Whatever you want to do, do it.

'I don't want to get away with it,' she said.

He moved one of his hands down, until it cupped the curve of her buttocks.

'Good, because you're not going to.'

He rubbed her skirt up and down, the light silky material rumpling over her bottom. Between her legs, the sensation quickened, causing her to hitch her breath and catch a little sigh.

'So, what are you going to do about it?'

'What am I going to do with you?' His hand rubbed again, fingertips tracing the cleft of her buttocks over the thin material of her dress. 'I'll give you three guesses.'

She'd never thought of herself as really kinky, although she'd had a few fantasies of being tied up and used, but the craving she had for him to raise his hand and bring it down hard on her bottom, just then, almost drove her out of her mind.

'Spank me?' she whispered, and it happened.

It was so sudden and so loud that she didn't feel the sting of it for a moment or two – too busy jumping out of her skin. But a handprint of heat soon seared through her and her legs came close to giving way.

'Ten out of ten,' he said. 'Clever girl.'

'That hurt,' she said, reaching behind her to tend to her sore spot, but he grabbed hold of her hand and held it tight.

'It's supposed to,' he said. 'But you can take a little pain, can't you? Especially when you know you deserve it.'

'You won't go too far, will you?' she asked, wondering how much force he had in him, if what she'd already had was just a taster.

'I won't bruise you. Unless you want me to. But I'll make sure you feel it for a while after. Trust me, babe. I'm an old hand at this.'

'Are you?'

'Uh huh. But this isn't the best position for it. I need to be sitting down.'

She followed him like a lamb as he led her into the kitchen, which contained a row of breakfast bar stools, ranged like chrome sentinels, with little black leather pillbox hats.

He positioned himself on one of them, even his long legs only just able to reach the floor, and slapped his thigh meaningfully.

Jenna, her hand held in his to prevent escape, felt as if she'd entered Looking Glass World. She'd never had a man treat her this way, would never have dreamt that she'd ever find herself in this position. But now she was here, she had to let the drama unfold, and it was more than mere curiosity urging her on. The place where Jason had smacked her felt good: it pulsed with excitement, and the need to feel it again.

She had to fight her natural urge to reject anything that smacked of abasement or humiliation, of course, but Jason knew that, and he tugged her closer then tumbled her over his thighs so that she didn't need to continue with that struggle any more. It was done. She was there, bum up, over this horrible, attractive bastard's lap, and there was nothing at all she could do about it now.

She could kick and flail, but her limbs came nowhere near the floor, and she was obliged to grab on to the metal legs of the stool to maintain balance, otherwise there was a real danger of sliding off his knees. Or, at least, there would have been, if Jason hadn't put a firm hand in the small of her back, holding her exactly where he wanted her.

'Keep your legs still or I'll have to go harder on you,' he said.

She let her muscles slacken at once and lay, shamefully docile, over her lover's lap.

The helplessness felt alien to her, and she had to adjust more to that than to the position itself, which was awkward and graceless but sustainable. To know that she could go nowhere, do nothing, without Jason's permission, gave a feeling in the pit of her stomach that wasn't quite fear – wasn't quite outrage – but included both of them. And yet the fear and outrage heightened the secret, shameful pleasure of it. A little nugget, hidden deep inside her, of intense realisation that she had been looking for this without knowing it. She had found it, the thing she had not known she wanted. Did she dare fully admit it to herself? Not yet. For now, she had to sigh and snuffle and complain and pretend that it was an ordeal for her. Even more so since she had the distinct impression that Jason had known she wanted this all along.

How dared he? He could he know her sordid, taboo

little secrets? It was unfair, and it laid her wide open to him.

She concentrated on her beautiful flooring; the polished granite tiles glowing and reflecting the subtle spotlighting. It looked good, even from this angle. Perhaps she'd mention that in her online review. Or perhaps not.

Jason was arranging himself on the stool, shifting into a more comfortable position. Anger seemed to have distilled into something else, judging by the burgeoning lump that made its presence felt beneath her pubis.

The hand on her spine moved to the hollow between her shoulders, while his other rested on her bottom, ready to deal more of what she had already experienced. How many? she wondered. And for how long? And how hard?

For a moment, fear claimed the upper hand in her turmoil of spirit.

'Are you going to hurt me?'

He patted her bottom.

'I told you. Nothing you can't handle. Just enough to show you I mean business. If it gets too much for you, just ask me to stop. I can't believe you wouldn't.'

Of course. It was obvious. But Jenna was shocked that this hadn't even occurred to her. She had swallowed Jason's authority whole, to the extent that questioning it seemed *verboten*. How had he done this to her, so effortlessly?

Her fear fell like a stone to the lowest reaches of her emotions. Now he was raising the skirt of her dress, revealing her knickers, causing her to squirm a little in his lap.

'Don't,' he said softly. 'Still.'

He lowered her knickers to her knees. She felt excruciatingly small and humble, reduced to her lowest status since childhood. She took the feeling and, instead of fighting it, sank into it, letting it seep into her overtired being. How light she felt now, how ready for what was coming to her.

When he laid the first stroke, she gave a sound that was more purr than plaint. Yes, she remembered it right, it had felt *good*. A wake-up call to her skin, to her flesh, to her sex and to that inner kernel of submissiveness she had ignored for all these years.

She knew he was holding back, testing her. The first few slaps were not much more than pats on her bare bottom, but together they joined and spread a festive warmth across her rump.

He paused to stroke her curves.

'Is that OK?' he asked, and she realised then that all the power was not with him. He had got her where he wanted her, but he wasn't going to abuse or overstep her trust. She was safe.

She nodded, then added, 'Quite nice, actually.'

'I knew it,' he said, laying a hard and hearty smack that made her yelp. 'I knew I was right about you. I'll stop pussy-footing around then, shall I?'

And he did. She had to hang on to that stool for dear life while he made her bottom scorch and her body flail and her sex melt into a flood of pure need. His palm was hard and his arm had a surprising amount of stamina, considering that it didn't do much more than hold a paintbrush most days.

But the longer he spanked her, the more she felt she could take. She didn't mind the sting, didn't mind the burn – in fact, she found it cathartic. She embraced it, pushing up her bottom for more. It was a good few minutes of solid smack-smack-smack before she began to struggle and emit breathy little cries. But still she didn't ask him to stop.

Towards the end, he started to speak to her, in gruff, broken sentences.

'So-won't-be-doing that-again, eh? Ask-me-next time.'

Words seem to coincide with strokes.

'Yes, yes, I will,' she gasped. 'Won't do that again . . . Owww.'

'Not so easy, now?'

An 'Ah' like the escape of gas was all she could manage.

He stayed his hand and laid it on her hot rounds, rubbing them.

'Bright red,' he said. 'I think the lesson got through, don't you?'

'Mm,' she said meekly.

'What's that? Didn't catch it.'

'Yes,' she whispered.

'So,' he said, his hands heavy on her sore flesh. 'What was the lesson?'

'I won't do anything that concerns you without talking to you first,' she said.

'Is that all?'

'Um?' She didn't know what else he wanted her to say.

'I mean, I think you learned something about yourself, didn't you?'

His hand slipped slyly between her thighs, much as she tried to clamp them together. Her face, she thought, must be as scarlet as her behind. He had the true measure of her. He knew that the way he treated her turned her on beyond her understanding.

'I don't know,' she whimpered.

He pushed his fingers in between her lips, soaking them.

'You don't know?' he said, dipping and stroking, slow and steady. 'Oh, I think you do. What happened here?'

'Ahhh.' The blessed relief of having her clitoris touched was enough to unstring every nerve.

'Tell me, Jen. Why are you so wet?'

He took his fingers away.

'No more until you tell me.'

Oh cruel, so cruel!

'It got me hot,' she blabbed.

'What did?'

'The . . . What you did got me hot.'

'What I did? Sit on a kitchen chair, you mean?' He let his fingers hover so close to her clit that she could almost feel them – almost. She tried to wriggle closer but he held her just that fraction apart from them.

'No, you *know*.' She knew he wasn't going to let her get away with it. If she wanted satisfaction, she was going to have to override her embarrassment.

'I don't,' he lied. 'Not until you say the words. What's got you so horny, hmm?'

She tried one last, agonised jerk then blurted out the words. 'The spanking.'

'Aha,' he said, and she half-expected the word 'Eureka' to follow, but it didn't. 'I see. Is that right? Does it really turn you on when I get you over my knee and smack your bum? Does it?'

He smacked it again to make his point, not hard, but enough to send tremors back down to her clit.

'Yes,' she wailed. 'Oh, please.'

'All right.' He had mercy on her, reaching into her once

more for a slow massage of her clit. 'That's good to know, Jen. Really good. Because I've got lots of tricks up my sleeve when it comes to spanking. Lots and lots.'

'Oh God,' she moaned. What the hell had she let herself in for now? Today, an over the knee hand spanking, tomorrow chained to the wall and bullwhipped? Not that he could chain her to any of the walls in this place. Now there was an idea for a decorative theme.

Her mind ran off its rails as her climax built, deliciously enlarged by the heat of her bottom and the excitement of her punishment. She felt like such a small thing as she bucked and yelped on his lap, reduced to her bare nature, known and understood and owned by him. It was terribly shaming, and the biggest turn-on of her life.

'OK,' he said roughly, handing her down from her awkward position on the stool. 'Come over here.'

He led her to one of the armless white leather dining chairs ranged about the table by the garden doors. He unbuttoned his jeans and ordered her to her knees.

She was happy to obey. She wanted to please him now, after everything he had given her.

When he sat down, his erection standing straight up in front of him, she leant forward, eager to wrap her lips around it.

But he put a hand on her shoulder, making her pause.

'Uh-uh,' he said. 'Ask for it. Nicely, mind.'

She shut her eyes and let the thrilling humiliation overwhelm her for a moment.

Then she spoke.

'Please, may I suck you?'

'Suck what?'

'Your cock. Please, may I suck your cock.'

'Thank you. You may.'

She did, deep and hungrily, while he tried his best to hold back for as long as possible.

He could ask anything of me, she thought, tremulous with alarm and adoration. He knows he has this power over me now.

What she had thought might be a secret, summer fling was moving far beyond her self-imposed limits, and fast.

What if I've fallen in love? It feels that way – as if he could kill me with a careless word. Oh, God.

She accepted and swallowed the quantity of bitterish liquid he spurted into her mouth, as gratefully as if it had been champagne from a king. Without being asked, she licked his shaft clean and kissed the tip, then bent her head and waited for him to speak.

He didn't for a while, lolling on the chair and recovering his breath.

When he revived, he bent forward and lifted her chin.

'Are you mine?' he asked.

'Yes.' She didn't need to think twice.

'I knew it. You're still on your knees. You're waiting for my permission, aren't you?' He stroked her cheek with his thumb, his gaze upon her so intense she thought it would shrivel her up. 'Good girl. Come on.'

He pulled her up into his lap and they snogged like teenagers, all tongues and fumbling fingers and clashing teeth, until her face was raw with stubble burn and there was nothing for it but to go back to the mattress and fuck each other into oblivion.

Her last words before they slid into well-earned sleep were, 'Am I forgiven?'

''Course,' he murmured. 'Cos you're mine.'

Her last thought was that she needed to get that bed delivered, and soon.

Chapter Six

Next day's *Bledburn Gazette* brought an unpleasant little shock with it.

TALENT TEAM COMES TO TOWN said the headline, then underneath, STARSPOTTER JENNA DIAMOND TO JUDGE LOCAL CONTEST.

'Oh, fuck!' she exclaimed, spreading the paper out on the kitchen table. Jason was painting upstairs, out of earshot, so she flipped out her phone and rang Lawrence immediately.

'Lawrence,' she said without preamble, speaking over his delighted noises of recognition. 'You've spoken to the *Gazette*. Why?'

'Why not?'

'I never agreed to this! I said I'd think about it.'

'But you were going to agree, surely. For Bledburn. For the kids.'

He seemed to put inverted commas around 'the kids' and it made him sound sarcastic, riling her up even more.

'How dare you railroad me? I didn't want publicity. I

was happy to do something low-key for the youth club but this . . .'

'Oh, chill out, Jenna. It'll be great. Let's meet up later and fine-tune it, shall we?'

'I can't promise anyone anything. I don't want to be hustling record and TV companies for the winner. That's *work*. I'm on a *sabbatical*. Don't you understand?'

'For God's sake, a couple of phone calls won't give you a nervous breakdown, surely.'

'And my name isn't Diamond any more. It's Myatt. Why didn't you tell them?'

'Oh, I'm sure I did, but you know the *Gazette* – hazy on the details.'

'That's another reason why you shouldn't have blabbed. Honestly, I'm really pissed off, Lawrence. Really, truly, pissed off.'

'Well, I'm sorry if I pre-empted you. I thought it was OK, honestly. I thought you were up for this.'

'You should have cleared it with me,' she said, suddenly understanding Jason's ire about her art gallery stunt of the day before. Perhaps she should take his approach and give Lawrence a good spanking. The thought made a tiny bubble of laughter rise inside her and she couldn't sound as angry as she wanted.

'OK, I should have. I'm sorry. But can we meet? We need to establish times, dates, prizes, details, all kinds of things.'

'I'm a bit busy,' she demurred.

'Well, what if I come to you? Bring a bottle and a takeaway, if you're free tonight?'

God, no!

'No, no, that's fine, I've got painters and decorators in,'

she lied, 'and the place is an unholy mess. I'll call you and we'll do something at the weekend, yeah?'

'But couldn't we—'

There was a hammering at the door, reminding her that she needed to fix the bell.

'Shit. Delivery – I have to go. I've already missed this one once.'

She ended the call and ran to the door. In the hustle and bustle of supervising the delivery of a fine big bed into the drawing room , she forgot her irritation and spent the rest of the day out shopping for sheets and pillowcases, and supplies for decorating the big front bedroom, her next project.

'Nice to have a bed to lie in, isn't it?' she said contentedly to Jason, the new furniture having been tested for strength and durability in the time-honoured manner. Jenna was wrung out, stinging between the legs and ready to fall into the sleep of the just, while Jason was sitting up, finishing off a half-bottle of wine.

'Yeah,' he said. 'It's been a while, for me.'

'I'll get started on that bedroom tomorrow, if you'll help.'

'I'll take a break from painting by painting,' he said.

'I know, but it is different, at least.' She yawned hugely. 'Aren't you tired?'

'Knackered,' he said. 'But I want to wait up and listen out for strange noises.'

'What?' She turned tired eyes to him.

'Last three nights in a row I've heard noises,' he clarified.

'What sort of noises?'

'Like somebody crying.'

'Shit.' She sat up, staring. 'Somebody told me this place was haunted.'

He gave her a pitying look. 'Don't be daft. I thought it might be rats or summat like that. There's a cellar down below, is there?'

'I don't know. I suppose it's likely. Wasn't mentioned in the deeds, though.'

'No? Cos it definitely sounds like it's coming from under the floor.'

Jenna tried to dismiss the cold feeling in her chest. Ghosts didn't exist.

'Are you sure it's not Bowyer, on the hunt outside?'

Jason snorted. 'Bowyer hunting, that'll be the day. Ever since you pitched up, the lazy fucker's more likely to chase a tin opener than a bird or a mouse. It's not coming from outside, I'd swear to it.'

Jenna racked her brains, sure she couldn't recall any mention of a cellar. But all of these big old houses had them, she was certain. Had she seen a trap door anywhere, or anything that might give access to some stairs?

'There was no cellar in the floor plan,' she said. 'And the agent never mentioned it.'

'Probably been shut off for years, abandoned, like,' said Jason. 'Maybe there's a murdered body down there.' He grinned, ghoulishly, and waggled his fingers in a spooky manner.

'Don't. It's not funny.'

'You're freaked out, aren't you? Aw, don't be. It's nothing. Just mice or summat.' He put an arm around her, resting her head on his shoulder. 'And I'm here. No bastard ghost would mess with me.'

'No, I'm sure,' she said. 'I'm going to look for a cellar

tomorrow. Not tonight though. Tonight I think we should just get some sleep.'

'Aye, you're right.' Jason snuggled down under the covers with her. 'It'll be nothing, anyway.'

All the same, she was slow to fall back into that lulling, pleasant weariness again, her ears seeming to pick up the lightest of sounds. The house being old, it tended to creak and crack all night long anyway, and each little clank of water pipe made her heart race. She heard nothing that sounded like crying, though, and she fell asleep without incident.

The next day they were too busy steaming and stripping off the ancient wallpaper in the big front bedroom to be much concerned with the possibility of hidden cellars, but when they broke for lunch and she put together her edamame salad (much to Jason's disgust) she looked down at her beautiful granite tiles and wondered if the elusive cellar entrance was below it. How awful to have to pull it all up again. She didn't think she'd have the heart, or the energy.

Jason, having grilled some bacon for his own lunch, slapped it into a bap and squirted generous amounts of ketchup all over it.

'One wall to go,' he said cheerfully. 'I'll finish this then I'll refill the steamer. Did you find anything interesting underneath yours?'

'No. What do you mean – underneath the paper?'

'Yeah. There was writing on part of mine. Said "I am lost" in that kind of old-fashioned, curly handwriting.'

'"I am lost".' Jenna felt that creeping feeling of chill again. 'That's . . .ugh!'

'Dead faint, like. Could hardly see it, but it'd been kind

of scratched in, so the ink was faded but you could read what it said still.'

'Christ.'

'Probably kids,' he said, shrugging and smiling at her consternation. 'Don't look like that. Whoever did it is long gone.'

Or still in the cellar, in spectral form.

But she had a stern word with herself before returning to the bedroom with her scraper.

The writing still upset her equilibrium, though, written as it was in a wobbly, old-fashioned hand. It had to be about a century old, maybe older.

'Who do you think wrote it?' she asked Jason, but he shrugged.

'Anyone who married into the Harvilles,' he said. 'Poor bastards probably didn't know what they were letting themselves in for.'

'Or children, being children,' she said, to cheer herself. 'Maybe a child playing hide and seek, genuinely lost in the house. A visitor.'

Jason turned to her and cast an appraising, amused eye over her.

'Blue-sky thinker, as one of my idiot teachers used to say. You don't like to think of bad stuff happening, do you? You want to make everything all lovely and nice.'

'What's wrong with that? It got me out of Bledburn, didn't it?'

'And now you're back here, because everything in La-La-land stopped being La-La. Stopped going your way. So you didn't want to play any more.'

Stung, she sucked in a breath.

'Is that what you think of me?'

'Controlling? Well, aren't you? Just a bit?'

'Jason, I'm *tired*. I've worked flat out for years. I deserve a break.'

'You're tired of moving people around like pawns,' he said. 'You want a break from that. Let someone else take the strain.'

'Like you, you mean?'

He held up his hands, one carrying a scraper.

'I'd be up for it,' he said.

'Fine, I'll give you my office number and you can take care of all the calls and texts then.'

'That's not what I mean, and you know it.'

'What do you mean, then?'

'Well, all right,' he said, putting down the scraper and folding his arms with a frown. 'If you want to know. The other night, when we had our little clash, you didn't seem too unhappy with how I dealt with it. Right?'

She looked at her feet in their battered Converse boots. 'Right,' she muttered.

'I'd say it came as a relief to you. And maybe even something that'd been missing from your life. Am I reading it wrong?'

'No,' she said, still focusing on the curls of old wallpaper around her toecaps.

'So perhaps you'd like to get a bit more into it?'

She looked up.

'How do you mean?'

'Well, not so much the handcuffs and floggers and stuff, unless you're into that, but the submission thing. You seemed to like giving in to me, like it took a weight off you.'

'That's how it felt,' she said, more to herself than him.

'Like a weight coming off. Not having to be responsible for everything. I never thought I'd want to give up control to anyone but . . . It's weird.'

'We're all a bit weird, duck,' he said, and she smiled at the local term of endearment. 'It's nothing to be ashamed of. It doesn't make you any less of a power broker in your outside world. But if you want to leave that at the bedroom door, well, why not? I'd be into it. And I think you'd be into it, too.'

She looked at him wonderingly, taking him in. For all his paint-spotted scruffiness, he looked like a man who could handle her. She'd never really seen that in a man before.

'I know what you're thinking,' he said, looking away for a minute. 'You're not sure if you can trust me, and I don't blame you but—'

'No,' she said. 'I wasn't thinking that. Which is strange, because I *should*, shouldn't I? But it never even occurred to me.'

His expression made her want to cry.

He held out his hands.

'Come here,' he said. 'I want to give you a hug.'

She walked into his arms and felt herself enfolded, encompassed, safe. This piece of Bledburn flotsam was so much more than he seemed. On paper, he looked like the worst prospect ever, but when she looked at him, when she touched him, he was everything she wanted.

'Thanks,' he said into her ear. 'That means more to me than I can tell you.'

She raised her chin and met his eye.

'I mean it,' she said. 'I trust you. I believe everything you've told me. I know the world's against you, but it'll have to be against me, too, because I'm on your side.'

She stood with her head against his shoulder, his hand in her hair, his cheek on the crown of her head, for a long time. It seemed neither of them wanted to break the embrace.

'So,' he said finally, unlocking them from their impasse with a pat on her bottom and a kiss on her forehead. 'What do you want to try first?'

'You mean—?'

'In bed. Is there anything you're curious about? Any little experiments you'd like me to take you through?'

'Oh, I don't know,' she said, with the dizzy feeling of being surrounded by shelves and shelves of sweetie jars, and no idea what to choose. 'Aren't you the expert? With your friends who worked in sex shops and all that?'

'I've tried most things,' he admitted with a cocky little smirk. 'You're in safe hands with me, love. And when I say safe, I mean . . .'

'*Hard*!' she exclaimed, thinking back to the spanking.

They both laughed.

'All right. You want me to take the lead? That seems appropriate.'

He pondered for a while, tapping his fingers against his lips as he did so, while Jenna tried very hard not to prance about like a cat on hot bricks, desperate to know what was going through his dirty mind.

'OK,' he said eventually. 'Here's a mission for you. Get yourself to the sex shop in Trentham. Buy yourself a vibrator and some bondage cuffs – any kind, I don't mind. Make 'em comfortable. Oh, and a flogger. Nothing fierce, just a suede one.'

'I . . .' She stood, staring, too many responses flying about in her mind for one to step forward.

'Go on, then.'

'But can't I order them? Online?'

'Well, you could, but then they wouldn't get here till tomorrow earliest, would they?'

'I suppose not.'

'And besides, I want you to go to the shop. I want you to take those things up to the counter, out and proud, baby.'

'But they'll all know who I am,' Jenna wailed. 'I *can't*. I'll die of embarrassment.'

'Don't be a div, Jen. Everybody buys sex toys now. Nobody's going to judge you. Much,' he said, with a little chuckly cough.

'But have you thought of what the gossip will be, beyond my being a kinky perv? They'll wonder who I'm doing it with. It could get in the papers, Jay.'

He shrugged. 'They aren't going to see you with me, are they? Not like we'll get papped going into nightclubs or owt.'

'I can't,' she said again, after a moment's pause.

'Listen, Jen. Don't think of it as a request. Think of it as an order.'

His voice was hard now, and he took a firm hold of her elbow, leaning down to her. She felt that fatal thrill, the weakness, the flutter.

'What if I refuse?' she whispered.

'I think you know.'

Time had slowed, everything around her was blurry and wonderlandish.

'OK. I'll go now. In these old jeans and vest, with my hair tied back like this and my shades on. There's an outside chance nobody will recognise me, or look twice.'

'That's the girl,' he said, kissing her nose. 'Do you want me to write you a list?'

'No, I think I can remember. Thanks.'

She left the room without looking back.

'I'll finish off in here, then,' he called after her.

Yes, she thought. You do that. You'll finish me off, too.

She put on her sunglasses and posed in front of the mirror, desperate to be as unrecognisable as possible. On TV, she always had big hair, but she didn't bother here in Bledburn, so that was one bonus. A different hairstyle was often as good a disguise as any. No make-up, boring clothes, flip-flops. A person would have to look twice and, in a busy street, most people wouldn't bother.

In a sex shop, though . . .

Oh, God. With any luck, it would be empty. Mid-afternoon on a working weekday had to be a safe-ish time to do this kind of thing. An idea occurred to her. She could pretend she was buying them for a hen party. Yes, that was how she would rationalise it. The stuff wasn't for her – it was jokey gifts for some bride-to-be. Excellent.

Thus buoyed up, she made the drive to Trentham in double quick time, parked in one of the little short-stay parks on the fringes of town, where the shop was situated, and hurried through the hinterland of corner pubs and charity shops until she found the unlovely 70s concrete mini-mall she sought.

It was near-deserted, apart from some mums of small kids, smoking and chatting outside a bakery while their little ones tore into sausage rolls in their buggies. None of them registered her and she passed as quickly as she dared without risking attention for being *too* quick.

The sex shop was in the corner unit. Its display was pink and floral, as if pretending to be a fashion boutique, but the only clothes in the window were very brief briefs and lacy basques.

Luckily, the door stood open, so she was able to flit inside without too much side-eyeing. She went over to an inoffensive display of nightdresses, pretending to take an interest in the flimsy negligees until the sales clerk looked away. It was quiet all right – too quiet. The woman at the till was clearly bored and would probably watch her like a hawk. She might even ask her if she needed any help. And then the possibility of being recognised loomed large.

She moved slowly past the nightgowns and into the lingerie. Most of it was quite ordinary; the kind of thing you could get from any department store. As she walked further towards the back of the shop, it began to be made of strange fabrics, like PVC and latex, and holes appeared at inopportune places, like the nipples and crotch.

She began to fluster. Had Jason been mistaken about this place? She couldn't see anything in the way of sex toys – the entire floor was given over to clothes, about a fifth of them really racy and the rest quite suitable for giving to your fun aunty at Christmas. Closer to the till, rack upon rack of stockings, fishnet gloves and little fluffy bits and bobs could be acquired. Some books and magazines. A shelf of glittery make-up. Nothing looked remotely like a vibrator.

She was almost at the back, with the shiny black catsuits and the leather corsets, when she noticed a staircase heading down.

MORE ITEMS IN BASEMENT read the sign on the wall above.

Ah.

Feeling as if she was heading along the Styx into Hades, she took the first few steps down.

She felt the sales clerk's gaze boring into her back as she made her descent. At least nothing was said.

In the basement, she was blessedly alone, and she needed to be because first sight of all that – God, what even *was* it all – was enough to bring her out in a cold sweat. She had an impression of lots of metal, and a noticeable smell of rubber. Chains and clips and cuffs and collars and . . . Oh, boy. It was all here, all right.

Vibrators were right there on her left, easy to find, but such quantities of styles and shapes and sizes and colours and materials that Jenna was sure she'd never be able to pick one.

She went to study the rows of samples, picking them up, weighing them in her hand, assessing them for potential fit and comfort. Why had Jason just said, 'a vibrator'? Couldn't he have been more specific? She was tempted to call him, except that she still had no landline and he had no mobile, so that would be a pointless exercise. Perhaps she'd nip into a phone shop, after this, and get him a cheap Pay As You Go.

In the meantime, she stared into a wall of flesh-coloured latex, interspersed with purple plastic and black glass and all variations in between. She was frowning at a long, thin number with a curved end, wondering how it worked, when a voice at her ear made her twitch and almost yelp.

'Do you need any help?'

'No, no, really. Fine.'

'It's just there's such a lot to choose from these days,' said the sales clerk sympathetically. 'I remember when you

had your rabbit or your plain plastic whatnot and that was
that. But now, well, you've got your bullet, your butterfly,
your g-spot, your magic wand . . .' She enumerated on her
fingers.

'Yes, quite,' said Jenna, trying to disguise her voice with
a quantity of coughing.

'I'll leave you to it. But give me a shout if you need a
hand.'

The offer struck Jenna as hilarious and she couldn't
help giggling, close to hysteria.

'Look,' she said, pushing her sunglasses back down
over her eyes. 'If I was to say I wanted a very basic model
– it's a joke present for a hen night, you see. I don't want
to spend a fortune.'

'Oh well, you probably want this, then.'

The sales clerk picked a plain, plastic flesh-coloured
number.

'Three speeds, only five pounds.'

'I'll take it. Thanks.'

'Can I help you with anything else?'

'Oh no, I think I can manage from here.'

The sales clerk turned to go, then stopped and glanced
back at her. Jenna knew that look. The 'where have I seen
you before?' look.

She scuttled hurriedly to the back of the room, making
it clear that further conversation was not an option.

Ah. Now here was something else on her list. The
flogger. And what a lot of interesting company it had.
Hanging on hooks, from ceiling to floor, were a cascade
of disciplinary implements, from slender, mean-looking
riding whips to sweet little heart-shaped, fur-backed
leather paddles. One of those might be nice, actually. She

picked it up and stroked the fluff. Another had letters cut out to form the word 'SLUT' on the recipient's skin. Beside them, a scarier range of leather straps in varying lengths and thicknesses made her both shudder and thrill. How would they feel? She weighed one in her palm and found it heavy, but supple. That would hurt a lot.

At the end, the canes stood menacingly in an umbrella stand, price tags tied around their whippy shafts. The floggers were arranged above them.

Jason had said she should go for a light one with suede thongs. She found the perfect specimen, with a thick handle and strands of purple suede so whispery soft she couldn't for the life of her imagining it hurting at all. It felt delicious as she dragged it across her palm, a promise, a caress. She looked forward to experiencing it on another part of her and she closed her eyes to picture Jason in the act of using it.

What if she bought Jason something to wear? But all the costumes seemed to be for women, unless they were harnesses or gimp masks, which hardly seemed right. She wanted something sleek and form-fitting but manly – not the sort of thing that would make her want to laugh at him. She'd have to look elsewhere for that, though.

There was something else on the list – what was it? She thought and thought, and then she looked up and saw. Cuffs. All kinds of cuffs. Velcro, metal, leather – what to go for?

She opted for a kit that described itself as 'Perfect For Bondage Beginners', containing a set of black velvet cuffs and an eyemask. It would have to do. She had spent long enough here and expected the sales clerk to burst back through the door, shouting, 'Oh, *now* I've placed you!' at any moment.

She took her goods to the counter, annoyed to find a pair of new customers in, riffling through the racks of frilly knickers and nighties. Luckily, they didn't bat an eyelid at Jenna's armful but carried on loudly discussing the disgusting service they'd had in another shop.

The sales clerk rang it all through without comment but, as she put the items in a bag, she said, 'Have you seen our hen night extras? These are popular.'

She pointed to a display behind her, of L-plates and scratchy lace veils and the like.

Jenna shook her head and snatched her bag.

'I'm fine,' she said, handing over her card to pay, realising too late that her old, married name was still on it.

The sales clerk said, 'Ooh!', then stopped short, seeming to understand Jenna's mood. No further words were spoken, and Jenna made a rapid escape from the shop, the dingy mall and the generally grubby part of town they both inhabited.

Damn, she thought, taking refuge in the car and putting the brown paper bag of sex toys on the passenger seat. She's going to tell all her friends I was in today, and what I bought and what I said . . . Oh God. Don't panic. It'll just be an anecdote for them. It won't make front page news. They'll have forgotten about it in a month.

While she worked on calming herself down enough to drive, she took out her phone and found an online men's clothing store, where she ordered a smart black jacket and trousers for Jason, together with a pack of three crisp, white shirts. If he was going to flog her, he wasn't going to do it in jeans or, worse still, trackie bottoms. He would have to look the part. A tie? Oh, why not. What about shoes, though?

She put the phone down, realising she didn't know his shoe size, and drove off out of town.

From the ring road around Bledburn, the estate was visible; a nest of red-brick housing, in concentric circles like a child's ball-in-a-maze game. At the centre, low-rise grey flats, the pub, the mini-market and the youth club. Perhaps she ought to call in on Kayley, give her a progress report about the bloody talent show.

Not today, though. Tomorrow. She cast her eye over the bag on the passenger seat and bit her lip. Whatever was going to happen at home, tonight, came first.

Clutching her paper bag, she ran up the front steps and let herself into the house. It was quiet, and motes of dust danced around in the late afternoon sunshine.

'Jay?'

No reply. She put her head into the drawing room and the kitchen – the obvious places – then went up to the bedroom they'd been stripping. The walls were now bare plaster and a great pile of paper scraps lay in the centre. Her eye rested on the little message and then she blinked rapidly, trying to expel it.

Jason was not here. He must be painting in the attic.

But the attic was empty too, the great mural paintings surrounding a vacant space.

Jenna told herself not to panic, to breathe normally, to stop assuming the worst. Descending the attic stairs, she called his name again.

When no reply came, she ran in and out of every room, her pace increasingly hectic, her hands increasingly shaky. He was nowhere to be found. Finally, just as she was about to drop to the kitchen floor and sob, she noticed that the back door was open.

She ran out in the wilderness of garden and found him, sitting on the low wall that bordered the kitchen yard, drinking a can of beer, with his shirt off and Bowyer purring at his side.

'Jesus,' she gasped, holding the lintel of the door for support. 'Thank fuck. Oh, God. Don't do that to me again.'

'Do what?' He squinted at her. She still held the paper bag from the sex shop.

'I thought you . . . I thought . . . Gone. Been taken. Or just gone.'

She doubled over, panting out the remains of her panic.

'Oh, come here, you daft thing,' he said, crumpling the beer can and throwing it, with deadly accuracy, into an ancient water butt. 'I'm not going anywhere, am I?'

She joined him on the wall, subsiding against him, welcoming the reassurance of his arm around her waist, cradling her head on his bare, sun-kissed shoulder.

'If you'd gone,' she whispered, 'I don't know what I'd have done.'

'Looked for me, I hope,' he said. 'Hush.' He kissed her hair, pulling her tighter into him. 'I only came out to look for Bowyer. He hadn't eaten all day and I was starting to worry.'

'He seems fine,' remarked Jenna dryly, observing the dark grey cat stretched out in the sun in a state of blissful laziness.

'Yeah, he's just found himself a favourite bush, that's all. Can't say I blame him.'

'Oh, stop it.'

'It's a nice day, though. Thought I'd join him, that's all.

Nobody can see into this back garden and, if they could, well, look around you.' He sang the opening bars of Guns 'n' Roses' 'Welcome to the Jungle'.

'It's a risk, though.'

'Barely. Better than when I was skip-diving, before you moved in.'

'I suppose.'

'What do you think of that?' He nudged his toe at a paving slab. It had a clump of weedy overgrowth on it that, when pushed aside, revealed a rusty iron ring.

'Oh! The cellar? Do you think?'

'Nah. I've tried pulling it up but it's no good. I thought it might be though.'

On impulse, she threw her arms around his neck and made him kiss her. He had no objections to this, and they smooched in the mellowing sunshine, until the paper bag slipped off her lap and on to the flagstones.

'You haven't showed me your shopping yet,' he said, with a sly smile.

'No, and I'm not getting it out here,' she retorted. 'Not in front of that cat.'

Jason laughed. 'He won't mind. That cat's seen stuff'd make his fur curl. I'm surprised it hasn't.'

'Don't tell me. I don't want to know.'

She shuffled off the wall, picked up the paper bag and walked demurely back into the kitchen.

By the time Jason followed, she'd emptied her purchases over the table, where they lay in stark relief on its sleek, stylish lines. Three cheap, garish sex toys, a long way from their natural home.

Jason picked up the flogger first.

'Purple, nice,' he said, running the strands through

his fingers, then winding and looping them around a forefinger. 'Did you have loads to choose from?'

'Yes. You said suede, though . . .'

'Yeah, I think I did. Anything else take your fancy while you were browsing? Any paddles, whips, straps, canes?'

'*Not* canes,' she said with an involuntary shake of her head.

'Oh? Why not canes?'

'They just look so painful.'

'That's kind of the point.'

'Not for me, it isn't. Not yet, anyway.'

'Fair enough.' He unwound the little thongs and gave the table a sharp, downward stroke.

Jenna found herself pitying the table. The sound of the flogger making contact with the Corian top had been startling and swift and, soft as the suede was, she could imagine it would have hurt on bare skin.

'This is nowhere near as nasty as the cane,' he said. 'It can tickle, too. You'll see.'

'I hate tickling.'

'Ah, see, you shouldn't have told me that.' With a devilish grin, he flicked the tails at Jenna's bare arm. She squeaked and tried to dart out of range, but he grabbed hold of her and began to drape the flogger up and down her back, lifting up her vest to let it feather over her exposed skin.

'Oh, don't,' she protested, squirming and trying to knee him away. 'It *tickles*.'

There was no way she could get away from him, though. She thought he must have been doing press-ups, or sit-ups, or something when she went out, because his grip was iron and his body felt solid against hers.

'Wait till you feel it further down,' he whispered.

'Nooo,' she moaned.

'You will,' he promised then, to her breathy relief, he put it back down.

The next thing he picked up was the cuffs.

'Not bad,' he said. 'And a blindfold, too. Is that a hint?'

She blushed. 'Might be.'

'Taken,' he said, reaching over and fitting it around her eyes. The velvet dark was instantly disorientating, making her more aware of the soft sounds of the summer evening beyond the kitchen door and the hot male scent of Jason.

'I think I'm ready for some experiments. Are you?'

He turned her around with a hand on her shoulder, and she heard sounds that made it clear he was putting the rest of the toys back in the bag. Then he guided her towards the hall. She heard the scrunch of the paper bag in his hands and felt the weight of his palm on her, heavier than usual. Was that the blindfold?

'Do you trust me, Jen?' he asked gently. She felt the flooring change from granite to wood. They were out of the kitchen, the smell of newness changing quickly to one of age and damp, mixed with polish and the vase of lilies on the side table.

'I think I can,' she said. 'I hope I can.'

'I'm going to show you. On that nice, new bed of yours.'

'Ours,' she corrected without stopping to think.

'What?'

'That nice new bed of ours.'

He bent and kissed her ear, stopping by the drawing room door.

'I didn't pay for it,' he said.

'No, but I think you're earning your keep.'

He nipped her earlobe.

'Aren't I just?' he said, nudging her through the doorway.

The smell changed again. Less musty, more lived-in, with a hint of her favourite perfume from where she had sprayed it into the air before leaving the house.

Halfway across the room, Jason came to a standstill and turned her around to face him.

'Arms up,' he said, placing his hands in her armpits as a prompt.

She raised her hands in immediate surrender and let him lift her vest up and off her, leaving her in bra and jeans.

'Should've got you to buy some of their pervy underwear,' he said. 'Nice PVC corset or something. Next time.'

He slid one hand into the small of her back, holding her steady while he used the other to trace the outline of her bra cups, then hold her breasts in his palm, rubbing and kneading them under the padded satin.

'You were never tempted to get a boob job then?' he said. 'These are one hundred per cent real.'

'No, no. I had Botox, and fillers, and a few bits and bobs but nothing major. Why, do you think I should have had my boobs done?'

'Fuck, no. Shagged a girl with implants once, was like feeling up a melon. Weird. I like a bit of give.'

'And a bit of take,' she whispered.

'Yeah,' he said, and she could picture the lascivious smirk on his face. 'A lot of take.'

He ran his hands over her ribs, her sides, her back and shoulders, then he edged her backwards until her thighs met the side of the bed and she tumbled into a sitting position.

Then he was unlacing her shoes and pulling off her socks, holding each bare foot and giving it a stroke that came perilously close to a tickle until she curled up her toes and tried to kick him off.

'Oi, feisty,' he warned. 'You need to watch yourself, madam. I'm the one with the whip.'

It was a good point. She twisted her ankles, as if using them to plead and wheedle. He pulled her back to her feet and unbuttoned the waistband of her jeans.

'What's in here, then?' he murmured, pushing his hand down inside.

She held herself as straight as she could, gasping as he delved between her thighs, forcing them apart. His fingers pushed up at the gusset of her knickers, making the cotton rub and bunch inside her pussy lips. She felt like falling backwards, her knees beginning to buckle, but he put a hand on her hip and kept at her, rucking the thin material of the knickers until it was fully inside her lips, a thick strip covering her clit.

'How many times do you think I'm going to make you come tonight?' he asked as he worked on her.

'I don't know,' she whispered, her thoughts reeling away from her.

'Guess. Go on. How many?'

He pushed the wedge of fabric up and down, making sure the friction against her clit was just enough to be maddening.

'Three,' she said at random.

'Oh, I think I can do better than that. Let's see, shall we?'

He took his fingers out of her crevice and pushed the jeans over her hips and down to her ankles. Once she had wriggled her feet free, he pulled her into an embrace and stood with her clasped to him, kissing her fiercely with one hand on her bottom, inside her knickers.

Once she was as hot and melty as she could be, he laid her on the bed, kneeling over her, and kissed her from her throat to the elastic of her knickers. On the way, he unclasped her bra and freed her breasts, treating them to a thorough tongue bath. She was twisting this way and that, her back arched, her gusset soaked, every cell of her body begging for more, harder, longer, when he rolled her roughly over and began the business of cuffing.

One velvet restraint was buckled on to her left wrist, then the connecting chain was drawn up and looped around one of the bars in the wrought iron headboard. Her right wrist received the same treatment, leaving her with arms spread out on either side of her head, and her hands quite helpless. She could waggle her fingers a little but, in effect, she was defenceless and bound. Now, she would find out how much she trusted Jason – and how much he deserved her trust.

This could go terribly wrong, and yet she had faith that it would not. Was it faith, or was it sheer excitement, tripping through her veins and sparking on her skin?

'Oh yeah,' he crooned, and she felt his knees press her legs together, the denim rough against her bare skin as he straddled her like a cowboy on his mount. 'My prisoner.'

He put his hands underneath her, coming between her nipples and the bedspread, holding her breasts firmly while he fed hot breath and kisses into her ears and neck. The mattress creaked softly as he rocked back and forth, pushing his still-covered erection against her bottom until it had made a considerable dent in the cotton, right in the crease of her cheeks.

'Have you ever done anal?' he asked.

She shook her head.

'No.'

'Wrong answer,' he murmured, right into her ear. 'The right answer was "not yet – but soon".'

She squirmed, feeling the tension of the cuffs on her wrists, and loving it. She was completely lost to this man, in thrall to the obscene education he was giving her. She wanted to pass all the tests, move on to the advanced level, make him proud.

'I'll have your arse,' he continued, his voice like filthy honey, sending its dirty sweetness way inside her. 'I'll make it mine, babe. All mine. You're all mine.'

He kissed her neck again and sucked it, reminding her of the old days, in back alleys behind tawdry pubs and clubs, with Deano. Those no-holds-barred, hands-all-over-everywhere days. God, they'd been good. How did they end? Why did they end?

He released her breasts and shuffled further down her legs, peeling her knickers off as he moved lower.

'Are you wet, love?' he asked, removing them completely. 'I think you are. Are you?'

'Mm-hmm,' she said, feeling the burn of her cheeks, even though they were buried in a pillow.

'Oh yeah,' he said, an explorer discovering his promised land – except in Jason's case the promised land was Jenna's pussy and the explorer was his fingers. 'God, dripping. So wet. And you reckon only three?' He chuckled. 'We'll see about that.'

He smacked the backs of her thighs, once each, smartly but not especially hard.

'Spread 'em,' he said, in bad imitation of a US cop show.

She parted her legs, trying to imagine what he could see. Everything open and available to him, nothing off limits.

'OK,' he said, and she heard the rustle of paper. 'Because you're such a bad girl, I'm going to start with . . .'

She guessed he was going to use the flogger, and clenched her buttocks.

He loomed over her from behind. She could almost feel his shadow.

'Relax them,' he said, rubbing her bottom with his palm until she obeyed and let her muscles loosen. 'I'm not going to beat seven bells out of you, for Christ's sake. It's supposed to feel good.'

The first stroke fell, a pleasant little spatter on her skin, not in the least bit painful. It was like being flogged with silk ribbons – the sting was only just detectable with serious concentration. But she knew he'd made it so deliberately, and that it could hurt a lot if he just used his wrist a bit more.

'Is that nice, hmm?' he asked. 'Want more?'

'Yes please,' she said, very quietly. He made her say it again, louder.

She eased into the play, enjoying the sweet sensation. First it was ticklish and made her giggle, then it began to confer a slow, sensuous buzz, sensitising her and making her crave more, and harder.

Jason was keeping a close watch on her responses, it seemed, for as soon as her breathing deepened, he stopped and laid the flogger across her gradually warming globes.

'Feeling it?' he asked.

'Oh, don't stop,' she said, the words coming out without her having to think about them.

'Don't worry, you'll get more,' he said.

But first, there was more crackling, and then a low hum. The vibrator.

Its curved tip was cold enough to make her gasp and jiggle her hips, at first, but it soon matched the temperature of her juicy folds once it had circled her clit a few times. Jason drew slow circuits, keeping his hand perfectly steady and his motion tantalisingly in check, never quite bringing her to the pitch she needed. She felt herself coil tighter and tighter inside, wanting him to press down, to place the buzzing tip on her swollen centre, but he wouldn't.

He took it away and began to ply the flogger once more.

She began to feel the edge of it, tiny cuts of heat stinging her. She liked it, she liked his heavier hand, his harder stroke. She pushed her bottom out, needing him to know.

'That's it,' he said. 'You're just as perverted as I am, aren't you, babe? You love this, don't you?'

'Oh,' was all she could say, brimming with over-stimulation.

He whipped her steadily until she tingled and glowed, then the vibrator returned, and this time it was pushed just a quarter of a way inside her – not enough, oh God, not nearly enough – while he picked up the flogger again and continued his work.

She could feel spasms higher up inside, her vaginal walls begging to be stretched while the damned vibrator buzzed lower down. But the lower shaft was fitted snugly inside her lips and it overwhelmed her, suddenly and very swiftly with a clitoral orgasm, while Jason was flogging her.

'Oh God, yes,' he exclaimed. 'You came while I was whipping you, you little star. I *love* it when that happens.'

'Glad to be of service,' she panted, trying to get her wits back together.

Jason took the vibe out of her, bent down and kissed her pussy, then licked and sucked at her clit as if to thank it for its good work.

'How's your bum?' he asked, stroking it. 'Feels nice and warm now. Does it hurt?'

'No. Just for a second, when you hit it, then it's gone.'

'Did it make you come harder? Being flogged at the same time, I mean.'

Flooded with shame, Jenna did not want to give an honest answer at first.

'I don't know,' she said, then, guiltily, 'I think so.'

His knowing chuckle made her cheeks flare all the hotter. He knew her secrets, didn't even need her to tell him. Her body did it for her.

'Good times ahead,' he said. 'Hold tight.'

She couldn't have done much else, spread-eagled as she was.

He put the vibrator all the way up inside her. It glided in as easily as if she were buttered. Once he had switched on the pulse to a medium setting, he began again to flog her.

This time it was harder. But that was good. She felt she had earned the smart, even when she began to sweat and writhe under the lash.

'You can take it,' he said. 'You need it.'

His calm words steadied her, and she concentrated on the way the pain splashed over her skin then moved deeper into her, setting a million sparks alight all over unexpected and unconnected parts of her body. Her nipples were stiffer, her clit heavier. The sated feeling from the orgasm she had already had evaporated, replaced by more tension, more need. She had never been able to build up again so quickly after one climax, always needing a break in the past. With Jason, everything was different. It was as if he knew her body better than she did.

After whipping her soundly to the point where she twisted in her cuffs and uttered helpless little cries, he put down the flogger and moved the vibrator inside her, using his fingers on her clit at the same time.

She was powerless under his touch and she stormed into another, stronger, orgasm, calling out his name as the sensation took hold of her.

'That's me,' he whispered.

He lay down on the bed beside her and stroked her hair.

'I could do this all night long, Jen. Seriously. I could do it until you couldn't take any more.'

'I know,' she said. 'I know you could. Oh God.'

Her face was wet and she realised that she had shed a few tears.

'I'll let you off tonight,' he said. 'But I just wanted you to know . . . if I wanted to . . . I could.'

'Are you going to untie me?' she said. The vibrator was still buzzing inside her, but she was too numbed to really notice.

'Not yet,' he said. 'First I want to fuck you, and I want

you just the way you are right now.' He kissed her face. 'I'll let you get your breath back first though.'

'So kind.'

'That's me. All heart.'

Some smooches and a lot of stroking later, Jenna had a pillow slid under her stomach, the better for Jason to enter her from behind.

He took her forcefully, but not painfully, jolting her closer and closer to the headboard until the cuffs were slack and she was able to grip the bars. His hands felt so good on her hips, gripping bruisingly hard while he thrust in, in, in, until he swore, and gasped, and subsided with a little sigh on top of her back.

'I want to stay inside you,' he said.

She could feel him beginning to soften, her stretched walls reverting to their normal diameter around the spent invader.

'Stay,' she said. 'I like it.'

'I wish I could keep a bit of myself inside you all the time,' he said. 'You could walk around with your pussy full. I'd love that. If only it could be done. Maybe one day.'

She snuffled out a laugh into the coverlet.

'You're weird.'

'Artistic temperament, yeah?'

'I'm sure that must be it.'

He drew out reluctantly and unbuckled her cuffs. She pulled off the blindfold and lay on her back, looking up at his misty face.

'You're quite something, you know,' she said.

'Not so bad yourself,' he replied.

'Thanks.'

'So—' He coughed, slightly nervously. 'I can't believe

I'm setting myself up for this, but . . . Who's the best you ever had?'

'Jason! You're fishing for compliments.'

'No, I'm not. I know what I'm hoping you'll say, but if it turns out to be someone else, I want to know why, so I can work on my own technique. If I'm not the best you've ever had, I'll make fucking sure I am next time.'

She took a deep breath. 'Bloody hell. You're something else.'

'So?'

'It's you, of course. By about this much.' She spread her arms wide in the air.

He was clearly extremely pleased with himself, and kissed her, but she was touched by a hint of insecurity when he made her repeat it.

'You're not just saying that? To be nice? Cos I'm here and the other bloke isn't?'

'No, no and no. Anyway, it's not a competition. I know you've slept with lots of women and I've no intention of asking for a comparison.'

'I've never shagged anyone like you.'

'What do you mean, like me?'

'Class. Peng *and* posh.'

Jenna laughed.

'What the hell is peng?'

'Fit, yeah?'

'Oh. Thanks for the compliment, then.'

'No probs.'

He lay back for a while and Jenna watched him from the corner of her eye as he stared up at the ceiling. She thought about getting a shower, thought about getting some food, but it all seemed too much effort.

'I could be falling for you,' he said, eventually.

'So could I,' she admitted.

'But what's the use?' He turned, leaning on one elbow, his huge dark eyes sombre. 'Where are we going, Jen? There's no future. Definitely not for me, anyway.'

'There is a future. There can be and there will be.'

'How? All I'm doing here is putting off what's inevitable. Sooner or later I'll end up in prison and you'll go back to America.'

'Jason, don't. You're innocent. You were set up.'

'All the evidence is against me, Jen, you know it. It's not that I'm scared of going to prison – I'm not. It's just . . . I don't know. I was starting to think my life was worth something.'

'Your life *is* worth something.'

'It's the first time I've ever thought so. It's like, I don't know if I dare. If I start thinking like that, then I'm going to fall harder, aren't I, when the time comes? Might as well go back to being what I was, just some chav with nothing going for him.'

'Jason, stop it. You aren't that. You were never that. Nobody is.'

'You'd have crossed the street to avoid me, if you'd seen me out of here.'

'No I wouldn't. I'm no different from you. I come from where you come from. I couldn't have made it out without Deano, I know that. I accept it. I built my career on his talent. It's not something I feel that great about, to be honest, but it's the way it is. You have *so* much more than that. You're a brilliant artist. You're clever, but you just never bothered with school. You're good-looking, you're engaging, you've got a great sense of humour.

You've got everything it takes, except self-esteem.'

'And a price on my head. Don't forget that.'

'What, there's a reward out for you?'

'Nah. I dunno. Might be. But it's not the best start to my amazing artistic career, is it? A five year stretch for possession with intent.'

Jenna sighed. 'There *has* to be a way to clear your name.'

'Leave it, Jen. Don't get mixed up.'

'Where's this house you were arrested in? Who owns it?'

'The council.'

'Yes, but you weren't the tenant, were you? Who was?'

'Mate of Mia's. I told you.'

'You didn't tell me it was a mate of Mia's. You said "some bloke".'

'Oh God, her mate's boyfriend or something.'

'What mate? What's her name?'

'Don't, Jen.'

'Tell me.'

'No.'

'I can—'

'No, I said, no.' Jason leapt out of bed and stomped upstairs to the bathroom.

Jenna sighed and went to the kitchen to put the kettle on. She had to find the answer to Jason's difficulties, otherwise he was absolutely right. There was no future for them.

Chapter Seven

The youth club was packed out: people sitting on the radiators, and piling into the tiny kitchen space, to get their coveted place at the meeting.

At the front, behind a table, sat Jenna, Kayley, the Head of Youth Services at Bledburn Borough Council, and Lawrence Harville.

The date for the talent contest had been set for three weeks' time, and every young person on the estate wanted a stake in it.

'Can we do skateboarding?'

'What, in here?' asked Kayley, to laughter.

'No, I mean, maybe set up some jumps in the car park.'

'No, it has to be something you can do inside, in front of the audience here.'

Disappointment rumbled and then died down as the next question was sought.

'We've got twenty people in our street dance crew, can you fit us all in?'

'I don't see why not, if you don't need the whole floor for your routine.'

The meeting was lively, and generally good-humoured, until one woman, sitting near the front, said, 'Why couldn't you have come a year earlier? My lad's the best painter in the county; something like this could've saved our Jase.' Electrified, Jenna leant forward. This must be Jason's mother.

'I'm sorry you feel we've left it too late,' she said, carefully, looking hard into the woman's bloodshot eyes. 'I hope we can make the difference we couldn't make for your son for somebody else. I hope you'll support us in that and I hope things work out for your son.'

Instantly, she realised that she sounded as if she knew Jason was still alive, when his mother had referred to him in the past tense. She swallowed and looked away, hoping nobody had picked up on this.

'I mean,' she mumbled, feeling that she was too late to fix her mistake but she ought to try, 'if that's possible.'

'I doubt it,' said Lawrence, speaking over the woman's attempt to reply. 'Jason Watson is known to the police and wanted for serious drug offences. No amount of artistic talent can get him off those.'

Jenna felt suddenly and intensely enraged with Lawrence and had to work like fury to keep her face and voice neutral.

'I'm sorry to hear that,' she said.

'It's not right,' muttered his mother, amid boos and catcalls. 'He hated drugs, did our Jase. Hadn't even smoked a joint for years.'

But nobody was listening and the meeting moved on to logistical matters around filming and sound systems.

At the end, Jenna broke away from Lawrence, who was eager to monopolise her, to catch up with Jason's mother.

'Excuse me,' she said. 'Do you mind? I mean, I was really sorry to hear about your son. Was it him who did the mural, on the wall over there?'

She nodded.

Now that Jenna was close, she could see the lines and broken veins on the woman's face, that made her look older than she was. Her badly bleached hair didn't help, either. If only her eyes were less red, though, they could almost be his.

'Drugs are killing this estate,' said Jenna. 'And the kids who grow up here. I'm thinking of sponsoring a project to help vulnerable youngsters in danger of addiction. Would you mind if I came to see you, to talk about your son?'

'I told you. He ain't no drug addict. He never took a thing, since he was a teenager. Took a shitload, back then, mind. Oh, he was a terror.'

'Could I, though?' Jenna persisted gently. 'I'd like to know more about him. Perhaps I could help.'

'Well, I don't see how. But all right then. Flat 5, Cloke Court, by the shops.'

'Later today? In about half an hour?'

'The house is in a state. I ain't been too well lately.'

'I don't mind. It's fine.'

'All right then. But don't judge me.'

'I promise I won't.'

It was difficult to get away from Lawrence, who seemed hell-bent on taking her out to lunch, but Jenna pretended to want a private word with Kayley and he gave up and left, promising to call her later.

'He's a bit full-on,' remarked Kayley, once they were safely hidden away in her tiny office. 'I couldn't go with a

Harville, though. Not that I'm trying to tell you what to do.'

'He's been chasing me since I got here, but I'm not really interested.'

'So, what was it you wanted to talk to me about?'

'Oh, do you know what? It's completely gone. Sorry, Kay. It'll come back to me. I'll call you. Mind if I go out the back way? Thanks.'

She was free and clear. She watched Lawrence's car negotiate the roundabout and take the high road out of the estate, then walked up to the shopping precinct.

A few of the teens who'd been at the public meeting sat around on the low wall by the off-licence, laughing, and flirting and showing off to each other.

Jenna skirted them, careful to keep herself out of view, and took the service road behind the shops to the small complex of square, low-rise flats that sat, ugly and squat, on the dried grass between them and the pub.

Cloke Court had a shopping trolley by the security door and two of the six flats were boarded up. Number five, when she was buzzed in, was at the rear of the building on the first floor, overlooking the pub car park.

This was where Jason grew up, she thought.

The front door was cheap wood, scratched, and the hallway smelled of stale cigarette smoke.

When his mother answered the door, she showed Jenna into a cluttered living room. It would have been just like any other place occupied by a person who had given up hope – dirty and neglected – if not for the remarkable artwork on the walls. Jason had painted the view through the window, over and over again, but each time it was different. In one version, the pub was a palace and the car park a gorgeous garden. In another, strange, zombie-like figures roamed the landscape. The pictures were so varied and so fascinating that she forgot to say hello to his mother until she coughed, and spoke.

'You see what I'm saying? Talented.'

'I'll say. These are incredible.'

'I'd make you a cuppa but the kettle's on the blink. I've got Coke. Or something stronger.'

'Oh, Coke'll be fine, thanks.'

She sat down, clearing a space on the sofa first. The window was open, but the place smelled of old cider and cigarette smoke.

Kathy came back with a can of Coke – no glass – and a lager for herself.

Although Jenna knew her name, she had to ask.

'Sorry, so you're . . .?'

'Kathy. And my boy was Jason.'

'And what happened to him?'

'He's gone. Don't know where, nobody does. He got busted, but it weren't him. I know it, I'd swear on my life. His life.'

'So he's in prison?'

'No, like that snake, Harville, said: he did a runner.'

'Have you any idea where?'

Kathy swallowed a swig of beer, shaking her head.

'Not a clue,' she said.

'If he was set up, who do you think was behind it?'

'I don't know, but I didn't trust that girlfriend of his further than I could throw her. Mia Tarbuck. She was playing around behind his back, I know that much.'

'Do you? Who with?' Jenna felt uncomfortably as if she was showing a little too much interest, but she had to ask these questions, had to find some answers from somewhere.

'I saw her with some other bloke in town, in the Wetherspoons. Don't know his name – I don't think he was from round here. Her and her no-good mates, all showing off their belly-button piercings. Never liked that crowd. They used to bully our Jase at school.'

'Oh, no, I'm sorry to hear that.'

'It were their fault he started getting into trouble. Trying to stand up for himself, trying to impress them so they'd leave him alone. He's a good lad, underneath it all, I swear.'

'I know,' said Jenna, then she caught herself. 'I mean, I'm sure you're right. And such a brilliant artist. How old was he when he started all this?'

'Tiny. He used to copy the cartoon characters when he were, what, three or four? Draw 'em, really good for a little 'un. It were good: a pack of crayons and some paper don't cost much, does it? It were a cheap hobby. I could afford that much.' She laughed, but it turned into a chesty smoker's cough.

'And from that start, he grew into this . . .' Jenna looked around her again. Barely an inch of the wall was bare of Jason's efforts. Judging by the mould spotting the ceiling and blackening the window seals, it was probably just as well.

'He could have done so well for himself.' Kathy shook her head and reached for the pack of cigarettes on the coffee table. 'D'you mind if I light up, duck? I wouldn't, but my nerves . . .'

Jenna shook her head, although she couldn't remember the last time she'd been in a smoky environment. LA was simply and utterly smoke-free, at least in the circles she frequented.

'So, this Mia was his downfall then, would you say?'

Kathy nodded vigorously.

'He was too taken up with her. I always felt she were laughing at him, taking the piss. He'd do anything for her, and she knew it.'

'Where is she, now? Do you think she knows where he is?'

'Oh, I dunno. Nobody saw her for a while, but now she's back in the pub most nights with her dodgy mates. She does the karaoke in the back room – that's her job. Goes round town with her machine of a night.'

'Where does she live?'

'I think she lives upstairs at the pub. You don't see hide nor hair of her all day, mind. She only comes out at night.'

'Like a vampire.'

Kathy laughed, wearily, at that. 'Yeah, you could be right, love. Perhaps she's a vampire.'

'Was he still living with you, when he disappeared?'

'No, duck, no. He was sofa-surfing, as they call it. I couldn't cope with him. I wasn't the best mother to him, I'll hold me hands up. I suppose he was what you could call neglected. But I love him, and I miss him, every day and I keep thinking he'll walk through that door with his big, cheeky smile . . .'

She broke off, and Jenna put a hand on her shoulder, feeling it shake beneath the lint-covered vest top.

'You know, I think he's all right, Kathy. Don't ask me how I know but I just have this feeling that he's fine.'

'You're very kind, love. I hope you're right.' She choked back a sob. 'He was such a gorgeous little boy.'

'Thank you for talking to me about him. Would you mind very much if I borrowed some of his artwork? I'd like to show it to a friend of mine who owns a gallery?'

'For real?'

'For real. It's so good. I think she'd like to see it.'

'Well, OK, duck. I'll go and get a few bits together. I can't give you any of these in here because you can see how I'm fixed – it's my wallpaper.'

While Kathy shuffled off to a bedroom to gather up some more of what seemed to be an extensive collection of Jason's work, Jenna had a surreptitious search of the living room. She could find nothing that might help Jason out of his predicament, though, so she took the armful of teenage masterpieces, thanked Kathy for her hospitality and determined to try Mia at the pub.

'She won't be up,' warned the landlord. 'What do you want with her, anyway?'

'It's business. She does karaoke, doesn't she? I was thinking of hiring her for my Gala, up at Harville Hall.'

'You're bringing back the Gala? Blimey, that's a blast from the past. Won't be the same, though, will it? Too much water under the bridge.'

'I thought it might cheer everyone up a bit. Bledburn's got that miserable since I left.'

'Well, you're not wrong there. I'll give her a shout, but she'll be dead to the world, I can guarantee it.'

The landlord disappeared upstairs, leaving Jenna with two inquisitive Staffies to look after. They panted and circled her legs, barking at each other, until the landlord returned, his face giving away the answer to her request before he had to speak it.

'No chance,' he said. 'She's not getting out of her pit for anyone till six this evening.'

'OK, well, could you pass on my number, then? Ask her to call me. Jenna Myatt. About the karaoke.'

'Will do.'

The landlord looked after her with bemusement as she left the pub. The people of the estate had got used to having a celebrity on their midst, and barely turned a hair when she appeared on the scene now. They had never been easily impressed, mind you. This estate was for people who could prove themselves in a hard world.

Hardly any of them even asked after Deano any more, although she was still regularly quizzed about whether Colin Samson, her nasty co-host, was 'really like that'.

She thought about Deano as she drove home. How was he, now? Did he miss her? Did he have regrets?

Only one man was on her mind when she arrived at the Hall, though, especially when she went out into the garden to find him hacking at the dead and overgrown rosebushes in nothing but his tight jeans.

She didn't tell him she was back, at first, but stood at a distance, behind some brown greenery, watching him. His upper arms were tight and strong, and his back and shoulder blades flexed as he sheared. He hadn't forgotten to put sunscreen on and his skin shone, taking on the beginnings of a tan. He could probably do with a haircut, she thought, watching him smooth it back when it fell in his face, but it wasn't in a terrible state. Unlike those rosebushes.

He dropped the shears and picked up a water bottle from the grass, tipping his head back to let it splash all over his face and glug into his mouth.

She crept up behind him, but he heard the crackle of the grass and spun around, the bottle held in his hand like a weapon.

'Oh.' He relaxed his grip. 'You're back.'

'You're gardening.'

'Why not? Weather like this, I didn't want to be stuck in that attic. It's not like anyone can see in here.'

'No. I'm not complaining. The place needs a good going over. It's been left to rot for too long.'

He smirked at that. 'Are you trying to tell me something?'

'Like what?'

'Like, you know, secret gardens that need seeing to. Thought you were giving me a hint.' He reached up to hold on to the branch of a low tree beside him, leaning into it, looking broad-chested, and slim-hipped, and ready to pounce.

'You've got sex on the brain,' she told him, pouting back at him, amazed at how quickly he could rev her libido from nought to sixty.

'I'd rather have it on the grass,' he said.

'You'll have to catch me first,' she cried, running off into the tangle of weeds and thicket that must once have been a beautiful garden.

He lunged after her, causing her to shriek with exhilaration, and gave chase. A spirited pursuit took them into the four corners of the grounds, dashing through rotting gazebos and dodging around moss-covered fountains.

'You might as well give in,' he panted, as they circled a summerhouse whose white-painted wrought iron had peeled while the floor was eaten away by woodlice. 'There's no way you can get away from me.'

'Oh dear, how awful,' said Jenna, in parody of a distressed cartoon heroine. 'Whatever shall become of me?'

'I won't be too hard on you if you give in now,' he promised.

'And if I don't?'

'If you don't . . .'

He made a sudden pounce, sending her screaming into the wilderness again, but she had given him too much leeway now and he caught her in seconds.

They fell to the ground in a tangle.

The dry grasses tickled Jenna's legs and she thought she'd sat on a thistle because something was prickling her bottom, but that was the least of her worries. On top of her, while she thrashed, and flailed, and giggled, and shrieked, was Jason, straddling her and holding her down by the arms.

'Oh dear,' he said, with undisguised relish. 'Somebody's in a bit of trouble here. Whatever is she going to do?'

'Get off me, you git.'

'Whatever is she going to *get*? I think she knows.'

Jenna tried to raise her knee, to shove him off, but there was no chance. Jason had been working, physically hard, over the last few days, with an obvious impact on his strength. He held her effortlessly, tickling her with a handful of grass stalks until she couldn't bear it any longer.

He flipped her over on to her front, once his sadistic enjoyment of this was past its peak. She felt the hard, warm ground crush her breasts, the thistle now irritating her upper thigh below the hem of the crisp cotton shorts she wore.

'Ouch,' she hissed, and he paused in his kissing of the back of her neck.

'What? I haven't started yet.'

'Something's prickling my leg. And what do you mean, haven't started? Started what?'

'Wait and see,' he said, reaching underneath her and plucking the thistle from the dry earth. That was better, at least.

His hands, now intent on pleasuring rather than tormenting her, lifted her vest and began to knead at her back and shoulders. They were still tense after her visit with his mother, and his touch brought out deep sighs of satisfaction as the knots unwound. He ground his hips over her as he worked, until she felt, quite unmistakably, his erection growing against her rounded backside. The gentle to-and-fro rocked her into a state of relaxed sensuality, heightened by the exhilaration of their earlier chasing game. She was caught, but she wanted to be, and now he was preparing her.

The thought was delightful.

'What are you up to?' she asked sleepily.

'Just getting you into the zone,' he said.

'What zone?'

'The zone where I can do anything to you and you'll love it.'

She was already there, but she didn't want him to know that.

'What do you mean by "anything"?'

'I mean,' he said, pressing his fingertips deep into her soft tissues until she moaned, 'anything.'

She wriggled her bottom, as much as she could with it wedged between his thighs, as a little signal that his work was paying off.

He took the hint, reached underneath her and

unbuttoned her waistband. Soon her shorts and knickers had been eased over her curves, baring her bottom to the mid-afternoon sun.

'What about sunburn?' she said nervously.

'I thought you didn't mind a red hot bum?' said Jason slyly.

'Not sunburn!'

'Nah. You're right. I'll put you in the shade.'

He took her shorts all the way off, then pulled her upright. She let him lead her, feeling very sheepish at being naked from the waist down, beneath the shadow of one of the few flourishing things in that desiccated garden: a plane tree.

The grass beneath it was softer and sweeter. Jason patted her shoulder.

'Get down on all fours, love,' he said.

'All fours?'

'That's right. Do you need a diagram?'

Slightly huffily, she dropped into the required position, her sheepishness blooming into full-blown shame at her exposed position.

Jason stood behind her, then crouched down and put a hand in the small of her back, forcing her spine down and her bottom up until she rested on her elbows.

'That's it. God, I wish I could paint you right now. Well, not *right* now, because there are other things I'd rather do, but in this position. Just like that – your skin and the way you're completely open to me. I'd look at it for hours.'

'I don't think I could keep this position for that long, to be honest.'

'No, I mean the painting. Well, or you. Both. But if

you're going to get tired, I'd better get down to it.'

She was about to ask what 'it' was, when her breath was taken away by the sound of him cracking his belt through its loops. She heard him walk up behind her and waited for the follow-up of the rustle of denim creeping down his long legs, but it didn't come.

Instead, she whimpered in shock at the feel of cold, soft leather drifting over her back and bottom. He was dangling his belt over her, letting it glide and whisper across her skin until it tingled.

'Feel that, babe? It's for you. It's coming for you. You need it.'

'Oh,' she moaned, fidgeting, every hair standing on end. 'Are you going to . . .?'

'What?'

'Use it on me?' she whispered.

He chuckled and she heard him crouch down behind her.

'Is that what you want?'

She gasped, feeling the leather strip pressed between her legs, flat against her lips. He rubbed it up and down for a minute and she knew she was getting it thoroughly wet and shiny.

'Hmm?'

She hadn't answered him, but she couldn't. She just couldn't tell him that she wanted that leather to fall on her bottom with a good, smart crack.

'Aren't you going to answer my question. Oh!' His exclamation came after he removed the belt from its juicy resting place. 'This is soaking. Well, I guess I don't need you to tell me any more than that, do I?'

The slick length of it was laid across both cheeks of her

bottom and held there, leaving a little residue of her own wetness when he took it away.

Its next appearance was under her nose, held there by him, wrapped around his knuckles as he proffered it.

'Give it a good sniff,' he said, crouching in front of her. 'Go on.'

She breathed in a lungful of its heavenly scent. If the leather itself had already been redolent of sex, now it was even more so.

'Kiss it,' he urged. 'Kiss the strap.'

She placed her lips upon it. He pushed it right up against her mouth, twisting it gently, as she smooched it in a growing fever.

'That's it,' he said. 'Kiss it harder. Worship it. Put your tongue on it. You know where it's going next, don't you?'

She moaned into the thick wad, which was now in her mouth, between her teeth.

Once it was licked into shiny wetness, he took it back, returned to her rear and then gave her what she craved – a long, hot bar of sting across her bottom. The noise it made was wonderful; much better than the flogger. But it hurt more than the flogger and she knew he hadn't hit hard. It had only been a flick really.

'How's that?' he asked. 'More painful when it's wet, I'm told.'

'Sore,' she said, but she put all the satisfaction she felt into her voice. 'But good. Really good.'

'Want more?'

'Please.'

'Well, since you ask so nicely . . .'

The second stroke was stronger, a solid rectangle along

the lower curve of her cheeks. She felt it sink in, then felt the hard smack of the third above it.

'Keep that bum high,' warned Jason, flicking at her thighs with the V-tongued end of the belt. 'Up as high as you can. No slacking.'

She gritted her teeth in her efforts to maintain her position. She wanted to feel more, wanted the heat to grow and spread through her body. She cried out with each stroke, but pushed her bottom up to show that she wasn't crying out in distress.

'Oh, you're so right for this,' he said, after the sixth or seventh. 'You're a fucking natural. Tell me when to stop.'

The leather scorched through her, and she took stroke after stroke, wanting more, even when he became more heavy-handed and cruel. She was in a kind of delirium, fascinated to know how hot and sore she was capable of feeling before it became unbearable. The answer, it seemed, was 'very', for she only called a halt after more than two dozen heavy strokes, once her skin felt tight and so sensitive the mere tap of a finger would make her wince.

He dropped the belt on to her bottom, from where it glided off into the grass, as if it had a life of its own.

She was still puffing out as if she'd run the length of town when Jason took off his jeans, dropped to his knees behind her and took a hold of her hips.

'You're bright red, babe. So hot. I've got to have you.'

He eased his hard erection underneath her and let it soak in her juices for a few moments before flexing back and lining himself up.

She was more than ready for him and she let out a deep 'ah' of welcome when he pushed into her at a stroke.

There, under the shade of the plane tree, he kept at her with a jackhammer pace, tightening her stomach until she was ready to let go again and surge into orgasm. But he made sure he kept her on that edge for as long as he wanted, pumping backwards and forwards until their skins were sheened with sweat and her bottom stung more than ever. The sting made it all brighter and fiercer and more intense, though, when her climax was finally allowed to burst through.

She plucked two handfuls of clover from the grass, the remnants clinging to her palms.

Jason's breathing took on a quality she recognised, a chaotic, laboured sound that meant he was close to his own moment of ecstasy. She pushed back against him, tightening her muscles to squeeze every iota of orgasm out of him.

He gripped her shoulder and thrust madly, in a kind of seizure, then fell on top of her, slack with the effort of it all.

'God,' he slurred, after a moment. 'S'too hot for all this. Think we should get a drink.'

She gloried in the way the kitchen bench made her skin feel raw and tender when she sat to drain her glass of water. Jason kissed her ear and asked if she'd rather stand, or get a cushion.

'You're a brute,' she said, but dreamily, happily.

'Only for you,' he said, getting up for another glassful.

'I feel special.' She laughed, a punctured, exhausted laugh, then her phone rang.

'Ah, dunno who that is,' she said, disliking this encroachment on their kinky version of domestic bliss. 'Better check.'

She went out to the hall where her bag hung with the phone inside.

Oh God. It was Mia.

Casting a guilty glance back at the kitchen, she hurried into the drawing room and shut the door behind her. She hadn't expected to hear from her until well into the evening. The landlord had been wrong when he'd said she wouldn't surface until six.

'Hello, Jenna Myatt.'

'It *is* you. Fuck me, thought Tommy was having me on.'

'Sorry, is this . . .?'

'Mia. Mia Tarbuck. You came to the pub earlier? About the karaoke?'

Her voice was soft and a little bit fluffy, like a Bledburn Marilyn Monroe.

'That's right. I'm after some quotes. Thinking of hiring one for the Gala.'

'What Gala?'

'The Bledburn Gala. I want to get it going again.'

'Oh, so cool. I wish they hadn't stopped having those. I was too young to go to any.' There was a sound, of gruff voices, in the background. 'Shut up, Nicker. I'm talking. Sorry. Annoying flatmates, don't you hate them?'

This made Jenna's hackles rise on behalf of the flatmate they had shared – Jason.

'I don't have any, so I can't really comment,' she said.

'No, of course, you're all on your own at the Hall. Doesn't it get lonely there? I mean, it's a bit creepy. Haunted and all that.'

'No ghosts, so far,' said Jenna briskly, though her thoughts returned to the knocking noises and the message underneath the wallpaper. 'Listen, can we meet and discuss quotes? I don't like doing business over the phone.'

'Well, I can email you,' the girl said doubtfully.

'No, I like face-to-face. Where can we meet? Tomorrow, preferably?'

'I could come to you, at the Hall.'

'No, best not. Do you know Sanderson's, on Mill Street? I'll buy you lunch.'

'Really? Sanderson's is . . .'

'It's just a glorified sandwich shop, Mia. Meet me there at one.'

'Well, if you're sure.'

Jenna felt a little sad at the wonder in her voice, as if a little café that put a rocket salad on the side of its plates was Le Manoir. She remembered being that girl, and the awkwardness she had felt in 'proper' restaurants and glitzy hotels. *I don't belong here.*

Deano, of course, had taken to it like a duck to water.

'Who was that?' asked Jason when she returned to the kitchen to find him soaking some couscous, ready for dinner. He understood couscous, now, though on first acquaintance he had simply stared at it and asked if it was edible.

'Ah, nobody. Business. About the talent show.'

She had small bruises on her bottom the next day and, when she got into the car, she shifted about on the leather seat, enjoying the feeling and the memories it evoked.

'Why was I afraid to explore this side of me?' she asked herself, not for the first time. She concluded, then as before, that she had been scared of what people would think of her. It was the story of her life. Always hiding behind other people and their star qualities, until LA had forced her into the spotlight with *Talent Team*. Her discomfort and anxieties about being a public figure had been, if she was honest with herself, part of what had led to the break-up with Deano. She'd become tense, snappy, defensive.

God, she had so needed to find a Jason.

But, now, she needed to let him out of deep cover. They couldn't live this way forever, much as it seemed like a fairytale for the moment.

She was early to Sanderson's, wanting to see Mia walk in and find out if she would recognise her. She would be younger than Jenna, probably prettier.

The girl who walked in at ten past one, still yawning and bleary-eyed, was pretty but unkempt. Her hair, dyed with henna, was scraped hastily back in a tight ponytail and she'd applied a lot of eyeliner quite clumsily so that she looked as if she'd been punched. Her skin was recognisably that of somebody who slept too little and partied too hard. Jenna had seen it countless times on her clients, Deano's friends, Deano himself . . . Baggy trackpants covered her lower half, but her layers of thin vests showed off some glorious tattoos. One of them, at least, looked as if it had been designed by Jason. His style was immediately recognisable in any format, a thought that made Jenna's heart beat faster, because it surely meant that he was as good as she hoped he was.

'Jenna?' she said, stopping in front of her. 'They said you looked different on TV. You do, a bit.'

'It's the make-up,' said Jenna. 'And the elaborate hairstyles. Take a seat.'

Mia sat down and slung an embroidered denim bag on the chair back.

'I'm starving. Haven't eaten since yesterday teatime.'

'I'm going to order the alfalfa and sesame salad,' said Jenna, handing the menu over.

'The Alf who? Do they do a bacon cob?'

Jenna smiled, thinking it had been at least fifteen years since she'd spoken of cobs – the local dialect word for a bread roll.

'I think they do a pancetta and sunblush tomato flatbread,' she said. 'Sort of distantly related to a bacon cob.'

'I'll have that, then. And a Red Bull.'

'Late night?'

'Yeah.' She yawned but didn't elaborate.

Jenna went to the counter to order, trying hard to calm down the butterflies in her stomach. She had to play this right, or Jason might never be free. If she could get Mia on side, get the real story out of her, everything could change.

But did she want everything to change?

What if Jason strolled out and went back to his old life? What if he was just with her because she was there?

Maybe she should leave it. Because she couldn't leave *him*.

But she had to try, or she would hate herself, despise herself, forever.

She turned back from the counter with her best breezy TV smile.

'So, Mia,' she said. 'I think I know one of your cousins. Terri-Lynn?'

'Yeah? She said she was at school with you.'

'How is she?'

'Living in Leicester now. She's a grandma.'

'Fuck off!'

The expletive flew from her mouth before she could stop it, and she clamped a hand to her mouth, her ears burning. You could take the girl out of Bledburn . . .

'Sorry,' she whispered, her eyes flicking around the clientele of bristling elderly folk, there for the vast range of teas, and a few hipsters. 'But she's my age.'

Mia giggled. 'I know. She had Cindy when she was sixteen and Cindy's just had Reuben, so . . .'

'Jesus.' She tried to shake the thought from her head. 'I don't feel mature enough to have one kid, let alone a grandchild. Do you have any kids?'

'Nah, not me. I don't think I'm cut out for it.'

'Can't say the thought's crossed my mind much. Perhaps I'm just not the maternal type. But I've been too busy to even consider it, mostly.'

'I bet. What with all your TV work and looking after big name stars. What a life.' Mia's voice dripped with good-natured envy. 'How did you do it?'

'I'm not sure. It was a whirlwind thing, once Deano's career took off. Looking back, it seems as if I went from the estate to the Ritz in about five seconds flat.'

'Must have been amazing.'

'Actually, it was quite frightening. I was such a small-town girl, in a world I didn't know or understand. I had to pretend to be this loud, confident person just to get through. You know, Eleanor Roosevelt said "Nobody can make you feel inferior without your consent", but I'm pretty sure she didn't come from Bledburn.'

'I've never heard of her.'

'No, I guess you haven't. So, anyway, you're Terri-Lynn's cousin and you run a karaoke. How long have you been doing that?'

'Not that long. Came into a bit of cash a couple of months back and bought the rig. Karaoke's big now, with all the karaoke TV shows. Everyone wants to be on them. Well, you should know, since you're a judge in one of them. What I do gives people a chance to see if they've got a bit of what it takes. Belt out the *Titanic* song in front of an audience – if it goes down well, they might apply for the next series of *Talent Team UK*.'

'It was a good idea. Good way to spend the money. What was it, an inheritance?'

Mia looked down at her knife and fork, and seemed immensely grateful when the food arrived, distracting them from the question.

'Bit poncey, this,' she said, grinning at Jenna over her upmarket bacon sarnie. 'I don't even know what that stuff is in yours.'

Jenna decided to try another tack.

'I love your tattoos,' she said. 'That one on your arm there is stunning. Is it a copy of an artwork?'

'Sort of. It was designed for me.'

'Who by? Leonardo da Vinci?'

She coloured so deeply that Jenna felt she'd drawn first blood. She could do this. It was possible.

'In a funny way,' said Mia, 'yeah.' And her eyes were misty and she looked so upset that Jenna had to work hard to keep her tone light.

'What, he came back from beyond the grave?'

'No, it was his nickname. The guy's nickname. The guy who did the tattoo.'

'Right. Well, he's very talented. Does he work in a parlour in town? I might be interested in getting one done by him, myself.'

'No, he's not the tattoo artist. He just did the design. The tattoo guy copied it.'

'Do you think he'd design one for me? If I paid him?'

'I doubt it.'

'Why?'

'He's, uh, he's dead.'

She pushed away her plate, only two bites taken out of the bread. She was very close to tears.

'Mia, I'm so sorry. I didn't mean to . . . Don't go. Stay.'

She sat back down and chugged at her Red Bull.

'That must be awful for you,' Jenna said. 'I guess you were close to him.'

'I was.'

'Was it him that left you the money? For the karaoke?'

Oh, the look on her face at that. Yes, it was sheer terrible guilt, mixed with a genuine grief. Jenna resolved to pursue her advantage, relentlessly.

'I never deserved him,' whispered Mia.

'Do you want to talk about it?' asked Jenna, gently, but Mia shook her head.

'The thing about life,' said Jenna, speaking quietly after taking a break to eat some salad, 'is that it gives a lot of second chances. If you do the right thing – even if it seems impossible to begin with – you get a chance to be the person you want to be again. Even if that person is poor, or unpopular, or even in prison or similar. At least you're something like the person you want to be. Instead of the person you despise.'

Mia went pale.

'What are you talking about? Do you know something? You know something about this. What are you on about?'

'I know,' said Jenna in very low tones, 'that somebody was set up. And I know that you know all about it.'

'What the fuck? Has Lawrence told you this? I know you're friendly with him.'

'Lawrence?' She knew Lawrence Harville, and apparently, Lawrence Harville knew more than he was letting on.

'Don't pretend you aren't shagging him. He's full of it. Jenna this Jenna that. He's a tart.'

'Is he . . . Are you and he . . .?'

'Yeah, I'm his bit of rough. Bit on the side. There, that's shocked you, hasn't it? Didn't know you were sharing His Nibs, did you? How are the mighty fallen.'

Mia's pretty face was contorted with spite.

'I'm not. There's no relationship of that kind between me and Lawrence. I can promise you that. If he's said otherwise, then he's a liar.'

'So why would he tell me?'

'To hurt you? To make you know your place?'

Jenna's mind was whirling. Lawrence was involved with the drug-dealing on the estate? Was he, perhaps, the mastermind behind it all? He owned the pub and the shops, so . . . Oh *God*, it was too much to take in.

'Oh, don't worry about that,' said Mia. 'I know my place all right. He never stops telling me I'm just his tart. But he pays well, if you know what I mean.'

'And that's enough for you, is it? Enough to make you betray somebody who—'

'Do you know where he is?' Mia's eyes were intense, shining from the rings of kohl like jewels. 'Jason?'

'Who?'

Jenna had to retreat. She couldn't let Mia know the full truth and place Jason back in danger.

'Leonardo,' she said meaningfully, tapping her tattoo. 'You know, Lawrence offered to pay for me to get it lasered off. But I couldn't go through with it. Just seemed like . . .'

Her voice caught.

'Let's get out of here,' suggested Jenna, leaving a banknote on the table between the plates. 'We can't talk with all these people listening in.'

'Oh, I'm going,' said Mia, snatching up her bag and marching out, but Jenna was quick and hurried along at her shoulder.

'You're not a bad person, Mia, I can see that. You've got a conscience, and it's bothering you. You can't live like that forever. You can't.'

They were on the towpath of the sluggish brown canal now, on to which Mia had sharply turned, in fear of passers-by being able to overhear.

'Oh, and what would you know about that?' she demanded, spinning to face Jenna, her black-ringed eyes bright as blue fire. 'What would you know about living back here? You escaped, somewhere proper. Most of us can only escape into getting high. You don't know how that feels.'

'You'd be surprised. No, not me,' she said quickly. 'But – swear you won't tell – Deano.'

Mia appraised Jenna's face. She might run. She might stay.

She stayed.

'Is that why you broke up?' she asked.

'It's one of the reasons. There are quite a few.'

'It's why me and Jase split up, too. He hated the drugs, but I couldn't kick them.'

'You split up?'

'Well . . . I never told him in so many words, but I'd been avoiding him for ages. I still cared for him, but when the pains are bad, you'll do anything.'

They sat down on a bench by the railway bridge. Trains clattered overhead but there were no barges on the canal, just big piles of junk and shopping trolleys baking in the sun.

'Mia, was he set up?'

'How do you know him?'

'I don't. I know his mum. I spoke to her after a meeting the other day. Poor woman. She thinks he's dead. But she knows he was set up. She's sure of it.'

'Yeah, well, she weren't much of a mum to him, when it comes down to it,' said Mia, resentfully. 'But she's right. Does she really think he's dead?'

She stared bleakly into the canal.

'Who knows?' said Jenna. 'But if we can convince the police that he's innocent, then perhaps we'll find out.'

Mia put her hands over her face.

'I can't,' she said, followed by a long sniff. 'I'll get killed.'

'By whom?'

But Jenna thought she knew.

'Don't ask me, please. I can't tell you. I wish there was something I could do.'

The young woman dissolved into sobs and Jenna, who had wanted to hate and condemn her, found that she couldn't. She was a confused kid, who'd got in too deep, and couldn't find a way out. Just like Jason. *Just like all of us.*

'I wish there was, too,' said Jenna, gently. 'Because then you won't have to go through your entire life knowing that you've sold someone you love down the river for the price of a karaoke rig.'

She stood up and walked away. Now it was up to Mia to come back to her.

But if she didn't feel she could confess, there was one other new, and rather disturbing, avenue to explore . . .

The explorations would have to wait until later, though, because when she arrived home, Jason ran down the staircase to meet her waving the newspaper she had delivered daily.

'Guess who's in the fucking *Times*?' he opened, and he didn't sound happy about whoever or whatever it was.

'What is it? Show me.'

He marched into the kitchen and laid the broadsheet out flat on the table, tearing through it until he reached the Arts pages.

'*Voi*-fucking-*là*,' he said, stabbing a forefinger directly in the photographed face of Tabitha Lightfoot. Beneath the headline, taking up the top third of the page, was one of the pictures Jenna had taken to show her at the gallery.

'Oh, God,' said Jenna. 'She never told me she was going to . . .'

She exchanged a look of dismay with a smouldering Jason.

'Are you sure about that?' he said. 'Sure you didn't cook it up between you? Get your little project off the ground?'

'Quite sure, thanks,' said Jenna, bristling at the implication that Jason thought she had learned nothing from their earlier disagreement on the subject. 'Let me read it. OK. It seems to have started life as a straightforward profile of Tabitha, but taken a turn somewhere into this mystery artist thing. Oh, Tabitha. I know you need publicity, but . . .'

'Jen, if someone recognises my work, she's going to have the boys in blue round there. It'll lead straight here. Fuck. I'm done for. I might as well go and give myself up.'

'Christ,' said Jenna. 'What can we do? There must be something. I'll call her.'

'What, and tell her to lie to the police? You can't ask her to do that.'

'I can ask her, Jason. I can't make her, that's all.'

'It won't make *any difference*.' He was shouting now, but Jenna still punched the number into her phone, wondering if she'd be able to string a sentence together when Tabitha answered.

'Oh, do what you want, I'm going to pack a bag,' he said, banging the table with his fist before storming out.

But his fist was not the only banging to be heard.

Jenna pressed End Call before Tabitha could answer, horrified by the hammering at the door. Was it the police already? Could it be?

'Let them in,' shouted Jason from the landing. 'What's the use? I've got "jailbird" stamped on my forehead already.'

'But—'

Jenna stood in the hallway, paralysed with dread, until she heard a voice call her name.

Not the police.

Without stopping to think, she opened the door.

'Lawrence. I want to talk to you.'

'And I want to talk to you. I hear you've been quite the private eye, around the estate.'

She tried to push the door back against him, but he barged his way in, causing her to stumble as he elbowed past her.

'How dare you force your way into my house?'

'*Your* house?' His face was ugly with rage. 'This is *my* house. My family's house, in my family's name. Harville Hall. You're just a tenant, until I can buy it back.'

'How's that going to happen?' Jenna followed him into the kitchen. 'My name's on the deeds now. I'm the owner, fair and square.'

'And look what you've done already. Ruining the place. It's like one of those crappy daytime DIY shows in here.'

'Lawrence, get out. This is my property and if you don't leave, I'll call the police.'

'Oh, will you?' Again, a nasty look in his eye. 'Really, Jenna? Is that wise?'

'I don't think it's me who has cause to fear the police.'

'What do you mean by that?'

'I mean that your name was mentioned in connection with something pretty serious to me today.'

'By Mia? A girl so out of her mind on ketamine that she barely knows what day it is? I think you'll have to do better than that, my dear. You know she called me the moment your little *tête-à-tête* was over, don't you? She's my bitch. She does what she's told.'

'You have a hold over her, I know that much.'

'And I have a hold over you, Jenna. Because I know you aren't alone here.'

Jenna had to fight to keep a quaver out of her voice.

'You know nothing. You can get out and stay out.'

'I'll leave when I'm ready, Jen. But I thought I'd stick around for the fun.'

Jenna grasped the back of a chair to steady herself.

'What fun?'

In reply, Lawrence walked out of the kitchen and went to stand at the foot of the staircase.

'Oh, Jason,' he called in a creepy mockery of a voice, his hand cupped around his mouth. 'We're all bored with hide and seek now. Come on out, wherever you are.'

Bowyer came scampering down first and wound himself around Lawrence's legs before being kicked aside. Jenna, furious, picked him up to protect him from further assault.

'Just get out,' she hissed. 'What do you want from me?'

'What I've always wanted,' he said, in a brief respite from calling Jason's name. 'My house back. But it's OK. I'm going to get it, now.'

'No, you're not!'

The screech of sirens sounded faintly in the distance, growing closer. Lawrence laughed with pleasure.

'Ah, the game is on,' he exclaimed. 'Aren't you going to open the door to our visitors?'

Jenna ran to the front porch and watched in horror as three police cars and a van pulled up outside, lights flashing. Within seconds, half a dozen uniformed officers were in the front garden – and they were all looking up.

Jenna ran down the stairs to see things from their perspective, and was horrified to see Jason standing on a parapet near the top of the house, above the great mullioned window at the centre of the façade. Bowyer, appalled by the noise and fuss, leapt from her arms and streaked off into the bushes.

'Jason!' she screamed, but her voice was drowned out by a police officer with a megaphone.

'Come down from there,' he called.

Jason shook his head and raised his arms so that he looked like a living statue.

'I'm innocent,' he shouted down, and Lawrence, now standing beside Jenna, laughed scornfully. 'The man you want is there.' He pointed down to Lawrence, who reiterated his scornful laugh, but with an extra forced quality.

'Come down, and we can talk,' shouted the policeman. 'Or we can come up to you.'

'Can I go up?' urged Jenna. 'Let me talk to him.'

'If he's suicidal, it should be a professional,' demurred the officer.

'He's not suicidal. He's just being dramatic. Let me talk to him.'

Jason picked something up from beside him on the ledge and threw it over the side. Paper fluttered down, like ungainly snow. His drawings.

'What's he doing?' one of the police officers wondered.

Jenna wasn't going to wait for their permission any more. She ran into the house and up the stairs, to the room that gave access on to the parapet. She could see Jason's lower legs through the little doorway and she hurried up to them.

'Jason, please come down,' she begged, her heart in her throat, which was dry. She wanted to heave.

'This is it, babe,' he said. 'Death or glory.'

'Oh, don't! You wouldn't. You can't. Jason, please, for me.'

'For you? Lawrence Harville's girlfriend? Please.'

'I'm *not*. You can't think that! I can't stand him, now I know what he really is. It was him, wasn't it, behind all the drug stuff?'

'Nobody can prove it, so why bother to mention it?'

'Because it matters. Your name *will* be cleared, I swear, I won't give up as long as I have breath in my body. Harville might have won for now, but the truth will come out. I promise you.'

'I'm sorry,' he said after a pause.

'What are you sorry for?'

'Mixing you up in all this. You'll get done now, for perverting the course of justice, and your life'll be ruined along with mine. I should've got off, that first night, left the area, left the country.'

'But then we'd never have . . . Please come in. Please, don't jump. I'll never get over it if you do. I love you.'

'Jen, don't.' His voice, which had been full of laconic bravado, now wobbled. 'You shouldn't. I'm nothing.'

'You're everything,' she whispered. 'To me.'

'I'm a no-good jailbird.'

'I'll wait for you.'

'Don't wait for me.'

'You can't stop me. I'll wait for you till I'm ninety if I have to.'

There was a pause, then a grudging laugh. 'I don't think the sentence is as stiff as all *that*. Besides, what about a hundred? Is ninety your limit then? Snuff out your ninety candles and then bugger off into the sunset with some old geezer from the pensioner bingo night? I thought you cared about me.'

'I more than care about you. I love you. Please, come down.'

She saw his feet flex on to tiptoe, then flatten again, then he shifted his weight from one to the other, before finally there was a mutter of, 'OK. For you.'

And then, thank God, he turned and stepped down from the parapet, back into the little upstairs room, where Jenna waited for him.

She flung her arms around him and he held her close, and both of them had tears in their eyes when the police officers came up and prised them apart.

Chapter Eight

They arrested Jason and, even though Jenna protested that surely there was no need, they put handcuffs on him before they led him away.

'I love you, Jen,' he said briefly, turning his head to her at the top of the stairs.

She could only run down after them, then watch, helpless, as he walked slowly but with his head high, along the front path. Passing Lawrence Harville, he stopped to give him a long, wordless look before letting the officers yank him onwards.

Jenna stood on the steps with her face in her hands, trying not to howl with anguish in front of the remaining officers and Harville. At least there were no press here – not yet. That was the one and only silver lining she could find to this huge, overwhelming cloud.

But that small comfort didn't last. No sooner was Jason out of sight than a gaggle of camera-wielders appeared at the gate. Harville would have called them, of course. He'd want his moment of triumph to be complete.

Suddenly, her hatred was more than she could bear.

She took a few steps down, then ran towards him.

'Get out. Get off my property. Get out now before I have one of these officers arrest you for trespassing.'

The cameras clicked and the shouts of, 'Over here, Jenna! Jenna!' came thick and loud.

Harville was laughing and she was about to take a swing at him when one of the officers, a woman, restrained her.

'Take it easy, love,' she said gruffly. 'You don't want assault on your charge sheet, too.'

She gaped at the officer, aghast. 'Charge sheet?'

'You'll need to come down the station with us, Ms Diamond.'

'Myatt. It's Myatt now.'

'Ms Myatt, then. We'll have to charge you with perverting the course of justice. We'll need a statement.'

'I haven't perverted anything! How dare you?'

'He's been living here, hasn't he, all this time? With your knowledge?'

'I'm saying nothing.' Jenna whipped out her phone and dialled her London lawyer. 'Penny, it's Jenna. I need to talk to you urgently. Can you call me back. Thanks.'

And then she allowed herself to be led away, to be photographed by at least twenty people, climbing in to the back seat of a police car.

'Tomorrow's front page,' she muttered to herself, as they pulled away from the pavement, and left Harville Hall behind.

She refused to talk or make any kind of statement until she'd spoken to Penny, so she was left in an anteroom to stare for aeons at posters about car theft and a helpline for sufferers of domestic violence. The one that drew her eye and wouldn't let go said 'Rat On A Rat: Drug Dealers

Ruin Lives In Bledburn'. Underneath was a number to call
to inform on suspects. Perhaps she could call it, mention
Lawrence's name. She was tempted, but before she could
get her phone out of her bag, it rang. Penny.

The conversation was breathless and frenetic, and
Jenna could barely take in what Penny told her.

'You'll have to take the duty solicitor in with you –
obviously I can't come up from London right now. But,
Jenna, say nothing. Just "no comment" all the way through,
until we can meet and discuss this properly. It sounds as if
they'll charge you. We'll talk it about it after that. Can you
be in London, tomorrow?'

'I guess.'

'Come to my office, then.'

She rang off. Jenna wanted to call her PR people, to
warn them, but she'd had her one phone call and now the
duty solicitor was here and it was time for the interview.

'I've been advised by my lawyer to make no comment
at this time,' Jenna warned them before she sat down, but
they asked the questions anyway.

'Did you know that Jason Watson was living in your
house?'

'Did you know that he was wanted by the police for
drugs offences?'

'How long has he been sharing a house with you?'

'Did you know him prior to moving into the house?'

'What's the nature of your relationship? Are you
lovers?'

To all of these she fired no comments with a dull-eyed
resignation until they gave up.

'OK, Ms Myatt, we're going to charge you with
assisting an offender and perverting the course of justice.

You'll appear before Bledburn Magistrates on Friday, so you'll need to sort out any bail arrangements before then. You'll get a letter with dates and times and so forth. You're free to go.'

'What about Jason?'

'He's in custody. I shouldn't think he'll get bail.'

'Can I visit him?' She knew she was giving away some of the answers they'd wanted, but she didn't care.

'No, I'm afraid not.'

'Is he here? Where will they take him?'

The officer shrugged.

'Nottingham, most likely.'

The officer held open the door for her. It was clear that there would be no further questions.

She made it to the door of the police station, then stopped. There were cameras set up on the pavement outside, and a curious crowd had gathered.

'Excuse me,' she said to the desk sergeant. 'Do you have a back or side entrance I could use to leave? It's a zoo out there.'

The sergeant bit his lip.

'I shouldn't, but, just between you and me, I'm a big fan of yours, and Deano's. Got all his albums. If you could give me your autograph for the kids . . .'

'Right. Sure.'

She signed a leaflet about dangerous dog breeds and the sergeant took her to a back door that led into a yard full of police vehicles. On one side, she saw an almost-blank wall with high slits of windows at the top. They must be cells. Was Jason in one of them? She walked over to that side and called his name. He wouldn't be able to answer her, but if he at least heard her . . .

'Jason,' she called. 'I'll get you out of there. I love you. I won't forget you.'

Then, fearful of being heard by the vultures at the front of the building, she ran quickly out of the yard and up the little side street beyond, in which a taxi office was fortunately situated.

She didn't want to go back into the house, not now, but there was nowhere else for her to go. She went straight up to the attic and lay down on his old sleeping bag, grabbing the ancient tracksuit he never wore any more, and hugging it tightly to her chest.

She cried until her throat ached and her eyes stung, then she sat up and made dozens of phone calls. Everybody had to be warned about this – all the PR people, the TV bosses, the record company executives, the world and its spouse. And Deano.

'What?' Deano sounded as if she'd dragged him from sleep or, more likely, a party, even though it would be about lunchtime in LA.

'It's going to be in all the papers tomorrow. It's probably on Twitter already. I've been arrested.'

'Yeah, you said, but I don't get it, Jen. Why? You're straighter than straight. Is this a joke or something?'

'No joke. I wish. You know I bought Harville Hall.'

'Yeah, you weirdo. Why do you want to live in the same place as those skanks?'

'Never mind that for a minute. I moved into Harville Hall and found that I had a lodger. A lodger I didn't know about.'

'What? Sounds like something out of a horror movie. How can you have a lodger you don't know about?'

'He was hiding in the attic. Turns out he was wanted

for various crimes. He's been found and arrested and I'm accused of harbouring him.'

'Yeah, but it's not your fault if . . . I mean, did you know he was there?'

'I don't want to get into the ins and outs of it. The point is, there's going to be lots of shit about it in the papers tomorrow and I thought I ought to warn you. That's all.'

'That's *all*? You've been arrested and . . . You're my *wife*, Jen.'

'Until the divorce papers come through.'

'But, babe, are you OK?'

She swallowed, touched by his unexpected concern.

'I'm good, Deano. Honestly.'

''Cause I can come and be with you, if you want. Support you. You know, like a husband's meant to do.'

'Oh, Deano, really, that's so kind but, no, it's OK. You can't just drop everything for a silly blip. That's all it'll be. It'll work out. Penny's on the case and you know how shit-hot she is.'

I'll instruct her for Jason. She can take on his case. She'll win it for him.

The little bubble of much-needed optimism this plan engendered cheered her up just enough to keep Deano sweet.

'Yeah, she's good,' he agreed. 'Are you sure, though? I can drop everything if I want – that's the thing about being Deano Diamond. People will fall in line for me.'

'I know, but they don't need to. Get on with your life, Deano. I'll be fine.'

'You're still as fucking stubborn as you were when I met you.'

He sounded so fond and exasperated that she was

reminded of those early days, that all-absorbing love and that tireless belief in his talent she'd had.

And now she had both of those for Jason. How would he react if he knew that?

'That's me, D. Stubborn to the end. Listen, I'll keep you in the loop, OK? If anything happens, I'll call you.'

'You do that. And remember – my offer still stands. Yeah, all right, I'm coming.' This last was to somebody in the background. Somebody female-sounding. 'Bye, then, Jen. Keep the faith, babe.'

'I will. Bye, Deano.'

She held the phone to her cheek, wondering how he would react when the full story came out. When he knew that the arrested man was her lover.

She lay back down with the tracksuit, then Bowyer came to join her and rested by her head, purring and nuzzling as if he understood how desperate her affairs were now.

She lay like that, in the dark, until her stomach rumbled and, even then, she couldn't bring herself to get up. Jason was gone. Jason was in a police cell, in a paper suit, with the laces taken out of his shoes. Jason was in Nottingham nick, in a cell with God knows who, lying on his bunk, alone in the world.

'You're not alone,' she whispered into the tracksuit. 'I'll do anything for you.'

Then she sat up, catching her breath, at the sound of feet on the stairs.

'Who's that?' she whispered to Bowyer.

She crawled across the attic boards and bent close to the trap door, looking down on to the landing. Jason had left a craft knife in his tracksuit pocket and she gripped it tightly, just in case.

The footsteps came closer, stopped on the landing below, then moved into one of the bedrooms, then out, then to another.

She thought of climbing down the ladder, but her legs were shaking so much she thought she might fall. She thought next of pulling the ladder up and shutting the trapdoor, then calling the police, but before she could do this, Bowyer sprang down to the landing and ran, tail high, off down the stairs.

'Stupid cat,' she hissed, clenching her fists.

She was about to try and pull up the ladder as quietly as she could when she heard Bowyer make the awful, strangulated sound cats make when they've had their tails trodden on.

'Fuck off!' a male voice roared.

Lawrence Harville.

She froze for a moment, then made her way down the ladder and on to the upper landing, aiming for complete silence, holding her breath until she had achieved it.

What was he doing here? And how did he get in?

His tread was back, and on the stairs. She had to confront him now. She ran to the top of the staircase.

'What the hell do you think you're doing?' she demanded, her fingers wrapped around the handle of the knife in her pocket.

He was disconcerted only for the merest flicker of a second, then his face relaxed into a laconic smirk.

'Just checking over what I might need to do to the place when it's mine again,' he said.

'You're trespassing. Get out.'

'What are you going to do, call the police?' he asked politely. 'I'm not sure you'd make what they call a credible witness, now. Not after what you've been charged with.'

'A crime's a crime, whoever reports it, and you're committing one. Get out.'

'Oh, I don't think so,' he said, the smile still in evidence. 'Come down, Jenna. Let's talk. I'd rather keep things amicable. There's no need for all this shouting.'

'I have nothing to say to you except to tell you to give yourself up.'

'I beg your pardon? Give myself up? What on earth are you talking about?' There was distinct menace in his tone now, the smile withering at the edges.

'You're behind all this. The drugs, Jason's imprisonment. You set him up. Somehow you've got Mia and her friends eating out of your hand, but you can't keep it up forever, Lawrence.'

'What utter rubbish,' he said, his face contorted with anger. 'He fed you all this, did he? Your jailbird lover?'

'No, I worked it all out for myself.'

'Well, better get back to La-La-land, my dear, because you don't seem to understand the real world. But I can teach you all about it, if you want. Come down.'

'I'm going to call the police.'

He made a sudden move up the stairs and she tried to pull the knife out but her skinny jeans were so tight she couldn't wrestle it out of her pocket quickly enough.

He took advantage of her impotent struggling to take hold of her elbow and drag her, yelling and kicking, down the stairs and into the half-decorated master bedroom.

'Sit down,' he snarled, pushing her on to the bed. He seemed to think she'd been reaching for her phone and hadn't bothered to take the knife off her. She fidgeted with it in her pocket, trying to ease it free of its confinement without Lawrence guessing what it was.

'Why couldn't you have just been nice to me, Jenna?' he asked, standing over her. 'I gave you so many chances, but you kept your distance, every time. I was kind to you but you threw it in my face. We could have been so good together. We still could.'

She laughed with disbelief.

'You can't be serious. I'd rather shag a whole pit full of snakes.'

'Bravado, Jenna, hot air. Stop lashing out and think. Use your brain, instead of what's between your legs. You were obviously hot for loser boy, but it would never have worked out, now, would it? Be sensible.'

'He's worth a million of you. And I bet he's better in bed.'

'Well, shall we find out?'

'I'd kill myself, first.'

'No you wouldn't. Come on. You and Watson – it's just a mismatch. You and me, though, we understand the finer things in life. We could work so well. And it would mean that you could keep this place. You could do what you liked to it, carry on with all the plans you had. I wouldn't mind, even though you've cut the heart and soul out of my kitchen.'

'But you aren't going to get this place back. I've no idea why you think that.' Jenna shook her head at him, all the time trying to make calculations as to her best chances of getting away.

'Come on, Jen. Bledburn hasn't worked out for you. You're up on a charge of perverting the course of justice – you'll get a hefty fine at the very least, prison time at worst. Just cut your losses and sell up. I can afford to buy it back now.'

Jenna was too furious to speak for a minute, then she managed to grind out, 'With dirty money, yes.'

'No comment, as I'm sure your lawyer advised you to say at your interview. You wouldn't want to be here any more. Have you seen the press setting up camp outside? You're going to be a virtual prisoner, anyway. Come with me to an hotel and we'll sort out the conveyancing tomorrow.'

'What's the hurry?'

'What's the sense in hanging around? Sell up and live with me here or fuck off to London. I don't really care.'

'I suspect my bail conditions will involve staying in Bledburn, actually.'

He shrugged.

'Whatever. It's your move. Literally.'

'I'm staying here. And I'm not selling, you can get lost now.'

He took a step closer and, yes, she could get the knife out of her pocket now. She clicked up the blade and brandished it.

He laughed.

'Not a smart move, Jenna. Threatening behaviour with an offensive weapon on top of your existing charges? My, my, they're going to throw the book at you, aren't they?'

'I'll throw this at you if you don't just fuck off,' she said with desperate clarity.

Lawrence lunged and she was about to jab the blade at his face when they were distracted by an almighty noise and rushing wind through the window.

'God, a helicopter,' she breathed.

'Some press outfit or other,' said Lawrence. 'I bet you're on News 24. Aerial shots of this place all over Sky. You should turn it on and see.'

'I don't have a TV.'

'On your phone then?'

'You just want to be a star, don't you, Lawrence,' she said with pitying sarcasm. 'Is that what this is all about? You don't have any talents of your own so you've decided you'll get a bit of fame by association with me?'

He was at the window now, looking out at the hovering copter. He seemed to have forgotten that Jenna had a knife, but he soon remembered when she came up behind him and put its tip to the side of his neck.

'Get. Out,' she said softly. 'Just turn around and walk out of that door, to the front door, then out of the front gate. You'll get your picture taken, and you'll like that, won't you? Your fatuous, grinning mug all over the front pages tomorrow. Except it won't be – it'll by my face, and Jason's, because you are completely irrelevant.'

'Put down the knife,' he said, his voice wobbly with fear.

'I could up the ante,' she said, pushing it that tiny bit further, just enough pressure to make him think his skin would puncture at any minute. 'I could say I won't put it down until you call the police and make a confession.'

'I have nothing to confess,' he said levelly. 'Whatever you've come up with about me is false. You've jumped to conclusions, because you don't like me, and Watson hates me.'

'Are you sure about that?'

'Just put down the knife and I'll go. I promise. Please?'

'OK.'

She moved it an inch from his neck.

He hurried out of the room and she followed him to the front door.

He turned back before leaving.

'You will sell this place to me,' he said. 'And if you don't, I'll buy it at auction after the repossession. Because you're finished, Jenna. So sleep on it. I'll still be around in the morning.'

It was a relief to see him go, but his words haunted her as she went to the kitchen to pour herself a stiff drink.

She was finished.

Coming back from a scandal like this would be incredibly difficult, both personally and professionally, but perhaps not impossible. Her mind ran over the situations of various celebrities who had ended up in hot water – you still didn't see them panhandling on street corners. Well, not many of them. Oh, God.

She drained the tot of brandy and went to lie on her bed, the trials of the day taking their toll, at last, on her reserves of energy. She felt sapped and wrecked, a shell of herself. But at least she lay on her own bed in her own house, whereas Jason . . .

The thought of him, standing on that parapet, terrified and desperate, brought tears to her eyes and she wept until she was spent, then went to the kitchen for more brandy.

There was no evidence against Lawrence, nothing she could do about anything. It was hopeless, and all was lost. She made sure her phone was switched off and drank brandy until she passed out.

Chapter Nine

She woke up with a fearful headache and Bowyer curled up on her chest. The weight of him had led to nightmares in which she was being pressed to death as torture to try and extract information about Jason's crimes. Waking up was both a relief and a torment.

She needed water, but the idea of lifting her head from the pillow didn't appeal. The idea of doing anything didn't appeal, come to that.

She could hear distant voices, unusually, because this place was so quiet and protected from the outside world. Of course it would be the press, manning their barricades, in case she came out to give a statement. Not bloody likely.

She shut her eyes again, thinking of Jason. For some reason, she pictured him in a suit with arrows on, eating thin gruel in a darkened dungeon. Obviously this wouldn't be the case, but the vision pierced her heart all the same.

Bowyer's hungry mews eventually forced her from her bed to feed him.

She drained a litre of water and took some painkillers. No food – she couldn't even face a sliver of dry toast. A sense of dread at what might happen when she switched on her phone hung over her. She postponed the evil hour by taking a long bath, but it couldn't be avoided forever.

Dressed in capris and a vest top, for another glaringly hot day, she pressed the on button and awaited the onslaught of text tones and missed call alerts.

There were many. She left the phone bleeping away to itself while she tidied the room and straightened the bed, then came back to it.

She had to return the calls from her people at work, her PR and her lawyer. The rest were personal or speculative contacts from various arms of the media.

The calls were long and heated and, by the time she had dealt with them all, her throat was dry and she felt hot all over, and wrung out.

In the meantime, the morning papers had been delivered. She turned them face down on the kitchen table so the England cricket team's latest woes were all she had to worry about.

'I don't want to know,' she muttered to herself.

She lay on the bed again, staring at the ceiling, screening phone calls, until finally there was one she thought she should take. It was from the police station.

'Ms Myatt? Sergeant Black from Bledburn Central Police Station. I've got a young lady here who wants to make a statement. She's asking if she can speak to you first.'

Mia?

An arrow of hope shot into Jenna's heart. Was it possible?

Without enquiring any further, she gabbled, 'I'll be there as soon as I can,' and hung up.

The next question to arise was how to get out of here without running the paparazzi gauntlet. The front door was clearly out of the question – was there any chance of vaulting over the back wall? She hadn't even made it to the end of the garden yet – at a certain point, two thirds of the way back, it became too tangled and overgrown with brambles to contemplate. But perhaps if she took a good, hacky knife and a stepladder . . .

She hurried to the kitchen and selected the most evil-looking of her Japanese Saji knives, grabbed the stepladder she'd been using to strip the bedroom wallpaper, and set off through the back patio doors. Stepladder under her arm, knife held out in front of her for optimum safety, she marched across the less neglected stretch of the garden, until she reached what had once been the orchard and was now a dark and twisted thicket, hosting who knew what.

She put down the stepladder, resolving to come back for it, because this would be hard and possibly dangerous work. Her knife sliced through the thorny branches with ease, but there were so many of them, and the distance to hack through so uncertain that she was soon disheartened. It was going to take far too long.

Perhaps she could just climb the wall a bit closer to the house? But, she thought, she would probably be seen. The beauty of going over the rear wall was that it backed on to the church graveyard, and she doubted that the vicar would allow enterprising snappers to set up their tripods among the lichened headstones.

But she was already scratched halfway up her arms and hot and itchy with the effort of what she had done, and still the wall was nowhere in sight.

She dropped the knife and took a deep breath. Her

priority was to get to the police station. Never mind all this ducking and diving.

She wiped her forehead and bent to pick the knife up again. Something lay, not far off from its glinting blade, at the foot of a withered apple tree. It was a coin, an old one, not in current circulation, with a hole bored into it, as if it had once been a pendant or keyring charm.

She picked it up and saw that it was a gold sovereign, of a design much imitated even now in the form of rings and other jewellery. This was no copy, however, but a genuine article. It had been a keepsake, perhaps a treasure.

And on the bark of the old tree, she noticed some initials carved. DH and FJ, with the classic heart around them. DH must be some olden Harville, she thought, and FJ his sweetheart. Perhaps they had married.

She resolved to look into the history of the Harvilles and try to identify these lovers, now long gone. But first, there were lovers in today's world to consider: herself and Jason.

She put the sovereign charm into her bag and turned back. There would be no wall-climbing today.

She put on a cardigan to hide her scratches and opened the front gate to the expected barrage. Clicks and shouts and rude, forceful figures standing in her way. She swept past them all, keeping her eyes to the front and her mouth shut.

Even as she climbed into her car, a camera was pushed in beside her, so that she had to struggle to get the door shut. She drove off, chased by a gaggle of the more desperate sorts until they could no longer keep up with her.

Wryly, she wondered how many had got their shot, and

which one would end up in the sidebar of shame. Not that she cared.

There were even a few stragglers at the police station, and these were the ones whose long wait was rewarded, for they would get a rarer photograph.

She ran up the steps to the front door and hurried to the desk. Annoyingly, there was somebody already there, making a very long meal out of reporting somebody parking over his driveway. The sergeant gave her an apologetic look and pointed towards a side room.

She expected to see Mia. She didn't get what she expected.

'Kayley! Hello. What are you doing here?'

Kayley looked sheepish and took a sip out of her cardboard cup of coffee.

'I've come to make a statement,' she said. 'But I wanted to talk to you first.'

'A statement?' Jenna struggled to overcome her disappointment, but it wasn't easy. 'Has there been trouble at the youth club? Something to do with the talent contest?'

'No, that's not it. Look, I had no idea about you and Jason. Obviously.'

'Is this to do with Jason?' Her heart lurched. She wasn't sure if it was up or down.

'Yeah. And before I tell you, I'm sorry. OK? I didn't know it would work out this way.'

'I'm all right. Where did you get the coffee?'

'Vending machine, out in the hall. D'you want one? I'll get it for you. Least I can do, in the circumstances.'

Jenna watched, nonplussed, as Kayley went out of the room, returning a minute later with another cardboard cup.

'So,' said Jenna, taking a sip of the scalding liquid. 'What's this all about, then?'

'I've come to tell them that Jason didn't know anything about what was going on with those drugs.'

'Have you really?' Jenna spilled a splash on to her hand. It hurt, and would leave a mark, but she could hardly have cared less. 'How come? How do you know?'

'All right, I'm going to go back a bit. I'm Mia's best friend from school – you met up with Mia yesterday, I heard?'

'That's right.'

'Well, me, Mia and Jase were all the same year at school together. They were the lovebirds of year eleven, and I got left out because they were always together, and I suppose I was jealous. I took against Jason from then. Just in a silly teenage way, I mean. There wasn't anything serious to it. I just wanted the times Mia and I used to have back. I missed her.'

'So you and Jason didn't get on?'

'No, I wouldn't say that. I put on a good face. We went to the same parties, socialised with the same people. In the end, I got so lonely I went out and got myself a boyfriend, just so I could do coupley things with Mia and Jase. We did everything together. And I mean everything.'

She gave Jenna a significant, slightly shamed look, and Jenna remembered what Jason had told her about the wild sex lives of the young people on the estate. She didn't want to know more.

'So, you know them. Is this what's going in your statement?'

'No, this is just the background. I wanted you to know the full story before you . . . Ah, whatever. Anyway

I ditched the boyfriend, because we had nothing in common, and decided to get a life. Went to college, did my youth work qualification, kept away from the dodgy parties. But I got invited to a different type of dodgy party by a lad on my course – a party up at Harville Hall.'

'My house!'

'Yeah, except it was Lawrence Harville's house, then. I didn't know it, but it was party central. The place was falling down around him, but you could get anything you wanted there, do anything you wanted, have anyone you wanted. It was a different world. Anyway, Lawrence took a shine to me. I think he liked having a bit of rough. We got together, in a way. I mean, I were never his girlfriend. He wouldn't have taken me out anywhere nice. But I got a lot of booty calls.'

'Oh God, I hate him,' muttered Jenna, unable to contain herself.

'I brought Mia along to one of the parties, and then he dumped me and went for her. Well, she is pretty. I'd kill for her looks. She got into drugs, big time, and – I don't know, I didn't want to know, I never asked – I think she started dealing for him, in the pub. She stopped seeing so much of Jason because he didn't know anything about it. I stopped seeing Lawrence and going to his parties. It was all starting to look a bit too sick for me. I just wanted a normal life.'

Her voice had a note of plea in it, and Jenna felt sorry for her, despite herself. She knew how easy it was to get sucked into dark places – she'd seen it over and over in LA. Some of her most promising talents were drying out, in psychiatric facilities, right now.

'Of course,' she said. 'And you've done well for yourself. You do good work at the Youth Club.'

'It's not enough,' Kayley said, hollowly. 'I've done something horrible and I can't stay quiet about it any more.'

'So what's the horrible thing?' asked Jenna, but she was starting to see the picture.

'I kept away from Mia, Jase, Lawrence, everyone, for a couple of years. I heard on the grapevine that Mia was getting more and more involved, and Jason was getting more and more pissed off with her. In the end, I think Lawrence just decided to get him out of the way. He turned up at my flat one night, and asked me to give him my rucksack.'

'Harville?'

'Yeah. I was surprised to see him – it'd been a while – and I asked him what the hell he wanted my rucksack for, and he got nasty. Brought out a load of photographs of me, off my face, and naked and whatnot at his parties. Send he'd send them to the Youth Service, and the local paper, unless I just handed it over, no questions asked and nothing to be said about it ever again. If the police asked me, I was to say I'd lent it to Jason, and didn't know any more than that. And then I was to get off the estate for the night and stay with a friend until morning.'

'Oh, God. You're the friend of Mia's.'

'Yeah, but I didn't know what was happening. Nobody told me, until I saw Mia the next day.'

'Lawrence took a lot of trouble to cover his tracks.'

'He used my rucksack, then got Mia to give it to Jason to deliver to the house – he'd had a tip-off that it was going to be raided, so he thought he might as well take

Jason down, since he was going to lose a lot of stock.'

'Whose was the house?'

'Just one of his goons. A pathetic druggie called Blister. He'd got him to take the full rap for it, promised him a better crib when he got out of prison, if he kept schtum about his suppliers and higher-ups.'

'And you knew all this, but you never said anything?'

'I couldn't. Lawrence had those photos. Plus he knows some bad people in Nottingham. Hitmen, even. I didn't dare.'

'But now?'

'I could keep my trap shut when it was just Jason on the hook. But you? You really don't deserve it. When I saw those stories in the newspapers, I felt like scum. I'd rather go down myself than let you go down for me.'

'Jason doesn't deserve it either,' Jenna said, still angry, but moved by Kayley's open and sincere confession. 'He has a life to live, and an amazing talent to give the world. You nearly deprived us of that.'

'I know. Believe me, I can't feel any worse than I do. If I could turn back the clock—'

'I know, I know. Everyone has regrets, but these are serious ones.'

'I had no idea you and he . . .' She gave Jenna a quizzical look.

'I found him in my attic. Can you believe that?'

'I can't believe you didn't scream the place down, then call the police.' Kayley smiled, weakly.

'I almost did. I'm very glad I didn't.'

'So is there, like, you know, you and him . . .?'

Jenna bit her lip and nodded slowly.

'Wow. That's romantic. Like a story.'

'It's romantic, right up to the point where he gets arrested for a crime he didn't commit.'

'And that's where I come in,' said Kayley, drawing a deep breath. She stood and went to the door. 'Shall we?'

Jenna could only wait in reception while Kayley was taken to an interview room. Time dragged, and stretched, and did everything it could to elongate itself. Jenna drank three cups of vending machine coffee, before realising that it wasn't really helping.

Her idea of looking at the news sites on her mobile phone proved to be unwise – in the hurly-burly, she had forgotten that she, herself, was front page news. She was shocked to see a headline ROUGH DIAMOND with a picture of herself and Jason, in the front garden, at the time of his arrest.

She wondered how supportive Deano would be feeling now.

She didn't have to wait long to find out.

A text came through and, seeing that it was from him, she didn't ignore it, as she had been doing all the others.

She opened it.

'U were shaggin him!'

Oh, dear. Outrage. She sighed, and deleted it unanswered.

A door opened somewhere in the hinterland behind the front desk. She pricked up her ears. Kayley?

She came to the front desk, winked at Jenna, then had to go through a number of forms with the sergeant before she could speak to her.

'What's happening?' asked Jenna breathlessly.

'I've been arrested and charged,' she said, as cheerfully as if she'd been telling her about a holiday booking. 'I should be devastated, but I feel really like a weight's been lifted. I feel *good*.'

'I knew that you would, babe.' Jenna quoted the old song, smiling back at her. 'So, what's the score now, with Jason?'

'They've got to look into it, of course. For all they know, I could be lying to save someone else's skin. And they need to get hold of Harville and Mia.'

'What have you been charged with?'

'Perversion,' she said grinning. 'It sounds so bad, doesn't it?'

'Not accessory?'

'No, because I didn't know what they wanted my bag for – though I could have guessed. And I was blackmailed into it. They might charge me later if they decide not to believe me, though. That might depend on Harville.'

She looked glum.

'I don't like the idea of everything depending on Harville,' said Jenna.

'Neither do I.'

'Mia, though?'

'Mia would fess up, I'm sure she would. She's all right, underneath it all. I don't think she's happy about Jason going down, either.'

'So, are you free to go?'

'Yeah. They'll send me the court details when they get a clearer picture of who else will be in the dock with me. Ugh. In the dock. I expect I'll lose my job now. Mum'll kill me.'

'You can work for me,' said Jenna without thinking twice.

'Oh, get away. I'm not a showbizzy type.'

'You don't have to be. I could find a place for you.'

'Could you, really?'

'Leave it with me. First of all, we need to pin down Lawrence Harville and Mia, make sure the police can get hold of them. We don't want them going to ground.'

'I think they were going to look for them straight away. Mia's easy – she'll still be in her pit, at the pub.'

'Yes, I bet you're right. As for Lawrence – well, I think I can deal with him. Will you come back to the house with me for back-up?'

'Oh, is this a covert operation?' Kayley was thrilled. 'Sign me up. I always fancied myself as a spy.'

'Excellent. What are we waiting for, then? Let's get going.'

They were allowed out through the back door, again, and hurried to the car, Kayley making sure she pulled the brow of her baseball cap down over her face in trademark shifty-villain style.

'There's press all over the front of the house,' Jenna warned her. 'I'm going to go in first, and you can wait in the car ten minutes, then come to the door. Tell them you're my financial advisor, if they ask.'

Kayley laughed out loud. 'I look so like one,' she said, looking down at her jogging pants and tattooed arms.

'That'll give them something to gossip about while we're working, then,' said Jenna.

The throng had not thinned while Jenna had been out – if anything, it was worse. Jenna had to elbow her way through them, keeping her head low and her mouth sealed.

Once in the house, she took out her phone and called Harville.

'Jenna.' He sounded surprised.

'Lawrence. I've been thinking things over, and I think you're right. I can't stay in Bledburn. There's no point hanging on to the Hall.'

'Right. Good. Well, how about a private sale, then? Get your lawyer to call my lawyer . . .'

'Can't we do things a little less formally? I'm up to my eyes in legal shit as it is. Why don't you come round? I'll give you the keys and get the hell out of here. I'll stay in a hotel, till the trial is over.'

There was a silence. He was bound to suspect trickery, she thought, but she mustn't start to beg or sound desperate, because that would be the biggest giveaway of all.

'Very reasonable,' he said, at last, 'for a woman who was completely *un*reasonable yesterday. Do you have something up your sleeve? Something like a kitchen knife, for instance?'

'Lawrence, I'm sorry about that. I was stressed. Can I wave the white flag? I'd like to make it up to you.'

She had put just enough subtle promise in her voice to hook him, it seemed, because he changed his tone straight away.

'Well, in that case, OK.'

'If you're nervous, you can bring a friend.'

'Oh, I don't think so. I don't think that would be appropriate, do you?' He chuckled softly then hung up.

Jenna punched the air.

A few minutes later, Kayley knocked and was admitted.

'He's coming,' said Jenna eagerly.

'Shit,' said Kayley. 'What do you want me to do then?'

'I want you to – have you got a phone? Good. I want you to go up to the attic and lurk there. As soon as you hear a knock at the door, call the police. Tell them Harville is here. The rest should be easy enough.'

Kayley did a mock salute. 'Yes, partner,' she said. 'Gorgeous house, isn't it? Shame Lawrence let it go to rack and ruin. You've got your work cut out for you.'

'I know. But I'll get there. Quickly, then – I have no idea when he'll get here. He's out and about a lot, is our Lawrence.'

Kayley bounded up the stairs, apparently given a new lease of life by her new criminal status. Jenna paced around the ground floor, trying to get her thoughts straight and her courage up. The idea that this could go horribly wrong insisted on inserting itself into her mind, filleting through her resolve.

Perhaps it was a bad idea, after all. Perhaps she should put him off.

She took out her phone, but it was too late. He was at the door.

His smile was pure, triumphant smarm as she opened it.

'Good girl,' he said. 'I knew you'd see sense.'

'Come in,' she said tonelessly, the urge to break his nose never stronger than now.

'Ah, the old place,' he said, filling his lungs appreciatively. 'Soon have it back up to scratch. Harville Hall for the Harvilles. If you want, you can stay over, any time you like.'

'I'll be sad to leave,' said Jenna. It occurred to her that perhaps she should take him out in the back garden, where he would be less likely to hear the police arriving. 'There's something I wanted to ask you about – something I found outside.'

'Oh yeah? I thought you were going to pour me a nice drink, and get comfortable.'

'We can do that outside,' she said, leading him through the kitchen and grabbing a bottle of wine and two glasses on the way.

'Oh, I've done it all out here, in my time,' said Lawrence, stepping out on to the blazing back patio. He took off his jacket and slung it over a rusty garden chair. 'Up against a tree, on the lawn, behind the bushes.' He chuckled. 'Can get a bit waspy, but if you pick your time . . .'

He put a hand on Jenna's shoulder, as if it were his God-given right.

She bristled, and put the drink things down on the low wall that enclosed the sides of the patio.

'The thing I wanted to ask you about,' she said, trying not to sound too steely. 'Come down and see.'

She found the paving slab with the iron ring that she and Jason had spotted before and theorised about the existence of a cellar.

'Here. It made me think you might have a cellar. But the deeds don't mention anything underneath the house.'

Lawrence put the toe of his shiny shoe against the iron ring and nudged it.

'It looks like it, doesn't it?' he said. 'But no. There's no cellar. I don't know why that ring was put there. Maybe one of my kinky ancestors liked to chain his women to it. Hm, there's an idea.'

The look he gave Jenna was equal parts lust and menace.

She looked around, nervously. Not that she'd be able to see the police cars coming.

'Or her men,' she suggested.

'Yes, I suppose so. Why, are you that way inclined?'

'Not really. But are you sure there's nothing underneath? It's such an odd thing to put there.'

'Like I said.' Lawrence sounded surly now. 'And I'm glad you're not a Miss Whiplash type. I don't like pain.'

'So, about the ghosts you were talking about,' she said, keen to keep matters away from his expected seduction of her. 'Do any of them have names, or stories?'

'Oh, yes, our dear Harville ghosts? Yes. I grew up with little Fay.'

'Fay?'

'Fairy Fay. That's what we called her. I think her name was actually Frances and she was the wife of my great-great-great-grandfather.'

'What happened to her?'

'She disappeared. She was there one day, and gone the next. Never found. Never explained. I thought you'd have heard of the case. It was a favourite scary story round here.'

'Somehow it passed me by. Perhaps it was only known to the circles you moved in.'

'That's probably it. Too good a story for the riff-raff.'

'Thanks. That would be me, would it?'

'Oh, come on, Jenna, don't take offence. We both know what we are. I'm old money, you're new money. I think we should get together and make middle-aged money.'

'Except you ran out of old money,' Jenna pointed out. 'Or you wouldn't have had to sell up.'

'Well, I took a few hits,' said Lawrence. 'Had a run of bad luck. But I've made it all back now, and more.'

'By selling drugs.'

He scowled and grabbed her upper arm in a painful grip.

'Don't start all that again, Jenna. It won't get you

anywhere. Now where's that good time I was promised?'

She tried to fight him off but he was stronger and managed to get her into a tight lock. His mouth was almost on hers, and she sensed there would be teeth, when an almighty bang on the door caused both of them to freeze.

'Who is it? Who are you expecting?'

'Nobody,' whispered Jenna. 'Let me answer it.'

The door banged again.

'Police,' bellowed a loud male voice.

'You bitch, what have you done? Set me up?'

'No, it's probably for me, perhaps they've charged me with something else. Let me get it.'

'I don't trust you.'

He wouldn't let go and she couldn't elude him, but both of them heard the footsteps on the stairs, and the opening of the door.

'What's . . .?'

Lawrence let go of Jenna as a squad of police officers burst into the house, truncheons drawn.

'In here.' Kayley's voice was high-pitched and urgent. 'He's got Jenna, in here.'

He was surrounded. There was nothing for him to do but to surrender himself into custody.

'This isn't over,' he snarled to Jenna as they led him off.

'No,' she shouted after him. 'I'll be giving evidence at your trial.'

There were more statements to be taken, heels to be kicked at the police station, photos to be papped, disgusting cups of coffee to be drunk, but eventually the story seemed to be straight, and understood in everyone's minds, and Jenna was sent back home.

Jason was released the next day.

Jenna's PR had been on the phone until she had earache from the number of entreaties not to go and meet him from prison, but she ignored them all.

The photographers were lined up along the road on either side of the prison gates. Jenna stayed in her car, parked a few hundred yards away, watching the great grey gates between the high blank red brick walls. There really was something about a prison that struck a unique kind of horror into the heart, she thought. And Jason had not just been observing it from a distance – he had been in there, inside those cold walls with their barred windows.

At least it was only for a couple of days. He had been prepared for a lot longer.

Her hands flew to her handbag, and a strange flame rose from her stomach to her throat as she saw movement at the gate. It was being opened.

She lunged for the door handle and her eyes filled with tears at the first sight of Jason, impossibly small in front of those huge grey spikes, accompanied by a uniformed officer who stood looking after Jason as he pulled his cap down over his face to hide from the press.

He ran the gauntlet of them, and at the end he found Jenna, who had abandoned her resolve to wait in the car until he found her and bounded out on to the tarmac, shouting his name.

'Jen,' he cried, spotting her.

The feel of him, his reality, in her arms again, lifted a burden she hadn't even been fully aware of. She felt light again, and capable of anything. There was nothing that could spoil this, nothing, ever.

'I love you,' she said, and he repeated the words back

to her before preventing further utterances by sealing her mouth up with a long, extravagant, passionate and very public kiss.

'Tomorrow's front page,' she whispered, breaking apart.

They had somehow staggered, lips still locked, across the forecourt to the car, in a hail of click-click-clicks.

'Who cares?' he said. 'They can print what they like. Perhaps it's just as well they're here.'

'Oh?'

'Otherwise I might have you right here, up against this car.'

She shivered with the thrill, letting him kiss her again with her back to the car door and his jeans-clad erection grinding into her, before they were interrupted by something other than the relentless photographing.

'Our Jay! Hello! Remember me?'

He buried his face in Jenna's neck, breathing a heavy sigh into it, before straightening up and turning to the voice.

'Mum,' he said. 'Have you met Jenna?'

'We have met,' she said, eyeing Jenna dubiously. 'She never said you two were . . .'

'He was supposed to be in hiding,' said Jenna. 'Or I would have mentioned it. I didn't want to lie to you.'

'You could have said he was alive, at least! I was in *bits*.'

'Look, can we have this conversation somewhere out of the public eye? Get in the car – we'll talk at the Hall.'

'Ooh, the Hall,' said Jason's mother. 'It's been a while. No, let me give my own son a hug. Thank you!'

Jason submitted to a quick squeeze, then sloped into the back seat of the car, keeping his head down as they drove off through the predictable phalanx.

The same predictable phalanx met them outside the Hall, but the three of them hurried past and into safety.

'Now,' said Jenna, shutting the world outside. 'I think we could all use a drink.'

'How did you swing it?' Jason was first to speak, taking a glass of red wine and sitting down at the kitchen table. 'I thought I were in for a five-stretch, minimum.'

'It was Kayley. She knew the details of the raid, and Mia and Lawrence's part in it.'

'She knew more than I did, then. What happened? Attack of the guilty conscience?'

'Pretty much, yeah.'

He stared into the glass. 'I'd hoped Mia might . . .'

'Well, she's being questioned, right now. I can't see her sticking to Harville's story.'

'So she'll go down?'

'I don't know. Possibly. Probably.'

He swished his wine around in the glass, his dark eyes fixed on it as if hypnotised.

'Have you ever put in way more than you've got out?' he asked.

'Yes,' replied both Jenna and Kathy.

He half-smiled at them.

'That was me and Mia.'

'That was me and you,' said Kathy with an ironic little laugh.

'That was me and, oh never mind,' said Jenna. 'You loved her more than she loved you. It happens. But it never stops hurting until you can take courage and move on.'

'She didn't deserve you,' said Kathy, stoutly. 'I never

liked her.'

'You never thought anyone deserved me,' said Jason, patting his mother's arm. 'Did you?'

'Well, I was right an' all. You're made of better stuff than that shower on the estate.'

'So you were always saying,' he replied. 'But that's what all mothers think, isn't it?'

'Not all of 'em have my grounds,' she said, a tad darkly.

'You are an astonishing talent,' Jenna reminded him. 'I saw some of your pictures on your mum's wall. Amazing stuff.'

'So,' said Jason after a pause. 'Harville's inside now? Hope he's got the same cell as me. My cell mate's a big lad with a short fuse.'

'It must have been awful for you.'

'Not much different from school, to be honest. Most of the same people, even. Food was better.'

'I always knew you were innocent,' said Kathy with a dramatic depth to her voice. 'I told everyone. My Jase isn't into drugs. It'll be that Mia, putting him up to it. But I couldn't prove it, of course. Was it really Lawrence Harville behind it all?'

'It really was,' said Jenna. 'Bastard. I hope he gets put away for a long time.'

'He'll wriggle out of it,' predicted Jason. 'Mia'll be too scared to say a word against him, even if Kayley isn't.'

'I won't be!' said Jenna.

'I bet they don't even call you,' said Jason. 'He's got good lawyers.'

'So have I.'

'You could've told me,' wailed Kathy, apparently not

happy to be left out of the conversation. 'Your own mother and you couldn't find a way to tell me whether you were alive or dead. I've been to hell and back, I have.'

'I'm sorry,' said Jason. 'I know. But I thought you'd know I was OK. You know me. I can look after myself. I've had to.'

The last words were a little pointed, a little resentful, but not quite enough to shut Kathy up.

'I've had it hard,' she said. 'You two can't imagine what it's been like for me. I've been let down in life, let down by everyone I ever knew. Even you, son. It's like a slap in the face.'

'Yeah, well, I'm back now, so everything's sound, right?' Jason sounded bored. 'Where's Bowyer?'

'In the garden, I should think. He deserves a treat, too. Let's have a little party, to celebrate your freedom, shall we? I'll get some food and drink in.'

'Sounds nice,' said Kathy. 'And I can get to know my boy's new lass. At last he's started to punch his own weight with the girls.'

'Mum, I think you ought to be getting home,' said Jason. 'You know what you get like when the booze is flowing.'

Kathy didn't take kindly to the suggestion.

'How dare you? Your own mother! I can't celebrate seeing my own son, what I thought were lying dead in a ditch, come back to life? You're heartless, that's what you are. Just like your dad.'

'Oh, not this again, Mum.' He turned to Jenna. 'Whenever I do something she doesn't like, I'm just like my dad. Convenient, isn't it, that I can't exactly argue, because I don't know who the bastard is.'

'The truth'll come out, one day,' said Kathy, rising from her seat and downing her glass of wine in one. 'Believe you me.'

'You don't know who he is,' said Jason, sounding bored. 'It could be any number of fellas. Probably some loser with a wife and six kids of his own. I've probably played darts with him at the pub.'

'You talk to me like that,' said Kathy, now full of wounded dignity, pouring herself another glass. 'But you'll eat your words one day, you'll see.'

'I'll give you a lift home,' offered Jenna, alarmed to see Kathy necking back the second glass in one.

'Don't you trouble yourself,' she said, the wounded dignity now so insistent that she was quite stiff with it. 'I can walk. I'm still a capable human being, whatever *he* has to say about it.'

She banged down her glass and shuffled out of the kitchen, followed by Jason.

'You'll come and visit your old mum sometime, will you? When you're not too busy with your love life?'

'I'll come round tomorrow. Stop being such a drama queen. Jesus. Anyone'd think it was you who'd just got out of prison on a false charge.'

She flounced out, banging the front door behind her.

'Oh dear,' said Jenna. 'I hope she'll get home all right.'

'She'll be fine. Two glasses is nothing to her. This was what it was like growing up. Everything was always about her. All "poor me" and veiled hints about some bollocks made-up story she's dreamed up about how I came to be.'

'That must have been hard for you.'

'Yeah, well, it weren't a picnic, that's for sure.' He swigged moodily at his wine, then his face softened as he looked properly at Jenna. 'But fuck that. It's just you and me, now, and this big old house. And I don't think we've had our proper reunion yet, have we? Come here.'

She smiled, her lips curving to fit the shape of the wine glass rim.

'What for?' she asked, teasingly.

'What do you think? What do you think was on my mind while I was lying on my hard prison bunk for twenty-three hours at a time?'

'Justice?' She wanted to eke out the predatory glint in his eye so she could gorge on it for as long as possible. 'Escape?'

'Escape, so I could get my hands on you again,' he said. 'Now, are you going to come here, or do I have to go over there and get you?'

'I thought about you,' she said. 'But I couldn't think about not being with you again for years. My brain wouldn't let me.'

'Mine neither. And we can be together whenever we want now. For example, this very minute. Are you coming, Jen? I warn you, I've got a lot of frustration to work out.'

'Sounds dangerous.' But Jenna put down her wine glass and pushed back her chair.

'Oh yeah, it's dangerous. Come and see how dangerous.'

She stood up and feinted a move around the table, changing her direction at the last minute, just as he lunged for her, to dodge out towards the hall door.

'Oh, don't you dare!' he cried, leaping up and chasing her to the bedroom.

But she had not been escaping at all. He found her sitting on the bed, her back arched to offer her neck and breasts to him.

'Why would I run from you?' she asked softly. 'When all I've thought about since you went away is having you back?'

'Yeah?' He pulled off his trainers and came to kneel opposite her, taking her hands and putting them on his chest, covered with his own fingers. 'I thought of you too. All alone in my cell. Nearly killed me to think of you, on your own, here, and to think of all the men, better men than me, who'd be round you like flies. I told myself I had to say goodbye to the idea of ever seeing you again, but I couldn't.'

'You don't have to,' she whispered, removing one of her hands from beneath his to stroke his cheek. 'You never have to worry about that. I ached for you. Nobody else would do for me.'

He shook his head. 'I don't understand it, Jen. But I'll take it. I'll take you, and I'll work for you – to deserve you.'

'You do, already.'

There could be no holding back the kisses after that. They fell against each other, wrapped around each other, a vampiric embrace that sought to drain the other of their deepest essence so that they could become one.

'Lie on your back,' he murmured into Jenna's ear. 'I need to pace myself. Need to calm down or it'll all be over too quick.'

'We can do it again, if it is. We can do it as many times as we like,' she reminded him with a catlike smile.

'Oh yes, that's going to happen,' he said, watching her lie down, in the light cotton shirt dress she had chosen to wear for their reunion. 'But there's no rush, is there? Just . . .' He settled himself in between her ankles and stroked her newly waxed legs lightly on both sides. 'Settle in,' he whispered. 'Get comfortable. And don't expect to be able to walk, tomorrow.'

'Is that a promise?'

'Hmm. But I know what's missing.'

He climbed off the bed and went to the drawer where they kept the sex toys she had bought. He took out the purple cuffs and brandished them at her.

'Oh,' she squeaked, her body's excitement – already considerable –intensifying at the sight. 'Now I'm nervous.'

'You should be. Give us your hand.'

He cuffed each wrist to the bedhead then resumed his position, lifting one of her legs so that the hem of her dress rose to the top of her thigh, and bringing her foot to his lips. He kissed it in random places: heel, instep, big toe, ankle. Then he laid it down and did the same with her other foot. She congratulated herself silently on the pedicure she'd self-administered that morning.

'I can see your knickers,' he said, still holding her left foot high, massaging it in strong, capable hands. 'You naughty girl. Do you show them to all the boys?'

'Only the ones who know what to do with them,' she said, squirming a little and trying to close her legs, which Jason would not allow to happen.

'Good answer. Well, I'll get to that. But first . . .'

He bent forward and began unbuttoning her dress from the top down. He dropped little kisses on her neck at intervals, sometimes turning them into wicked nips that made her gasp.

'Matching bra,' he commented, kissing the furrow in between her breasts, in their covering of polka-dotted silk. 'Pretty.'

He pushed the dress a little way down her shoulders, so that her bra was fully exposed, leaving the lower buttons still done up.

'Did you choose this specially?' he asked, running a finger inside the lace edging, tickling the slopes of her breasts as it glided along.

'I thought they'd be cool in this heat. Silk.'

'You knew you'd be getting hot, then?'

'Uh huh.'

'And what happens when you get hot, Jen?' His thumb rubbed the hard protrusion of her nipple in the middle of the silk, causing it to swell further.

'You can see what happens,' she whimpered, longing for him to press harder, or take it between finger and thumb and squeeze.

'This is getting nice and big and hard, isn't it?' he said. 'Popping up to say hello to me. And the other one.' He circled both nipples, lazily, enjoying himself. 'I could do this all day.'

He could, too, she thought, and the idea made her squirm again with frustration.

'What? Don't you like that idea?' He laughed.

'Mmm.' Inarticulate vocalisations were all she could manage. 'Please.'

'Please, what? What do you want?'

'More. Harder!'

'Poor Jen,' he whispered into her ear. 'She needs it bad.'

He loomed over her again and pulled the silk cups down, baring her breasts to the warm, circulating air.

'Now I can see how hot you are,' he said. 'They don't get much fuller than that.' He kissed and sucked each tingling, swollen nipple until she could feel the furtive

wetness in her knickers and the corresponding throb of
her clitoris. She ground her hips to try and get a tiny bit of
friction between the damp silk and the pulsing bead, but it
was not enough, nowhere near enough.

'No, no, no,' chided Jason, clapping a hand on her hip.
'You don't get to sort yourself out today. That's my job.
Believe me, I'm going to work you.'

She believed him.

He bent back down to her nipples, sucking until they
were sore and tight while his hands cradled her buttocks
underneath, cupping and squeezing them in their stretched
silk cladding.

She felt totally bared to him, more so than if she were
naked. She knew that she had no defence against him and
she knew, also, that he would do whatever he wanted to
her. The third piece of knowledge – that she would love it
– added a zest of shameful excitement to her vulnerability.

'Oh, you're gorgeous,' he said, breathing hard. 'Even
more than I remember. I'm going to have you every way
under the sun, babe.'

He unbuttoned the lower portion of her dress and
spread it wide, so it lay on either side of her.

'There now,' he said, gazing down at her, his eyes
roving from her head down to her feet. 'All mine. What
shall I play with first?'

He lowered her knickers, very slowly, kissing each new
expanse of uncovered skin until he reached her neat pubic
triangle, newly trimmed and tidied in his honour.

'I think you knew these were coming off,' he said,
smirking at the sight. 'Didn't you?'

'Yes.'

'Did you hope they were?'

'Yes.'

'What if I decide you should keep them on?' He feinted pulling them back up.

She pouted and kicked her heels in protest.

'OK.' He pulled them down to mid-thigh. 'I can see what you want.'

He put his hand over her denuded pussy, cupping it proprietorially.

'Did you touch yourself here?' he asked. 'While I was away?'

She shook her head.

'Couldn't. I was too wound up. Couldn't even think of it, except to dream of the day when we'd be together again.'

'So it's been waiting for me, all neglected?' He lifted his hand and kissed her mound, then spread her lips with his thumbs to inspect his territory. 'Can't be happy without me, is that it?'

'That's it,' she concurred.

'Because you're all mine, aren't you?' He began to rub and stroke inside her lips, very lightly and softly at first, but with the promise of more to come.

'God, yes.'

'I think that deserves a reward.'

He kept at her, his touch quickening, deepening, while other fingers slid inside her, one at a time, until she was filled. She kept her legs wide open, straining to show him that nothing was off-limits, all of her was his. His diligent fingers built her up while his mouth closed over her breasts, her neck, her shoulders, her face, her own mouth, thrusting his tongue inside in rhythm with his fingers. She lifted her bottom off the bed, driving herself further on to him, giving him all of her.

When her first orgasm came, it began with a flutter then quickly overwhelmed her, a soaking flood of pure sensation, its tide carrying her out of the tensions of the past and into a beautiful new future.

'I want you,' she said, as the last drops were wrung out of her.

'What's that, love?'

'Please. Want you. Want us together.'

He kissed her forehead and looked into her eyes with a kind of sadness.

'I wanted to keep you coming and coming and then finally get inside you,' he said. 'But fuck it. I can't wait. I want you.'

He pulled her knickers the rest of the way off, uncuffed her wrists and wrapped his arms around her. They rolled this way and that, kissing feverishly, twisting legs and arms into impossible configurations until Jenna got him on to his back and clamped his hips with her knees.

She was brisk and businesslike about getting his jeans and pants down to his ankles. He sat up and helped, no less eager than she was for their coupling to begin in earnest. They pulled and tugged and panted and laughed with frustration at the obstinacy of denim and elastic until Jason was ready, unsheathed and unmistakably hard.

He held on to Jenna's flanks and helped her lower herself on to him. She smiled, her eyes half-closed, as he filled her, inch by inch. Oh, that feeling could never be replicated in imagination. The gorgeous bursting fullness of it was to be savoured and dwelled upon for as long as possible.

But Jason was in more of a hurry. No sooner was he in to the hilt than he flipped her over and began to thrust with hungry urgency.

Everything was in this act. It was both lustful fuck and tender lovemaking, and all points in between. There was passion and intimacy, need and raw, animal want all tangled up together, melting into steam. It was almost a rite, Jenna thought, almost a sacred experience. She and he, one flesh, one being, one purpose in their minds.

She had never felt so close to any human being. She touched his skin and felt, in its damp heat, all his emotions combined. He was flawed and perfect, rough and beautiful, unschooled and brilliant, and he was the man she loved.

Everything of her was poured into their union, wanting him to know that she left nothing hidden to his eyes. She wanted him to know he could trust her.

The thrusting banged the headboard against the wall and made a cloud of plaster dust shower over the pillows. A curious bird, settling on the windowsill, was frightened off by the panting and moaning, flapping away to its nest. Knocks on the door and bleeps of the phone were all ignored, all unheard. Nothing existed but them and their lust and their love and their oneness.

Before he came, he asked her if she wanted it and she said yes so many times that she couldn't stop saying it, the word repeating over and over as he emptied inside her.

Afterwards she was lightheaded and aching all over, but it was a lovely ache, one to treasure. They held each other and told each other that they were loved and dozed for a while until the door was knocked again.

'Ignore it,' said Jason.

'I was going to. I don't want to see anybody for at least

the next forty-eight hours.'

'Forty-eight hours of shagging?' he said hopefully.

'Do you think we could do that?'

'I reckon we could.'

There was a full, fat, sated silence, then Jason yawned and said, 'You're not kicking me out then?'

She propped herself on her elbow.

'Don't,' she said, her voice catching.

'Don't what?'

'Just don't. You're here and you're with me and I want to believe it's going to stay that way forever. Let me have that, even if it's only for tonight.'

He laughed uncertainly. 'Why would it only be for tonight?'

'Don't.'

'OK.' He shrugged, and lay back down, while she tried to calm the storm-force thoughts in her head.

He's a free agent now. He can go where he likes and do what he likes. Why would he want to be some celeb's Kept Man? He has his pride, after all. And he's young and handsome and can have who he likes. He'll leave . . .

'Jen,' he said. 'I love you, you know.'

Her doubts were tossed into the back of her mind. She reached for his hand.

'I love you too.'

'You were all I thought about when I was in there. Whether you'd still be there. Y'know. Afterwards.'

'You thought I might not be?'

'Well, a woman like you, why would you hang around? I know I'm not a fucking rock star, or a millionaire, or anything close.'

'Sh. I don't want those things. I want you.'

'But now it'll be in all the papers. I was worried you'd be, y'know, embarrassed. Ashamed of me. It's one thing when it's all a big secret and another when the whole world knows your business. I don't think many people'll understand it.'

'They can get lost, then. I don't care what they think. You can stay as long as you want. And maybe you aren't a rock star or a millionaire but you're a genius and you're a good man, which is worth more than all of that.'

'I'm not a good man! I've never done anyone any good in my life.'

'Maybe not, but you can be. You will be. I have every faith in you.'

He leant over to kiss her and his dark eyes brimmed.

'Thank you,' he said. 'Nobody's ever believed in me before.'

The moment, poignant and laden as it was with emotion, was interrupted by a loud yowl from outside.

'Bowyer,' said Jason, leaping up out of the bed to stick his head through the half-open sash window. He whistled. 'Here, boy. Where are you?'

'I haven't seen him since breakfast,' said Jenna. 'He's been in that garden, all day every day, lately. I bet it's wall-to-wall dead mice under all those weeds.'

'I can hear him but I can't see him. I'm going down.'

He turned to pull on his jeans.

'You'll need sun protection. It's baking out there.'

'Slap it all over my skin, then, babe,' he said with a wink.

'Hang on, I'll come with you. Just let me get dressed.'

Outside, she rubbed the sunscreen into his back and shoulders, reaching up to cover the back of his neck.

They'd cut his hair in prison, and it was shorter than she was used to, a no-nonsense V finishing at the base of his skull. His jeans were slung across his hips and she was tempted to slide a hand down inside, to cup a tight, taut buttock.

A plaintive miaow put off such lascivious thoughts.

'He's over there somewhere. Bowyer! Come on. I've got a tin of tuna with your name on it.' Jason walked through waist-high weeds, heading towards the sound.

It took them past the slab with the iron ring they had thought might lead to a cellar, but had been unable to open. On the far side of the kitchen, the back wall recessed, some disused reception rooms and a library lying behind the shuttered windows. But before that, there was a little alcove set into the brick, and this was where Bowyer could be found. He was sharpening his claws on something – a thick length of rope hanging from the rather high-set tap. Its end was mere shreds, either as the result of age or Bowyer's antics, but attached to the top was something metallic and brassy that clanked against the rusty tap.

'What is it?' Jenna wondered, removing the rope from its hanging place. 'Oh. Look.'

The clanking metal item appeared to be a combination lock, with four brass rings numbered 0 to 9 around their circumferences, and an iron hasp.

'What does that open, I wonder?' said Jason, peering over her shoulder with a disgruntled Bowyer fighting to leap out of his arms and go back to his claw-sharpening.

'Do you think it's anything to do with that iron ring in the ground? Do you think there really is a cellar, despite what Harville said?'

'If Harville said there wasn't, then there probably is.

Ouch.' Jason let Bowyer leap away into the long grass. 'You don't know of any other locked doors or cupboards in there?'

'No. I've had a thorough poke around and everything else is accessible. I wonder . . .'

She went to find the iron ring. Mere pulling at it had done nothing, but perhaps there was another way. A closer look at the thing revealed a little bar near its base around which the hasp of the lock could fit quite snugly.

'It seems made for it,' she said in a low voice to Jason. 'I wonder if it can unlock something?'

'Well, perhaps, if you find the combination. But that might take forever. Come on, let's get that tuna out for Bowyer.'

But she held up a hand, intent now on her course. She tried a few combinations without success, aware that she was unlikely to stumble upon the right number by accident. Giving up for the moment, she gazed up at the sun and saw, built into the chimney above, a brick with the date of the Hall's construction on it. 1836.

Well, it was worth a try.

She clicked the numbers 1-8-3-6. There was an answering click, somewhere down inside the slab.

'Jason,' she cried, reaching up to grab his hand. 'Something happened.'

'What?' He crouched down beside her.

'It felt like something was unlocked. What if we pull the ring now?'

But nothing happened.

'No, hang on,' said Jason. 'What if we try to turn it?'

He put both hands to the ring and tried to steer it anticlockwise. It moved. Not without a grinding stiffness, but it definitely moved.

'Oh, God. Keep going,' urged Jenna.

He had to strain every sinew to keep the ring turning, but eventually he got to the point where there seemed to be a movement, a freeing of something, a lock opening.

He looked at Jenna, panting, his forehead sheened with sweat.

'I'm going to pull again,' he said.

He heaved at the ring and this time the slab began to rise, on a hinge. It was a slow process, the stone seemingly glued up with moss and silt and the muck of years, but it gradually unwedged itself and came free at last with a great shower of dirt, to reveal a square of absolute darkness, reaching down who knew how far.

Jason pushed it fully open and peered into Stygian gloom.

'Reeks down there,' he said. 'Damp and . . . I don't know.'

'I'm going to get a torch,' said Jenna. 'Hold on. Don't jump in.'

'Not fucking likely.'

Shining the torch down, Jenna saw that there was a series of iron rungs set into a narrow cylindrical shaft. At the bottom, she could make out a brick-laid floor.

'There's a kind of room down there. It's definitely a cellar,' she said. 'I daren't think how many spiders are living in it.'

'Could explain our weird noises,' said Jason. 'Rats or owt. Getting in some old pipes or something.'

'Ugh.'

'I'm going to take a look.'

'Jason, don't.'

But he had grabbed the torch from her and within seconds he was lowering himself down, rung by rung, torch in his teeth.

'Is anybody there?' he shouted, and it echoed impressively.

'You don't know what's down there. Come back. I'll call a professional in.'

'What, a professional secret-cellarer? Don't be daft. OK, I'm down. Let's take a look.'

She watched the top of his head and saw him cast the beam of torchlight in front of him, into the part of the chamber that was invisible to her.

'Piles of books,' he shouted up, apparently unimpressed. 'And old crap. It's quite big. If I'd known I could've hidden out here. Miles better than that attic.'

'Just books and stuff?' she called down. 'We'll have to bring them up and have a good look at them. They could be valuable.'

'Yeah, mainly books and some . . .shit!'

There was a silence.

'What? Jason?'

More silence.

'*Jason!*'

'It's OK, it's probably nothing,' he said, but his voice suggested otherwise.

'What is? What have you found?'

'Wait on. I'm coming back up.'

He climbed the rungs slowly and she could see that his hands slipped on the iron. They were shaking and his face was milky pale as it emerged from the darkness, his eyes like dark bruises in his skin.

'What is it, Jason? What did you see down there?'

Coal dust and cobwebs clung to his lotion-sticky upper torso. He tried to brush them off, compulsively, as if they were stains on his soul.

'There was a rolled-up carpet,' he said. 'Or something. A rolled-up something. I didn't see it, tripped over it and it unrolled a bit. There was something inside it.'

'What? What was inside it?'

'I can't swear but it looked like . . .' He looked up at her, shaking his head as if he wanted to deny the words. 'Bones. Human. Bones.'

Enjoyed *Diamond*?

Read on for a scintillating extract from

FALLEN

Also by Justine Elyot

**BLACK
LACE**

Chapter One

A small crowd was gathered outside the premises of Thos. Stratton, Antiquarian and Dealer in Rare Books, of Holywell Street, Strand. Largely composed of legal clerks taking their lunch hour, it jostled and catcalled beneath the Elizabethan gables from which one still expected to hear a cry of 'gardy loo' before slops were emptied onto the cobbles.

Some would argue that the shop itself was little better than those aforementioned slops, an abyss of moral putrefaction and decay. Despite the passing of the Obscene Publications Act some ten years previously, many windows still displayed explicit postcards and graphic line drawings. The object of the crowd's interest today was a tintype image of a young woman. She was naked and sprawled in an armchair, luxuriant flesh hand-tinted to look warm and inviting. One of her legs dangled over a chair arm, revealing split pinkened lips beneath a dark bush of hair. Her nipples had been touched up, too – in a figurative sense – improbably roseate against alabaster skin. Most shocking was the positioning of her hands, one of which cupped a breast while the other delved inside that displayed furrow. If she had derived any pleasure from her explorations, it did not show on her face, which was blank and stony. But nobody was looking at her face.

A woman, smartly but not showily dressed all in black, cut a path through the grinning throng. The young men fell back naturally, tipping hats and begging her pardon. A less formidable-looking woman might have found herself joshed or even groped, but nobody would have dreamt of doing any such thing to this lady.

She paused to evaluate what had been creating the sensation and the men around her looked away or to their boots, suddenly sheepish.

'For shame,' she said, then she put her hand to the door of the shop and entered to the dull jink of rusty bells.

A pasty young man whom nobody had cautioned against the excessive use of pomade double-took at the sight of her.

No woman had ever crossed the threshold of the shop before.

Panicking, he came out from the behind the counter.

'I think you may have the wrong address, madam,' he said, placing himself between her and a display of inflammatory postcards from which a portly woman wielding a whip glared out.

'I wish to speak with Mr Stratton.'

'Oh.' The youth found himself at a loss, his eyes darting wildly around the room at all the potentially feminine-sensibility-violating material on display. 'He is out.'

'When do you expect him back? I am able to wait if he will not be too long.'

Two of the clerks entered, throwing the shop boy into worse throes of confusion.

'Oh dear, customers. Perhaps you might wait in the back room? But it is not comfortable and . . . oh, it is not a place for a lady. Pray, put that down, please, gentlemen, it is not for common perusal.'

He spoke the word 'perusal' with absurd emphasis, as if bringing out a rare jewel from the duller stones of his workaday vocabulary.

'What, is it too dirty for the likes of us?' said one, sniggering.

'Please bear in mind that there is a lady present,' begged the shop boy.

The lady in question simply swept onwards into the back room.

Oh, if the clerks could have come in here, then they would see how tame, how positively innocent the self-loving young lady in the window display was.

The woman in black sat by the grimy back window and cast her eye over a box of postcards. Far from averting her gaze, she picked one out and examined it. A woman in a form of leather harness knelt behind another, younger, girl. This one smiled sweetly and broadly towards the camera whilst on her hands and knees. And behind her, the other woman pivoted her hips forward, ready to drive a thick wooden phallus directly into the rounded bottom of her playmate.

The visitor's lips curved upwards.

'Lovely,' she breathed.

The rooms above the shop had been used, over the years, for various purposes. They had been stock cupboards, brothels and family dwellings but never, until that late spring day in 1865, had they been used as a schoolroom.

On that afternoon, however, James Stratton had tidied away all the ink-stained papers from his well-worn desk and replaced them with a slate and chalk and an alphabet primer, with which he was doing his utmost to teach the buxom young woman beside him to read.

'I do know me letters, though, Jem,' she said, declining to place her finger beside his underneath the *A*. 'I can tell that much. It's just putting 'em together I 'as trouble with.'

'So if I wrote a simple three letter word, such as this . . .' He paused to write the word *cat* in as perfect a copperplate hand as the sliding chalk would allow. 'You could tell me what it said?'

She leant closer to him, very close, so that he could smell that cheap musky perfume all the fallen girls wore, mixed in with sweat and last night's gin and last night's men and, way beneath it all, a faint whiff of soap. He knew why she was doing it. She wanted to distract him with her breasts, and very fine breasts they were too, but today he was fixed in his purpose and he intended to achieve it.

'Why, that curly one's a *c*, I think, and the middle is definitely an *a*. Yes, definitely. The one at the end, I don't know, it might be an *f* or a . . . but *caf* don't make sense, so it must be a *t*. *Cat*!' She spoke the word triumphantly, beaming up at him with teeth that were still good, lips that were still soft and plump.

'Very good, Annie. I'll make a scholar of you yet.'

'That you won't. Who wants a whore what's read the classics anyway?'

'You'd be surprised,' he said, his lips twitching into a smile. Annie always had this uniquely cheering effect upon him for some reason, though what kind of a man this made him he didn't dare explore. She'd made her living on her back since she was fifteen and now, at twenty-two, she was quite an old hand at the game, yet somehow she refreshed him.

'Would you think better of me if I could quote yards of Latin while I rode your cock horse?'

'Hush, Annie,' he tutted, regarding his slate with resigned despair. It was clear she was not in the mood for concentration.

'Besides, I've usually got my mouth full when you're around,' she continued cheerfully.

'Now, I won't hear this,' he said sternly, jabbing a finger at the primer. 'Eyes down, Annie, or I shall have to take measures.'

'Ooh, "take measures"? Like in them stories you write? I'd far rather you read me one of those. Go on, Jem. It's too hot for this, and I didn't get much in the way of sleep last night and me head's all stuffed with rags. Tell me one of your stories.'

He ran a hand through luxuriant dark hair, exasperated at how easy it was for her to tempt him off his virtuous path. Truly, the road to hell was paved with good intentions, and he drew ever closer to the fiery void. But she was right. It was too hot and the buzzing of a fly against the grimy window played his nerves like a fiddle.

Besides, he needed a final read through of that latest story before he dispatched it. Annie made a splendid captive audience, always hanging on his every word. Perhaps she could be captive in more than one sense, if he bound her wrists to the bedstead . . . but no. Much as she pestered him for his latest chapters, she had never shown the slightest sign of sharing his darker proclivities. She was a girl of simple tastes, at heart.

'Oh, all right,' he said, closing up the ranks of upper and lower case letters with a thump. 'But tomorrow we must study in earnest, Annie, and I will accept no excuses. Do you mind me?'

'Of course, sir,' she said, the sweet little word of deference stirring him more than he cared to admit.

'Good. Well, then. Go and sit on the bed and I shall bring it to you.'

She scampered up, her gaudy skirts swishing, and climbed up on to the high bed that took up the greater part of the room, plumping up pillows behind her.

James opened a desk drawer and took out a sheaf of papers, all covered in his tightly packed script, tied with a scarlet ribbon.

'Is it the one about the dairymaid who went to the bad?' asked Annie, unlacing her much-patched boots and throwing them off the end of the bed. 'That's my favourite. Poor girl, though.'

'My clients pay a premium for exquisite distress,' said James, taking his place beside her. 'This unfortunate dairymaid has kept me in shirt linen and port wine for upwards of a year now. Speaking of port wine, would you care for a drop?'

'Oh . . . maybe afterwards. Come, I want to know what will happen to her. Had she not just been tied to a fence post and whipped by four swells on a spree in the country?'

'Indeed she had.' James released the papers from their ribbon and held them before his face.

Annie laid her head on his shoulder, settling into his chest with a comfortable sigh. He had to put one arm around her so as to have the freedom of its movement.

He cleared his throat and began to read.

'*A high-set sun illuminated the meadows and hedgerows, its rays roving over the breathing and the inanimate alike. It bathed cow and sheep, parsley and nettle in its golden warmth, but today, could it but know it, there was a fascinating addition to the bucolic serenity—*'

'Never mind that, what about Emma?' said Annie.

'Don't interrupt, or you may find that you share her fate.'

She wriggled delightedly against him and James wondered, not for the first time, why his idle threats excited her so.

'*How pitiless that post-noon heat felt to Emma as she tried in vain to extinguish the fire that raged at her rear. Those fellows, all four of whom still stood about her, leering and laughing at her fate, had plied the whip with a most diabolical will and her poor little round bum was all welted and throbbing, as if stung by a swarm of bees.*'

'Poor creature,' murmured Annie, but James chose to ignore her this time.

'*As if it were not enough that the quartet's insolent eyes roamed at will over her naked body, Emma feared that any moment a cart from one of the neighbouring farms would pass by, its wheels throwing up a cloud of dust, while the men on the box would see her bare, whipped bottom and, should they choose to alter the angle of view, her breasts squashed against the post to boot. Worst of all, the ringleader of that devilish coterie had made her spread her thighs apart, so that he could flick the tip of his whip lazily over the soft flesh located within, thus opening her tender little cunny to the gaze of whomever chose to feast upon the sight. And such a passer-by would see the swollen lips and the fat red bud that nestled inside, all downed with Emma's pale, sparse hairs. They would also see that little portal, once so tightly guarded, now the happy resting place of many an eager cockstand while Emma lay on her back or her belly, welcoming all to her glistening quim.*'

'Heavens, Jem, how does it all come to you? It's too rich for me. I never thought my ears was delicate, but you make me blush.'

'Should I stop reading?'

'Oh no, go on, do.'

'*No matter how she strained against her thick rope bonds, she could not alter her shameful position, nor could her hands, tied high above her head, reach down to shield or soothe the agonies of her posterior.*

"*Sirs,*" *she begged,* "*I have paid the price for my wanton behaviour at the inn last night, and heavy toll you have exacted from my poor sore bottom. Won't you please release me now and I will thank each of you on my knees, with my mouth.*"

"*Why, that's a fine offer, naughty maid,*" *spoke the chief of the swells.* "*But we have another means of showing your gratitude in mind. For when a man helps a maid understand how she has erred by applying merited chastisement, he has surely earned the right to take such payment from her as he desires.*"'

'What client is this?' asked Annie. 'Who reads this story?'

'I have no idea,' said James truthfully. 'My uncle makes all the arrangements, by correspondence. It could be anybody.'

'You don't know their names?'

'I know nothing about them. I picture a lonely, wealthy old gentleman alone at a bureau, for some reason, but it could be anybody. I write what I myself would care to read and, by some stroke of fortune, it appeals to people I shall never know nor meet.'

'But it ain't made you rich, or you wouldn't be living here.'

'No,' he said, with a tight smile. 'It will never make me rich. But it pays my bills while I am writing my other material.'

'Oh yes. Your novel. You'll remember me when you're as famous as Mr Dickens, won't you?'

'Is that sarcasm I detect?'

'No, indeed! I believe you will be famous one day. But I hope you won't put me in none of your books.'

'I might put you in this one. Then perhaps I will have the means to whip you into silence.'

Her mouth formed an 'O' and she sucked in a breath, her cheeks flaring red.

'Carry on, I'm sure,' she said.

'"*Oh, Sir, I wonder what you can mean," the fearful dairy girl said. For never before had her offer to bathe a manhood in the luxurious warmth of her mouth and tongue been rejected. Many dozens of pricks had she sucked in her dissolute life, and many gallons of their creamy issue had she swallowed, licking her lips with satisfaction of a task well completed.*'

'Stop there.' Annie's voice was a whisper.

'Is it not to your taste?'

'It's dreadful hot in here. Help me loosen these stays.'

'Annie . . .'

James knew what his neighbour was about when she knelt before him, thrusting out that plump white bosom of hers, but he tugged at the thinning lace all the same with a world-weary air.

'I reckon that Emma doesn't have the lips for it,' said Annie, holding James' gaze with bold intent. 'Those black-guards would've been queuing up to get in my mouth. Don't you reckon?'

She puckered her generous lips and James, having pulled the sides of her bodice apart to free some of that tight-bound flesh, patted her cheek.

'Really, Annie, I don't expect payment for teaching you. There is no need.'

'It wouldn't be payment, Jem. It'd be for friendship. For comfort.'

'Comfort,' echoed James, looking down at the delicious slopes of her cleavage.

'You know I've always liked you.'

'And I you, Annie, very much, but don't you tire of it?'

'Tire of . . . well, in the ordinary way. But this ain't the ordinary way, not when it's you and me.'

She dared a little dart up and a peck on the lips.

He grabbed her by the elbow and held her face close to his.

'You're too good to me, Annie,' he said. Their mouths brushed, tasting closeness, a salt-sweet flavour.

'I want to be good to you, lovey,' she whispered. 'I want you.'

Surely, thought James, it would take a man of stone to resist a pretty girl's offer to slide her pink, wet lips down the length of his shaft and suck it to completion. And he was no man of stone.

He made no move to stop her when her fingers began tugging his chemise from his waistband, nor when she unbuttoned his braces.

'That Emma should come to me,' she said under her breath. 'I could show her how to keep her lips always soft with beeswax.'

'Beeswax?' said James, tickling her behind her ear with his forefinger.

Annie had his trousers and undergarments around his knees now.

All he had to do was lie back and . . .

'Feel the softness,' she breathed.

He did. He felt the softness, as she kissed him from tip to root and then with her saucy tongue bathed his heavy sacs.

'Oh, you're too good,' he muttered when the wet ring of her lips sealed itself around his girth.

He shut his eyes, slowly feeding every inch of his erection into her, imagining it as something medicinal that would benefit her health. It was what she needed, a good mouthful, a swallow of cream to keep her warm for the rest of the day.

He opened one eye and watched her head of brassy ringlets bob up and down. The curls were falling loose after the exertions of the night before and needed re-twisting into papers before she put on her working clothes again. James liked the effect, though; the metaphor of it. He was like one of those ringlets, once so coiled and taut, now snaking down into perfect laxity. Where would it end? Where would his life go, now that it was all in a day's work to write obscene literature and get himself sucked off by his best friend, the whore next door?

He put his hands to her head, positioning her so that he could watch her hard at work, see that scandalously painted mouth staining his cock red with whatever bizarre compound of beetroot juice and berry she had put on her lips before coming to his room.

Lord, but she was a good little cocksucker, getting his blood up to just the exquisite degree he liked before he plunged into that final rush. And here was his crisis, high up above him, way down beneath him, meeting in the middle and roaring out of him.

He took a fistful of ringlets and emptied himself into her, feeling his strength drain out of him in short bursts until he was fatally sapped, wasted by pleasure again.

Spent, he watched her take his cock from her mouth and swallow ostentatiously. Then she lay down on her back, stretching like a cat, and looked up at him, licking her lips.

'Yum yum,' she said.

She reached up and grazed his whiskers with her knuckles.

'Was that good?'

He bent to kiss the mouth that tasted of him.

'You know it, minx,' he said.

He felt for the hem of her skirts, all mud-spattered and stained from the street, and began to raise them, knowing in advance that she would not be wearing drawers underneath.

'What you got in mind, my bad boy?' she asked, eyes like mischievous saucers.

'Less of the boy, if you please. I'm five years your senior.'

'Old enough to know better then.'

'Old enough to know.'

He placed his fingers on her exposed thigh. How soft the flesh, giving the illusion of spotlessness, a virginal air that would deceive the worst of roués. He bent his head and kissed the marble-like skin, his lips drifting up and further up.

'Oh, Jem,' she whispered, leaning back, throwing her arms above her head.

Last night's men.

A loud rapping on the door broke and swept away the vague disgust that had made its unwelcome presence felt via his nostrils.

'Christ,' he hissed, kneeling up and shaking his head at a crestfallen Annie. 'Who is there?' he called.

'It's me, James.'

His uncle – his employer, landlord and instigator of his Faustian pact.

'What do you want?'

'I have a visitor for you.'

'Oh?'

James tugged down Annie's skirts and hauled her off the bed, sending her back to the desk with a pat on her rump.

Standing by the door, fastening his clothes back into a state of decency, he said, 'I don't expect anybody.'

'I dare say, but please let us in.'

James opened the door halfway and peered out on to the gloomy landing. He almost didn't see his uncle's companion, so perfectly did her black attire blend with the lightless surroundings.

'A lady,' he said, nonplussed. 'Please come in.'

'I see you already have company,' sniffed his uncle.

'Annie, you may leave now. Put the book away until next time.' He smiled weakly at his guests. 'I am teaching her,' he said.

'No doubt,' said his uncle.

James' eyes fell, rather injudiciously, to his crotch, just at the very moment his uncle's did. The younger man coloured and looked away, watching Annie skip from the room with a wink.

'Does she have much to learn?'

The question, phrased in a low, ironic voice, diverted James' attention immediately to his female guest.

'Please, take a seat,' he invited, pulling the spindle-backed chairs away from the desk and offering them to the woman and his uncle. He sat himself on the edge of his bed, the only other available place.

'Thank you.' She was perfectly economical in her movements, he noticed, as she tucked her black skirts neatly behind her and lowered herself into the chair. Her spine was straight, her shoulders set a little back, her chin raised to display a slender neck.

The face, with its heart shape and quiet grey eyes, possessed an ageless quality – a stillness. James felt he could look into it endlessly and not tire, like looking out to the silver expanse of a calm sea. He supposed himself to be ten years her junior, or more, but she could be anything from twenty-five to forty-five.

'Excuse me,' he said, standing again and holding out his hand. 'I don't believe we have met. James Stratton.'

'Yes,' she said, failing to reciprocate his gesture. 'Your uncle told me your name.'

'And might I ask . . .'

'You might ask, but I'm afraid I cannot tell you my name. If you wish, you may address me as "Madame".'

He looked at his uncle for any clue as to what the purpose of this meeting might be.

'Let me explain,' said Madame. 'Please, sit back down, Mr Stratton.'

He subsided back on to the bed, watching her keenly.

'I am here on behalf of my mistress. She is a wealthy single lady, a client of yours.'

'A client?' For a moment, James could not imagine what she might mean. 'You cannot intend to tell me that . . . a lady . . . commissions my work?'

'I intend to tell you precisely that, Mr Stratton. Furthermore, this lady has formed a desire to make your acquaintance.'

'To make . . . my . . . acquaintance?'

James looked between his uncle and Madame, increasingly bewildered.

'Before I extend any invitation, I must impress upon you the requirement for absolute discretion. Nobody should ever be told of this visit. You must sign a document swearing secrecy. Do you agree to these terms?'

'I, er, well, yes. Yes, I think I do.'

'You must do more than think,' she said severely.

James, by now thoroughly itching with curiosity, simply held out a hand again.

'Give me the document. I will sign it.'

She took from her reticule a small folded paper and gave it over to James, who read it at the desk.

It was clear and simple enough. He, James Stratton, would never speak of what occurred tonight, the 27th inst., to a living soul, the details to include the location of the meeting, the persons met and everything that should transpire.

With a pleasant sense of embarkation on adventure, he signed with a flourish and presented the paper to Madame for her approval.

'Thank you,' she said. 'You will present yourself on the corner of this street and the Strand at eight o'clock this evening, where My Lady's carriage will be waiting to convey you to her place of residence. Do not be late. And dress properly.' She frowned at his shirtsleeves and loosened neckcloth.

'Oh . . . of course,' he said, tightening his collar straight away.

The lady wasted no more time in pleasantry but excused herself, Uncle Thomas Stratton bowing and scraping all the way like a human comic aside.

Also by Justine Elyot:

FALLEN

A lady of pleasure...

In the backstreets of London in 1865, James Stratton makes his living writing saucy stories for anonymous clients. But then he receives an enquiry of a far more personal nature.

Lady Augusta Heathcote is blind and has lived a very sheltered life, overseen by her watchful companion Mrs Shaw. But Augusta has a yearning to experience the intimate pleasures of dominance and submission and she makes James an offer he finds impossible to refuse...

BLACK
LACE

Also by Justine Elyot:

SEVEN SCARLET TALES

A sizzling collection of linked short stories by the highly acclaimed author of the ebook sensation, *On Demand*.

They include the actress/director of a new production of *Kiss Me Kate* discovering the fun of a real life 'taming', a sizzling BDSM ménage, an innocent's first day at a private fetish club and a very kinky encounter with a famous screen star.

BLACK
LACE

Also by Justine Elyot:

ON DEMAND

I have always been drawn to hotels. I love their anonymity.
The hotel does not care what you do, or with whom.

The Hotel Luxe Noir is a haven for sensual pleasures. But as
young receptionist Sophie Martin witnesses the hedonistic
liaisons of the staff and guests can she also learn to master
her own desires…?

BLACK
LACE

Also available from Black Lace:

WICKED

By Sylvia Day and others

Wicked showcases some of the best erotic writing, bringing together a collection of unashamed, wildly entertaining tales of sensual holiday encounters. This is the perfect sexy summer-reading collection and includes 'Magic Fingers' by the international bestseller Sylvia Day, author of the *Sunday Times* bestseller *Bared to You*. It also includes stories by favourites such as Primula Bond and Alison Tyler, among others.

BLACK
LACE

Also available from Black Lace:

THE DEVIL INSIDE

By Portia Da Costa

Just what the doctor ordered...

Alexa Lavelle is engaged to a man who doesn't truly excite her. But on holiday in Barbados she experiences a mind blowing sexual awakening courtesy of a sexy doctor and the devilishly handsome Drew Kendrick.

Back in London Alexa is determined to keep her newfound passions alive, especially after she runs into the enigmatic Drew...

From the *Sunday Times* bestselling author of *In Too Deep* and the 'Accidental' trilogy

BLACK
LACE

Also available from Black Lace:

THE DARKER SIDE OF PLEASURE

By Eden Bradley

Prepare to enter a provocative, scintillating world where three women are about to take ecstasy to the limit and beyond.

Jillian and Cameron will do anything to save their marriage, even if it means experimenting with a little bondage.

Meanwhile Cassandra answers an ad for a female submissive, ready to surrender to her body's deepest yearnings. Finding love is the last thing she anticipates…

And finally journalist Maggie expects her interview with a sensual extremist to be business as usual. Instead she finds herself submitting to the dominant desires of a handsome stranger...

Sensual and mysterious, this captivating collection by Eden Bradley, the *New York Times* bestselling author, is sure to seduce you, page after page....

BLACK
LACE